# I

# LIED

# FOR YOU

AVA DUNN

# DEDICATION

To all aspiring authors out there. You've got this...

# ACKNOWLEDGMENTS

This book has been part of my life for many years. I am extremely grateful I could take a year off from teaching to focus on getting the novel onto the page and achieving my lifelong dream of becoming an author. For that opportunity, I must thank my fiancé Rick for his encouragement and support. Thank you to my parents for being proud of the work I do, and letting me honour Nana's name. Thank you to my friend Kristine Dalgarno for reading all my stories over the years. Thank you to Rhiannon Dunn and Becky Wicks for reading my book and letting me know what worked well and what needed fixing. Thanks to Angela Baldi and Rose Crozier for all your encouragement over the years. Thank you to Elysia Clapin for your beautiful cover design and tips on the publishing industry. You went above and beyond to ensure I got this book right, so thank you. To my amazing editor Katia Ariel. This book would not exist without your insightful corrections and suggestions. Thank you for being an advocate for Cody and for helping me see my strengths as well as my weaknesses as an author. Thank you to the best writing teacher I've ever had: Nathan King – I know it's been a few years since I studied under your expert guidance, but my oh my – what a difference you made to my life.

# 1 RILEY

The beach was quiet, until it wasn't. My footsteps echoed as I sprinted along the private pier nestled in the horseshoe bay. Monday morning became brash. I pounded the wooden slats and they rocked and clattered, sending bangs up to where the mansions sat like beacons. No pause, no gasps for air as I leapt off into the frigid water of Port Phillip Bay. Air bubbles surrounded me and I hovered between life and death, up or down, before I kicked my legs like propellors and jetted back to the surface, knocking my long brown hair off my face. Numb fingers and numb toes, but burning inside.

Each time I dove off the pier, I imagined I was running away from my father. One day I'd be free from him and his abuse. Whatever it took to get away, I would do it. But until that day came, I would swim.

I swam every morning at sunrise. A light fog lifted off my father's yacht that bobbed in the gentle water of the still morning. Crystal like a lake, the water welcomed me but punished my bare skin with the needles of the late winter cold. One leg kick and one arm stroke at a time, my heart chose life. Adrenaline could stop it, though I had to trust that it would keep beating, even with the violent electric shock that rippled through me upon each morning's dive.

The sun peeked her rays over the trees, signalling that it was time for me to go in. I padded up to the house to get ready for school, and passed one of the security cameras on my way back inside. My head remained down, despite my wishes to smash that damn camera against the patio and jump on it until it shattered.

Inside, Mum sang her favourite songs, and Dad whistled to the coffee machine's hiss and chug. He drank his coffee, espresso with no sugar, with his eyes on his phone. Mum adjusted the belt on her satin dressing gown and tapped her peroxide blonde curls, making them bounce. We ate breakfast as a family, after my bolus load of insulin. My long hair dripped down my back and made a puddle where I sat. I'd wipe it clean later. My father kissed the side of my mother's head and caressed her cheek with his meaty hands.

He once threw her down our flight of stairs. She fell and broke her arm. I saw the whole thing from my bedroom opposite the landing. Their raised voices had taken my eyes to where my father gripped my mother's arm. He pitched her; she hit the edge of the banister and tumbled with cracks and wails that made me yank on my hair and grit my teeth. Be quiet or I'd be next. I hid under the bed and quivered until I threw up.

This morning, his blue eyes, the eyes I inherited from him, were locked on his phone, until I scraped the stool back and placed my dishes into the sink with a loud clang.

'Riley,' he warned. 'Clean up before Adam takes you to school.'

Adam Marshall was his assistant. He was the coolest guy I knew. He was in his twenties and he took care of me. He was going to get me away from my father.

I nodded to Dad; my face hot thinking about Adam. I washed and dried my dishes, and put them back in their correct place. Dad watched me to make sure I didn't miss a step. Each step, my every move, was monitored, by his eyes, the eyes of the sixteen cameras around the house or by the eyes of Adam, technically employed by my father to keep me and my mother safe from outsiders – but really, he kept us safe from my father.

I dressed in the dicky uniform I had to wear, not bothering to shower. Wrung my hair out on the balcony of my bedroom, under the eyes of yet another camera, tucked up under the drainpipe. I kicked at the rails of my balcony with my school shoes. I leant over the balcony rail that loomed over the patio and gazed at the sea. It glittered, as if beckoning me back. I licked its lingering taste from my cracked lips and paused to pick off a bit of skin. I went downstairs expecting Adam to have arrived, but he wasn't there.

'Where's Adam?' I asked Dad.

He checked his watch. 'Late.'

'I can walk to school…or catch the bus?' I'd never been allowed, but I tried anyway.

'Over my dead body,' he snapped. His chest puffed up and he pointed an accusing finger outside at the backyard. 'There are guys out there that would snatch you or rape you. You're only fifteen.'

I took a step back and looked down at my shoes. He was probably right. He said it all the time. There were bad people out there who did horrible things. He liked me to be at home. Safe. Secure.

The front door slammed. Adam Marshall called out, 'Yello?! Sorry I'm late, boss.' My mother readjusted her robe again with her thin mouth turning downwards.

Adam nodded at me. 'You ready, kiddo?'

I nodded and grabbed my school bag, packed with my medication and school work for the day. My father pinched the sleeve of Adam's leather jacket, then lowered his face closer to his. I lingered so I could hear.

'Don't be late again.'

Adam tapped my father on the side and said, 'No worries.' He turned to me. 'Go on then, kiddo. Get.'

I couldn't help smiling as he followed me. Time with Adam was a time to breathe. He drove me to school along the coast, the still waters of Port Phillip Bay. The sea melted with the cloudy Victorian sky, barely distinguishable from the canvas of the leftover stars from the night. Adam hummed the tune of *La Mer* and I closed my eyes, the sun flickering through the trees on the highway onto my face. With him, I was the safest, most secure girl in the world. He was the only person I could trust. He didn't keep any secrets from me the way my parents did. Adam told me everything. Everything. One day, he was going to get me out of that house and I'd be safe.

Once we arrived at school, I got out and started walking to the ivy-covered archway. 'Hey, Riley,' Adam called so I looked back. 'Remember…no talking in class, and no talking to boys.' He grinned and his big blue eyes glittered. He sped off back to work for my father which he'd done for the last four years, since Mum broke her arm.

My father pretended I didn't know what he did to make his millions of dollars that granted us an affluent life. He liked to pretend we were old money, like most of the other families. His high class, bumptious attitude exuded in public, while in private he tethered me and my mother, his chattels. I didn't belong in this world; it was an institute. Nobody would ever understand me, the weird girl, the drug dealer's diabetic daughter.

Living with Dad had taught me one thing: everyone was a potential threat.

The next day after school, I sprawled on the couch instead of studying. My blood sugar had been low for most of the day, making me sweaty and nauseous. I shoved the couch cushions off and willed my body to sort itself out. Control is a mirage when it came to my body. I ate a small piece of chocolate to bring up my blood sugar, but it left a sand-like sensation on my teeth. I turned on the television to have something to distract me from my heart fluttering.

'Hey, Riley.'

I started and looked up to see my dad standing in the arched doorway to the kitchen and eating area. I mumbled, 'Hi,' and turned my attention to the show that I hadn't even been watching.

I heard him sucking on his teeth. He had a stiff upper lip under a moustache that rarely moved, but a lower lip that drooped; he made sucking noises when he was thinking. My eyes went to the couch cushions. I picked them up before he could punish me for making a mess. 'Sorry, I wasn't feeling well. Had a hypo,' I explained.

'You all right now?' he asked, still in the doorway like a looming dementor.

It needed to be between four and seven to be ideal. I checked. '3.9. It's gone up from 3.6.' I smiled. 'It's all right now.'

He asked, 'Seen your mother?'

If he didn't know where she was, the cameras must not have been working, unless he hadn't checked them. He usually knew where Mum and I were at every second of every day.

I shook my head. 'No.'

He stuck a toothpick into his mouth and nibbled. 'I'll go check the boat. You be all right here by yourself?'

I nodded and watched him go out to the back patio and across the lawn. The lawn was clipped so short it had a brownish tinge to its shallow tips, as if it had been burnt. Dad walked through the wooden gate that squeaked. I stood at the French door and watched his outline make his way down the narrow path of ti-trees to our private pier. He moored his superyacht there and it was his prized possession. We were not allowed on his boat without him, so why on earth would my mother be on his boat?

I shook my trembling hands and went to his office, at the back of the staircase and to the left. The door was open and I went to the computer monitor to see if the cameras were working. They were. I watched the one in the bottom right. The cabin of the yacht. My mum was standing, gesticulating, pointing to the door. The back of Adam's head came into view. He shook his head and left, stuffing a mobile phone and a Ziploc bag into his jacket pocket, wearing a sour expression on his usually guileless face. My mother followed him, her mouth moving and her face snarling.

I left my dad's office how I had found it and galloped back to the French door to watch them all return.

I sat back on the couch just in time as my mother barged inside, shouting. 'He's stealing from you, Dominic. He is a liar!'

I froze, hoping nobody would notice me.

'He's not stealing.' Dad tried to calm her down.

'He was getting into your gear!' she hissed. 'I followed him. Look at him! His nose is covered in it!'

Adam brushed his nose clean and caught my eye before turning to my father. 'It's from my own stash that I paid for, fair and square.' He showed my dad the bag. 'Hm? Scouts honour. Go and weigh it.'

'Why is he doing it down on the boat, then, huh?' my mother snapped.

'I didn't want the kid to see me,' he said through gritted teeth. 'She needs to be protected – if you remember, that's part of my job description.'

Dad patted Adam on the shoulder. 'Wait outside, Adam.'

'But boss!'

'Go.'

Adam stepped outside. I stayed silent in the next room, stretching my neck to observe what happened next. Dad gripped Mum's neck and pushed her against the window. He stroked her face.

'Rachelle, darling…stay off the boat, stay out of the business. To protect you, we keep these things separate. You can't be involved. It's too dangerous.' He let her go and she choked a sob. 'Don't get involved. I love you.' He kissed the top of her head. 'But stay out of the business.'

Dad went outside to be with Adam and I watched my mother lower herself down onto the floor. I stood; my movement caught her eye and she looked up at me in horror.

'Oh, Riley, honey…I didn't want you to see that.'

I waited by the couch. She ran her hands over her face and stood up, touching her neck where Dad had grabbed her. I went to her and gave her a hug, inhaling her vanilla perfume, and the scent of coconut and mango from her shampoo, her blouse wrinkling under my touch.

'I'm sorry. I shouldn't annoy him so much.' She sniffed.

I wanted to tell her she was wrong. It wasn't her fault. She was wrong about Dad. She was also wrong about Adam. We could trust him, but she refused to. He could get us out of here – yet she stayed with fear.

I remained quiet. After all, tomorrow it could be me being gripped by the neck for doing something my father deemed as wrong.

'You were just doing what you thought was right,' I murmured.

'Who am I kidding?' she wailed. 'I can never do anything right.'


Dad wanted to make it right between Mum and Adam. It was a 'simple misunderstanding' or so he claimed. Dad made a barbeque for us on the beach. A sausage in a serviette dripped grease on my jeans. Mum drank too much champagne, her rigid shoulders got looser and swayed by ten in the night.

The clouds cleared and Adam gasped loudly, pointing up at the full moon. 'It's so beautiful,' he yelled. He swigged from his bottle of alcohol and then squinted up at it. His eyes glazing and narrowing. 'Is that…coming closer?'

Dad laughed. 'No.'

I wrapped a blanket around myself even tighter as Adam insisted, 'No, it is! It's coming down!'

Mum giggled and put her arm around me, the two of us safely cuddling up together while Adam imploded. Dad stood with one foot perched upon the esky and one firmly on the sand, laughing at Adam as he ducked and stumbled, righting himself.

'It's hurtling towards us!' he yelled. His eyes widened and his mouth opened before he started sobbing. 'We're going to die!'

Dad wrapped him in a hug and held him, shushing him like a baby. 'It's not coming towards us. It's only an illusion caused by the light reflecting off the water and Earth.'

'I'm gonna die,' Adam huffed into my dad's torso. 'I don't want to die living this life.'

'You're not going to die at the hands of a rock.'

While Adam calmed down, I gazed up at the moon he was so concerned about. It did seem to loom towards us, but Dad was right. It was an illusion.

Mum lit a sparkler. I took it from her and waved it back and forth, watching the glaring flare of light illuminate my father. He held Adam and stroked his hair like he was a baby and chortled with amusement at how hard the drugs had hit him.

Dad lit a succession of fireworks. They pierced the sky and exploded with a deafening pop and whine. Colour rained across the cobalt sky then cascaded, disappearing into the black bay. I watched them boom and scatter, sweat on my brow, leaving a lapping hush of the shore break and the cacophony of darkness. Fireworks by the pier, sparklers and barbeques, hugs with my mother under a blanket, a greasy stain on my jeans all under the shine of a looming moon. All a simpler time before Tempany walked in and ruined everything.

# 2 ADAM

It wasn't like it was hard or anything. Watching over the wife was easy. Being there for the kid was easy. Doing what the boss wanted me to do was easy. I do what people want me to do and go where people want me to be. It wasn't hard. What was hard was having to be there in the middle and watching it all happen.

My name is Adam Marshall and I used to be a good guy. A perfect guy. Now I was worried that I was beginning to become as bad as the people I worked for.

The boss was desperate to keep his family locked away, to keep them safe from the outside, where I came from. The mother was desperate to stay in his favour, to stay in the money and to be important to her husband. The kid was desperate to be a kid, just like we all were at fifteen. So assured we have a handle on how it all works, and it's as we paint it with our innocent eyes. It was my job to keep her from the outside world and it away from her. Her dad wasn't one to give up on his child, that was the truth; miles apart from my own dad.

I had told my dad I was dropping out. I was getting lost in the world of drugs. I had to give it up, yes. I got a new job. I was good with my hands, sure, so I wanted to do something with cars. *A mechanic*, his lip had curled, and I'd nodded and said that was what I wanted to do — good, honest work. He'd laughed in my face and asked me if I liked being called a grease monkey and told me only rehab would fix my problems. I found myself in Ben's Bar.

The bartender, Jess, asked me what I was doing. Wasn't I that doctor's kid with the perfect grades and perfect attendance who had been two years above her? My retort was hadn't she been that perfect girl? The one with a scholarship, going to be the next female astronaut, but here she was working in a bar?

'Touché,' she had laughed. 'You after a job?'

'I don't have my RSA,' I had said.

'Not serving, you moron; peeling potatoes in the kitchen.'

I nodded. 'Sure.'

By the end of the night, she lit a cigarette outside. I bummed one from her and coughed until I almost vomited on my shoes. Her face lit up with amusement. 'You really are a boy scout, Marshall.'

'Don't call me that,' I wheezed. 'It's just Adam.'

'Got ya,' she said. 'You need a ride home?'

I shook my head. 'I'm not going home. I can't go back there. My dad'll be livid.'

She blew out a stream of smoke and squinted at me in disbelief. 'You're running away? You're rich and could have anything you want…and you're happy to throw it away?'

'Be happier to throw it away than be miserable and keep it.'

She crossed her arms and leant back against the door, smiling. 'You're really going for the trifecta today, eh.'

'The trifecta?'

'Quit your course, start smoking ciggies and now homeless.'

I laughed. 'Yeah, I guess so.'

She dabbed the cigarette, flicking ashes at my feet. 'Shit, eh…' She smoked in silence for a while before she said, 'You can stay with me for a while, if you need to. I have room.'

'Yeah? That'll be really good. Thanks. I'll pay rent.'

'You won't make much peeling potatoes.'

I stared at her, waiting for her to change her mind. Instead, she asked, 'What if I told you I know a guy who wants somebody for a job? Will pay a hell of a lot better than peeling potatoes.'

'I wanna be a mechanic,' I told her and had another go at the cigarette, finding it went down easier this time. 'Use my hands. Fix things. Help people.'

She nodded, deep in thought. 'Yeah…you'll be doing a bit of that. Want me to set it up for you?'

I nodded. 'What have I got to lose?'

See. It wasn't like it was hard. I may not have been a mechanic like I had told my father, but I did use my hands. I made deals and collected money. I fixed people's mistakes and bad choices. But most importantly, I helped people – which was what was important.

I kept Riley Flynn safe from the outside world. I kept away the people in it that would hurt her. I also lied.

I didn't love it, though. Let's get that clear. It made my skin crawl to be there when the boss lashed out. Deep down, I saw him for the person he was. He did care, sure. He was not really a bad man…not a really bad man. He kept tabs on his kid because he didn't want her to end up like me. I was that loner falling into powerful men's laps. It was understandable why he wouldn't want his child to grow up like me.

The day after he strangled his wife for accusing me of being a liar, he went and bought her a necklace. Spent millions of dollars on it. It was a braid of smaller diamonds with a large diamond centrepiece. Surrounding the diamond were sapphires and pearls, all connected with gold. So, she had a price. It took that much to win her back over to him. My girlfriend was a bit cheaper. A line of the product here and there and telling her how I couldn't live without her. Sliding between the sheets at least once a day and letting her lick the product off my skin had me, for moments, believing her when she told me loved me.

In the four years I'd worked this job, I'd managed to buy my own place. A little red-brick house with two bedrooms and a neat box hedge in the front yard. A TV and a stereo. A car. A large sum of money to back up for the inheritance my dad had stripped me of when I didn't return home the night that I'd told him I was off course. He'd called my phone asking where I was, and didn't I know that Cody needed picking up from baseball practice?

A headache stifled my breath when I thought of the last day that I saw my brother Cody. I downed a line to erase the pain in my head. He had been thirteen years old when I had picked him up from baseball practice. I couldn't bear that he had been left alone. Our mum had passed away when Cody was a baby. I was ten, and he was one. It had just been us, the Marshall Men, and whatever cheap Au Pair Dad could find year to year. My younger brother went to the same school as the boss's daughter Riley, but the boys were kept in separate classes to help them focus on their studies. But I wondered if they knew each other. I kept my eyes peeled for him every day when I took Riley to school, but had never seen him.

The night I left him at baseball practice was the last night I ever saw Cody. I had walked into the clubroom and he, a smaller version of myself, had been swinging his legs under the bench. Those legs would no doubt be as long as mine now.

'What took you so long?' he had whined.

'Sorry, mate. I was tied up.' I walked him home, carrying his backpack for him. At the gate, I handed it back to him and bent over so I was at his eye-level. 'I'm going, little man. I'm not coming in.'

'Well, where are you going?' he asked.

'I'm going to stay with a friend, and then check out a job in town. Don't worry. You'll see me around.' I hugged him. 'I promise.'

I left him that night, standing at the gate of the house as I walked up the hill of the narrow street. I hummed *La Mer*, a song our last Au Pair had taught me. Tears streamed down my cheeks and the winter wind breezed across my face. Of course, I'd lied. I'd become a liar that day. I had once been so open and honest, a good kid. I hadn't seen him since. I worked for the boss and kept his family together all the while obliterating mine. I had to do something good for all the things I was doing that were wrong in the name of doing something right.

The boss was a big deal. A big *dealer*, anyway. He sold the highest quality cocaine in the southern hemisphere, this side of Sydney anyway. Imported, supplied, dealt out, sold, snorted. I'd tried it for the first time when I'd gone for the job. Met the boss at his house and met his stunning wife in her skimpy red dress. Cigars in the office. Motioning to the monitors, I'd asked, 'What are you watching your family for?'

He'd touched his moustache as if stroking it flat. Strut over to the screen and gestured to where they were both talking in a room. 'My girls mean the world to me. There are a lot of shit cunts in this business. Shit cunts that always want to replace me. Take the gear.' He sucked on his cigar and added, 'I keep an eye on my prize.'

I stepped closer and studied the garage camera. His car was a masterpiece. 'I love your car.'

'It's not bad,' he said with a flippant flick of the wrist before pointing to the yacht. 'This! This is my baby.'

'Wow,' I said.

'You sail?'

I nodded. 'I can.'

'You take the stuff?'

I raised my eyebrows. 'The stuff?'

He grinned and pushed a tray across the desk to me. Lines of white cocaine. I laughed and shook my head. 'Nah, Mr. Flynn. I've never taken it.'

'You can try it, or not. I don't mind.' He looked back at his boat with soft eyes. I stared at the lines. Best in the southern hemisphere. If I knew how it was, I could sell it better. I counted to three silently and then went for it, snorting it up with one finger on my nostril and the other flat on the desk. My nose itched and burnt for a second and I felt phlegm in the back of my throat for a moment until I swallowed hard. Mr. Flynn nodded at me. 'What you think, eh, Marshall?'

I coughed a little and sniffed. 'Yeah, it's great...but it's Adam.'

'Call you Adam, eh...son.'

I didn't speak. I felt the snot on my nose catching fire and fuelling the blood in my limbs. 'I can do this job, sir. I'll be really good at this job.'

He smiled. 'Welcome to the family.'

Keep the wife safe. Keep the kid safe. Move the product. Get reparations. Get paid a lot of money. Be the hero. Be the villain, too. Ah, shit. I guess it *was* harder than I thought.

# 3 RILEY

The next day, Dad kept me home from school because I'd woken up with a hypo that took its sweet time clearing up. Usually, my bolus load in the morning sorted me out within fifteen minutes, but it stayed at 3.5 so Dad slapped his hands on the table and said, 'You're staying home today.'

Adam walked in, wearing large reflective sunglasses, and sidled into a seat at the table. 'Good morning, everyone.'

'Some night last night.' Dad smirked.

'I...apologise...for my...' Adam cleared his throat. 'Bad behaviour.' He took his sunglasses off and squinted at me. 'I hope I didn't scare you. I was just playing around.'

'It's okay,' I mumbled and began peeling an orange to help boost my sugar. 'No big deal.'

Dad interlaced his fingers in a steeple upon the table. 'So, Adam, Riley is not going to school today because she is having a low blood sugar. But I need to meet some suppliers, and Rachelle is already at an appointment with a cosmetic surgeon.'

Adam's eyes widened and he sat upright. 'Suppliers? Where? Who?'

Dad said, 'Melbourne.'

'Who?'

'Huh?'

'Who are the suppliers?' Adam asked.

'Does it matter?' My dad scoffed. 'Can you look after Riley, or not?'

Adam blinked. 'I'll look after the kid, boss. No worries.'

Dad stood. 'Excellent. Stay off the boat.'

He nodded and I squeezed my fingers in my fists as we were left alone together in the kitchen with a slam of the garage door and the hum of his BMW starting.

I grinned. 'You were wasted.'

'Ah, shut up,' he laughed.

I ate a segment of the orange and beamed at him.

'So, what do you want to do today, kiddo?'

'What time will he be back?' I asked.

'He's going all the way over to Melbourne. He won't be back for at least three hours.'

'...and he can't check the cameras?'

'He'll be driving for an hour and a half each way, at least.'

'Let's go to Ben's Bar.'

He took out a cigarette from his pack and said, 'Let's wait 'til you're at 4 at least, first.' He smiled. 'Can't have ya blacking out on me. Your dad would literally kill me.'

Ben's Bar was an old tin shed fixed to a wooden cabin in the early settler years. It served as the local watering hole for alcoholics and the meeting place of cocaine users. It was not officially a bar, more of a backyard set-up by the millionaires who owned the winery down the road. Open day and night, it was a hovel shack down a back alley, caressed by cypress pines that dripped sap all over the walls.

I loved sitting by the warm coonarra with a hot tea in winter, or an icy soda water under the whirring ceiling fans in summer. It was never well-lit but I liked the darkness; it reminded me of being under water. The hum of conversation and the claustrophobic space when it was busy made my heart beat to a rhythm of the living. The bartender who

I liked a lot was working: a waif by the name of Jess, with her shaved head dyed peroxide-white, a nose ring too large for her rattish face.

'Adam, you've brought my favourite person in again!' Jess grinned, and immediately got us drinks.

'What's new, Jess?' I tried to act cool by shrugging and sliding into a booth at the back of the room.

'Nothing new, doll, nothing new; just making my way in this crazy life,' she sang. I laughed and accepted the soda water she handed me.

'Tempany here?' Adam asked, looking around.

'She will be; she's here most days now,' Jess said with an unsmiling face.

I glanced from Adam to her, then back to Adam. 'Who's Tempany?'

Adam gaped at me as he paused, rubbing his nose. 'Somebody I know.'

Jess smirked and winked at me. Then she nodded at the door, and Adam and I turned to look. A woman in her early twenties walked in, wearing knee-high boots over her black jeans. Long legs, thin and with a big smile with blinding teeth, a small gap between the front uppers. Adam greeted her with a hug. She flicked her hair back as she grasped his face into a meaty kiss, lifting a leg to wrap around his thigh.

'Sit down before you fall down,' Jess muttered, then glanced at me and moved away. I stared at Tempany and my jaw hurt. She turned to me once she stopped sucking on Adam's tongue and blinked her big blue eyes at me. She had a mole beside her left eye, that looked like a bedazzle jewel. Her thick eyelashes batted. 'You must be Riley.' She had a French accent and even as she spoke English, her thick lips puckered into an o-shape.

'I'm Tempany. Tempany Dillion.' Tem-pa-KNEE Dee-Yonnnnnnnn. Her name rang in my ears. I shook her hand reluctantly. Her skin was so smooth. 'I'm Adam's girlfriend. Nice to finally meet you.' She grinned at me with her big teeth. *Horse mouth*, I decided. She had a mouth the size of a horse.

I smiled politely. 'Nice to meet you, too.'

On arriving home, I went to my bedroom and paced up and down on the beige, coarse carpet. I shoved my swing, ripped the pink comforter off the bed and flung it on the floor. Why did Adam have to go and get a girlfriend? Why couldn't it just be us? I threw myself down on the bed and hugged my cushions, screaming into them.

'Riley?' Adam's voice came through the door. 'You okay in there?'

'I'm fine!' I called back, my throat hoarse. 'Stubbed my toe.'

The camera hummed in the corner of the room, the little red eye gleaming like a laser. I wedged myself under the bed. I held a razor I kept hidden under there to my arm until little pricks of red burst out. I smeared them with a gasp and chewed on my long sleeve until the pain went away.

Mum came along with me to school the next morning, along with Adam of course. She wanted to do some shopping along the main street – Dad had told her he wanted her in a new red dress for some charity gala on the weekend. Celebrating the donation of $100,000. Dad always said it was an honour to help others. If he was busy playing the good guy, they'd never see the horns under his receding hairline. The dress was on special order. All Mum had to do was try it on and find a boa that would match it to cover that bruise on her neck that she had woken up with yesterday. Adam was silent as he drove. Mum sat very straight and murmured, 'I'm looking forward to the gala.'

Adam nodded. 'Should be good, Mrs. Flynn.'

'Please, Adam…Call me Rachelle. Please don't be sickening.' She waved her hand at him in dismissal. 'Just…Rachelle.'

Adam's mouth narrowed and he kept his eyes on the road ahead.

'You're going to look beautiful in your dress, Mum,' I said quietly from the cramped backseat. 'I wish I could go with you.' I imagined the dress that Dad would have me wear if I had been allowed to go. It would be something long and high-chested, protecting me from the glances of the perverts that only wanted one thing. I was brought back into reality by my seatbelt catching on my pod, placed on my lower stomach. 'Ouch,' I muttered and readjusted the seatbelt.

'Are you all right, darling?' Mum asked.

'Yeah, fine. I'm fine,' I sighed. Adam's eyes met mine in the rear vision mirror.

The orange beams of early sunlight made me squint. The car said it was six degrees outside and there was a white cloud on the distant hills, hills I'd never been to. I wanted Adam to take me into those hills. I wanted to go there when it was foggy, with the sun rising. Dad fast asleep and not knowing we had gone. I smiled with the plan all the way to school.

It was, of course, not how I had pictured it. Adam had asked my father if his girlfriend could come over. She'd been a nanny in France, so she'd be good to look after me if any work issues came up. Dad had closed his mouth and nodded. 'Sure. But keep it clean.'

'Absolutely, boss.'

Tempany walked in on Saturday afternoon wearing a white lace shirt, tight black pants and stiletto heels. Her hair was wavy, in a half-up high pony. Red lipstick highlighted her thick lips. Mum stopped and stared. I stopped and stared. Dad froze.

'Hello,' she said, laughing her way through the awkward interaction and shaking our hands, acting as though she'd never met me. Dad brushed her arm and said, 'Bonjour,' which Tempany giggled at with exasperated eyes.

'So, uh…what are your plans this evening?' Dad asked, folding and unfolding his arms in front of his chest.

'We're all going to have a nice dinner, then come back and watch some Netflix,' Adam replied, putting his hand in the small of Tempany's back.

I nodded and said, 'Sounds great.'

Mum hugged me and Dad shook Adam's hand. 'Right. See you tomorrow – we'll be back at ten tomorrow morning.' He gestured at the camera. 'I'll be watching.'

We waved them off down the driveway. Once they were gone, Tempany squealed and her arms skyrocketed into the air. 'Adam, this house! Oh, my goodness! It is a palace!'

I pointedly said, 'Thank you.'

She jogged up the stairs, running her hand along the wall. 'It is stunning. I am so…impressed.' She grinned and twirled at the top of the stairs. 'Riley, show me your room!'

Adam shoved me. 'Go, kiddo.'

'Sure,' I muttered.

I took Tempany into my room and she gushed and lay on my bed as though she owned it. 'Oh Riley. You're the luckiest girl alive. To live in this…place.'

My eyes went to the camera. She would think it was a great place to live unless she had that hovering above her bed at night, stifling and strangling her freedom.

Her eyes followed mine. Her eyes narrowed and she swallowed before she sat up and gathered her hair and pinned it all up with a barrette so her back was exposed. No bruises, unlike my own back and my mother's. 'So lucky,' she sighed.

Tempany stood up and walked out, leaving me to follow her. Out in the hall, she looked around at the ceiling and the walls. She found her way to the bathroom. The only place a camera didn't cover. Her eyes still roved around the room, checking. They found nothing. She blinked slowly at me, standing in the doorway with my arms crossed.

'Such a…sanctuary,' she said.

I didn't reply, only smiled serenely at her as though I agreed. 'Show me downstairs,' she said. She grabbed my hand. 'Show me everything.'

Adam and I showed Temapny around the house and she gasped with everything she saw. The floor-to-ceiling glass windows, the marble benchtop, and even the pool room that housed an empty pool, the deck and the spa that hummed in the night. The crispy lawn, down the zig-zag track through the ti-trees, the rickety steps to the golden sand that met the sea. When she saw the yacht, she put her hands on her head and muttered, 'Shut up.' Her eyes went everywhere and glittered, even to the mundane walls, cupboards and photographs, as though she saw her future.

We went out to dinner to the fanciest restaurant in town, where the lighting was so bad you could only guess what you were eating. Adam held Tempany's hand and I trailed behind like a dog. Home by 8:00, on the couch with Netflix by 8:05.

Tempany went to the bathroom and came back with a sniff. Adam went and came back with a sniff and a sideways grin at her. I got up and went to the bathroom where I searched until I found the traces of powder in the grout with my finger. I held it close to my eye so I could see it shimmer and rubbed it between my index finger and thumb. I considered tasting it so I could see what the hype was about, thought about what would happen if Dad ever found out. Washed my hands, and washed the sink down so he wouldn't find out that Tempany and Adam had done cocaine in his bathroom. I needed to keep Adam around so it was no good to me if he was fired.

I announced I was going to bed early. I'd see them in the morning. I waited for them to turn in to the guest room, talking quietly to one another, only falling to faint sounds when they were sure I would be asleep. I covered my head with my pillow and slammed my eyes closed. I didn't want to hear it. I hated her and wanted her gone.

Mum and Dad returned exactly by ten the next morning. I checked over Mum for any new bruises or marks but she looked bright and actually happy, with her cheeks pink and her eyes bright. She kissed his cheek and went upstairs with her overnight bag. Dad's eyes went over Tempany with a slight smile. 'All good here, I see.'

I glared at him and snorted. He straightened up and licked his lips. 'Problem, Riley?'

23

I shook my head quickly and went upstairs, hoping he wouldn't bring it up once Tempany was gone. All night I'd wished she was gone, yet now I hoped she lingered as long as possible to put off the inevitable. Dad calling me out for having an attitude problem. When he came up to room once she had left, I coiled my muscles, ready to leap away.

'You had something to say.'

I shook my head. 'No.'

'What was that look?'

'It wasn't a look; it was a...thought.'

'A thought about what?' he said in a low voice.

'Men like her,' I whispered.

His eyes got dark and he stepped towards me. 'You think I'd cheat on your mother?'

I said quietly, 'Wouldn't you? I saw the way you looked at her.'

He lunged towards me, but I was ready and fast. I ducked under his arm and hurtled down the staircase, landing at the bottom and rolling my ankle. I raced to the back door and skipped down the rickety steps to the beach. I bolted through the sand and splashed into the water. I gasped with shocking cold that electrified my body from my legs to my chest, shivering. Turning my head over my shoulder and submerging myself to my neck, observing Dad. He stood on the beach with his fists balled and the vein in his forehead thumping.

'You can't stay out there all night,' he called.

'Yeah, but you can't swim!' I shouted back, sucking in some salt water and spitting it out at him. He shook his head and walked back up the steps to the house. He was right. I couldn't stay out long. The pod wouldn't let me. Someday, I'd be able to get away from him forever, but it wasn't that day. Best I could do was let him cool down inside with his whiskey, neat, take some of his pills, and hope he didn't take his mood out on my mother when she at least seemed happy and safe.

I tread the surface of the water until Adam came down. He waited for me to meet him on the sand where he wrapped a towel around me.

'I thought you left with Tempany.' My teeth chattered.

'I did,' he replied. 'Your dad called me back.' He lit a cigarette at his mouth, shielding it from the wind with his hand. He inhaled and blew the smoke away from me but the wind caught it and blew it into my face anyway. 'Listen, kiddo…' He hesitated by kicking the sand away from his shoes. 'I'm here for you. If you need me. *When* you need me.'

I nodded. 'I know.'

'But I can't help you if you're pissing him off on purpose.'

I shoved him away from me. 'It's not my fault he's an abusive cock sucker!'

Adam took my wrists and pulled me closer to him, the towel flapped and slid off my shoulders. He held me tightly and sucked on his cigarette. I slackened. He lifted my arms to either side of him and swayed like he was dancing with me, smirking with his cigarette dangling from his lips. I gave in and leant on his shoulder, and sighed, gripping his back with my palms.

Back at the house, I found my mother sitting at the counter in the kitchen, crying, with a red face. I hurried to her side. 'What happened?'

'I can't take it anymore,' she whispered through a wail. 'I didn't do anything wrong.'

My dad appeared from the living room. 'Oh, come on. Stop acting like you're so hard done by!' We flinched as he swiped the fruit bowl off the bench with a shattering echo. 'Rachelle, you have no money. No skills. Riley would end up in a foster home at the mercy of some bloody dirty rapist, and you'd be in prison for all the shit you've done. You both have no idea the lengths I go to just to keep you both safe! You'd both be fucked without me!' He stormed off, muttering about us being ungrateful.

Adam loitered at the door; his grey tee wet from where I'd been pressed against him. He hesitated, then came to lead me away from my mother. 'Come on, Riley. You have to go have a shower or you'll freeze to death.'

I looked back at Mum, her face streaked from her mascara, smiling weakly through her tears at me. 'Get warm, honey,' she said. Adam ran the shower for me and ushered me in, with a quick glance at the camera in the hall. He shut the bathroom door, leaving the shower running.

'You can't be in here while...' I began, but he held a finger to his lips.

'Your dad is under a lot of pressure,' he whispered close to me so I could barely hear him over the running water. 'There are a lot of bad people out there that would hurt you and your mum to get to him. You know that's why I look after you. I know he blows up, but he's trying to keep you safe.'

I shook my head.

'I know you don't trust him, but do you trust me?'

I stared at him. His bulbous eyes blinked at me like a deer, and his forehead pinched in the middle. I hesitated and then nodded. He squeezed my arms and smiled. 'Good. Get warm, kiddo.' He left the bathroom and I locked the door behind him.

While I showered, I tried to remember life in the time before Dad had hit me. It had only been in the last four or five years he'd been physical with me. He hadn't always hit Mum either, but it had been shoving and swearing at her for as long as I had been around. Raising me was my mother's responsibility, but I had good times with Dad, too. He used to take us out on his boat for weeks at a time, sailing all the way up the east coast and watching the whales off Eden.

We'd sailed to Tasmania, but he hadn't liked the Bass Strait for its terrifying shifts in weather and swell. Even on the super yacht, the ups and downs had felt out of control and Dad had white-knuckled it the entire trip. His lower lip had been jutted forward and his teeth welded shut. I'd seen that look on his face recently too. The way he'd run after me just now and four years ago when he had broken my mother's arm by flinging her down the stairs.

I switched off the water, finally warm again and stood under the heated light. I wondered who had him as scared now as the threat of going down in his boat.

# 4 ADAM

I woke up to the sound of rustling beside my bed and a dry mouth. A silhouette searched through my jacket pocket then reached for my pants. My clothes were flung across the floor.

'Babe, what are you doing?' I croaked, rubbing my eyes as I turned the lamp on. The lamp lit the room with an amber glow that made the edges on things hum.

Tempany caressed my face and kissed me. Her hands shook as she said, 'Looking for my phone.' Her pupils were larger than usual. 'I think I may have left it somewhere. Have you seen it?'

I sat up and felt the hum that the light gave to edges reverberate through my head. I looked at the bedside table and saw that it was there. I pointed. She kissed me again. 'Thanks, baby. Be lost without you.' She picked up her phone and started tapping, with the occasional sniff.

I lowered myself back down and felt the heat from where I'd be lying on the bed. I said, 'I'm still popping,' I murmured and smiled to myself, closing my eyes again. The energy tickled under my skin. 'How good is this batch.'

Tempany sniffed and nodded, pacing the room. 'Okay, I can't sleep. My heart is racing. I've got to go. Bye, baby.' She threw on her cardigan over her naked torso, pulled on her jeans and jogged out of my house, leaving me alone. I got up and put the air conditioner on because I was so damn hot. I thought Tempany would run a block or two, then return back to my place. But I woke up in the morning, and the bed was cold beside me. I rubbed where her body should have been and frowned.

I got up and got dressed. While I brushed my teeth, I checked my jeans pocket for my bag of gear. I had planned to take a line after I dropped Riley off at school. I had a big meeting today so needed the buzz. I fingered the pocket and its void. I remembered Tempany rifling through my clothes in the middle of the night then bolting. She took it.

I sprinted out of the bathroom with a mouth full of toothpaste, calling her on the phone. I swallowed and gagged as she answered, 'Hey, baby.'

'Where the fuck are you?' I yelled, snatching my car keys and slamming the house door. I cradled the phone in my neck so I could lock the house.

'At home,' she replied with a sigh. 'Sorry. I know you're mad. I was coming off it. I needed it.'

'Then you fucking pay for it!' I shouted, getting into my car. No doubt the neighbours, all retirees, would be turning their noses up at me for shouting obscenities at 6:20 in the morning. 'I'm coming over now and I'm getting the rest of it.'

'It's gone,' her quiet voice said after a pause.

I clamped my eyes closed and rubbed the back of my neck. 'Gone.'

'I'm sorry,' she mumbled.

I should have been more wary. Of course, a drug addict would steal from me. She couldn't help it. Compelled by her addiction and rule of the Id. I hated that I was beginning to understand what it was like to act on a compulsion because you needed to, you wanted to – you just had to!

'It's okay; just ask next time,' I sighed, looking down my street. The houses on the street all looked alike. They had neat nature strips, that were mowed every Saturday morning in a chorus of motors that

29

diminished all hope of a lie-in. Each nature strip had a squat paperbark tree as a feature. Brick homes, wide driveways. Their residents all charming, hard-working people that had settled down with someone that loved them and had some kids. Raised them right. The entire suburb was a 'raised right' kind of town. There was a public primary school around the corner where we voted and attended town meetings. The seaside was a few blocks away so the occasional pelican soared over the rooves of the brick houses. The fish and chip shop on the corner was like Burke Street on a Saturday night, buzzing with all the families that got take-away after their sons played cricket or footy, and their daughters did ballet or pony club or whatever the hell daughters did. Riley and Tempany were daughters. Tempany liked to fuck and snort drugs. Riley liked to swim in the sea until she was blue. I didn't get girls. I didn't get this town and it sure didn't get me.

I went to work, knowing I'd have to buy a bit more off the boss so I could face the meeting I had that morning. The big shot Aldo Iacopetta from Melbourne had summoned me for a meeting. My hands shook as I sped through the streets to the rich part of town where the Flynns lived. Sea cliffs towered above the beach and the roads followed their winding turns. The road I turned into was a narrow lane, similar to a goat track lane, squeezed by tall privacy hedges and high security gates. Your neighbours could be two metres away but you'd never see them.

The gate opened with the code 1006 and I parked in front of the front door, ready to take the kid to school. She was ready, in the kitchen, as usual. Bag at her feet, her school skirt past her knees, her hair smoothed flat and her pale face blank. The boss was massaging his wife's shoulders, delighting in the way her head rolled back and kissing her lips. See, he could be *caring*. He looked up at me as I walked in. 'Ah, Adam. Good morning.'

I nodded at him. 'Mind if I chat to you in the office, boss?'

Riley looked at me with her grey-ish blue eyes with intrigue as the boss and I went into his office.

'What is it? Problem?'

I wrung my hands together. 'Ah…I'm out.'

He looked as though he didn't hear me properly. 'You're out?'

'Out of stuff.'

He crossed his arms and watched my face, as I started to sweat. 'You can't be out. I gave you your usual. Enough to give you a buzz morning and night. That's it. That's all you get.' He lowered his voice. 'Any more than that, Marshall, it becomes a habit. A disgusting habit. A habit I can't have around my daughter.'

'It's not a habit, I swear,' I gulped. 'It's just…I…' I laughed to myself as I pulled out a cigarette and lit it. 'I shared it with my girl and, she, uh…she took it.'

The boss nodded, his eyes glazing. 'Right. Your girl.' He leant closer to me. 'If she wants to buy some, she needs to come directly to me. She can't be using you.'

I shook my head and waved my hand. 'Oh, nah, nah. She's not using me. She just…took it without realising I need it,' he raised an eyebrow at me so I added hastily, '…for today. Not *need it*, in general.'

The boss grit his teeth but smiled. 'Of course. Honest mistake she made. Taking your gear.'

I nodded.

He took a deep breath. 'Sorry, son. I can't spare another bit unless you're paying. Got the two grand for it right now?'

'Uh, no,' I coughed.

He shrugged. 'Then you best tell your girlfriend she needs to see me if she wants some. All right?' He looked at me intently and touched my shoulder. 'All right, son. Off you go.'

I walked out with trembling legs. How was I going to meet this guy without the gear to give me the boost that my nerves needed? *Oh shit.* The dread twisted and writhed in my chest and I couldn't keep my focus straight. I was packing it for the meeting. Iacopetta's authority loomed over me and I shivered in their shade.

As I went to turn the car around to take Riley to school, I stalled it, then ran over the concrete swan in the garden. Riley looked at me with big eyes and raised eyebrows. 'Are you okay today, Adam?'

I wiped my nose with my sleeve and grinned. 'Yeah, 'course, kiddo. It's all good.'

I sped along the tree-lined street to her school, doing eighty in a fifty zone, she told me that her mum and dad were going better than they ever had. He hadn't hit either of them in a while. I spun the wheel to turn into the school yard and braked hard, causing Riley to lurch forwards and slam back into her seat. She laughed at me. 'You drive like such a lunatic, Adam!'

'Yeah, I know,' I said, looking around for a boy that looked like me. 'Have a great day, kiddo!'

'Bye!' she said with a big smile and left. I scanned the school yard. No sign of Cody again. I didn't even know what I would do if I did see him. I sighed and steered the car back out on the road, and drove to 64 Lyall Avenue, where I'd be meeting with Aldo Iacopetta.

I chucked my car into reverse and sped backwards, then braked hard to avoid crunching against the concrete wall of the undercover parking lot that was number 64. I lit another cigarette and bounced my leg up and down, trying to drum up the high that the gear usually gave me. Aldo Iacopetta had a different kind of power than the boss. I shoved my window down and blew the smoke out the window, peering out of the window, the windscreen and the back window, tapping my fingers on my steering wheel. It was almost nine am, so I got out of the car and waited by the K marker like Iacopetta had told me to do.

Iacopetta was not one to be on time, so I waited while leaning against the pillar, and lit another cigarette that I'd tucked behind my ear. Iacopetta and I mainly communicated in text messages. I'd only met him a couple of times over the years.

'Adam Marshall?' a voice echoed across the carpark. I looked up. A man in a grey suit with blonde hair appeared from the elevator to the shops.

'Yeah?' I called back.

'I'm Thomas,' he stretched out his hand and I took it. 'Aldo Iacopetta sent me to check up on you.'

I squared my jaw and tried not to identify too much with him. 'There's not much to check up on. We have the turf and the whole peninsula is his. I don't know what else I can tell you other than stay in your lane and I'll stay in mine.'

Thomas smiled gently, and his grey eyes twinkled. 'I don't think you understand. I'm here to warn you.'

'Warn me? What are you talking about?'

'We know of someone that has been following your work for quite a while. Iacopetta wants me to let you know that he has a great deal of respect for you, but he wishes to send you his humblest offer in order to convince you to leave your employer.'

'What do you mean? Give up?'

He grinned. 'Something like that.'

I shifted my feet. 'What do you know about the people that have been watching?'

'We can only do so much for so long. Mr. Iacopetta is concerned it has been too long.'

I chewed my lip. 'But what about my job?'

Thomas tilted his head and said, 'I can't disclose that here.'

'What if I say no?'

He grinned. 'You're not going to say no.' I eyed off his muscles. I had to look up to meet him in the eye and I could feel the dampness in my armpits. He shook my hand again. 'We'll talk again. Think about it.'

'What is there to even think about?' I snorted.

Thomas started to walk away but pointed back at me. 'Be in touch.'

I stood alone in the carpark and watched him leave, wondering what in the hell had just happened.

# 5 RILEY

I studied the expensive necklace around my mother's neck and wondered if it would fit me. If my mother could be placated with an expensive necklace, where was my placation? Hadn't I earnt one too? My dad fawned over my mother with gentle caresses and she crumbled to his touch, melting into him and declaring how much she loved him. What the hell was wrong with her?

After school, Mum had another appointment with a cosmetic surgeon. Dad left me to do my homework and retreated to his office for a meeting. I had my chance to try the necklace on. I snuck upstairs and crept to Mum's dresser, where she had placed the necklace on a stand. I put out my trembling hands and picked it up. It was heavy. I sat at the stool and put it to my neck. It elongated my neck and hardened my jawline. I smiled at my reflection. It looked better on me than it did on her.

My eyes scanned my mother's makeup collection until I saw a plum shade of lipstick that looked good on Mum. It might look good on me, too, so I applied it and puckered my thin lips at my reflection version of myself. I bounced my hair like Mum often did hers, to add body to it, but it lay flat like my self-esteem. I pinched my sallow cheeks and stuck my tongue out at myself. I took the liquid eyeliner and thought about putting it on the rim of my eyes, but instead hovered it to the left of my eye. A beauty mark, like Tempany's. I painted it with a jerky hand, looking side to side in the mirror to see how it worked. Was this the secret to sexiness?

There were footsteps on the stairs, accompanied with the hushed giggles of a female. Thinking it was Mum and Dad coming up the stairs, I hurriedly took the necklace off and placed it on the stand. I rushed to the door but had no time to leave, so rolled under the bed, amongst some discarded heels and some hair ties. I covered my mouth to hide my breathing.

I heard smacking and thumping, soft moans, that were not my mother's. I peered out. My father was having sex with a woman against the dresser, her hands so close to the necklace. I fought the urge to throw up. I bit my lip, smearing the lipstick against my teeth and drawing blood. When my father swung the woman around to put her on the bed above me, I saw the beauty mark on the left of her eye. I curled into a ball and waited for it to be over. After they were done, Tempany asked, 'When do I get it?'

'You don't waste time, do you?' my father puffed with a laugh.

'No.'

'Get dressed. Stay here. I'll get it for you.'

'Merci.'

He left the room and Tempany got dressed. I watched her feet as she walked around the bedroom. She studied the room just as she had the other night when Adam and I showed her around. There were no cameras in this room either. She sighed in French, 'Riche bite.'

I listened to her tapping away on her mobile phone. She picked up my mother's perfume and sprayed it on herself and sniffed, then gave an unimpressed grunt. Dad returned and gave her an envelope. 'Thanks,' she said.

I watched Dad hold her by the arm. 'If you want it, all you have to do is ask.'

'I will,' she said and left the room. Dad set about making the bed and I held my breath, hoping he wouldn't see me. Once he was gone, I clambered out to stand. Breathing hard, I caught my reflection - at how I had tried emulating Tempany ten minutes ago. I spat on my finger and rubbed ferociously at the fake beauty mark until the side of my face was a smudged black. My eyes fell onto the necklace and my chest heaved. I had something. I actually had something against Dad right then. If he was willing to pay 12.4 million to apologise to Mum for being an arsehole, what would he be willing to give me for keeping his secret?

That night at dinner, I stayed quiet, as I always did, but this time my mind ran through the things I could say to him. He had his eyes on my mother as she spoke, but every now and then, he would look down at his plate and I caught the boredom in his eye as though it reflected from his pasta. I kept looking at him until he must have felt my attention and looked at me. I didn't look away fast enough and he crossed his arms upon his table and narrowed his eyes.

'Something you want to say to me, Riley?' he asked, licking his lips. Mum stopped mid-sentence and looked at me, her eyes wide and the side of her eye twitching.

I took a deep breath, thinking quickly. Should I hint that I knew what he'd done or save it for later? Should I tell him? I couldn't actually risk Mum finding out before Adam could get us out.

I said slowly, 'I'm tired. I want to go to bed.'

'How's your blood sugar?' Mum asked in a high-pitched voice.

I stood up and said, 'It's fine.'

Mum stood up too. 'Darling, do you want me to come lay with you for a while?'

'No, it's…' I snapped. 'I'm fine.

Dad said, 'Sit down, Rachelle. She said she's fine. Go, then, Riley.'

I went to walk off but he added with a low voice, 'If you talk to your mother like that again, you'll regret it.'

I looked back at Mum and said with numb lips, 'Sorry, Mum.'

'That's all right, Darling. I'll come check on you once your father and I have finished here. I love you.' She blew a kiss to me and I smiled weakly.

I stalked away but Dad called out, 'By the way, you've got something on your face.'

I rubbed at the smudge again then whispered, '…and you've got something on your dick.' I paused, waiting to see if he had heard me. When he didn't react, I left and retreated to sitting on the bench on my balcony.

Mum came in to check on me. She knocked gently before entering and sitting with me. 'Are you going to tell me what's bothering you?'

I shook my head.

'Was it something that happened at school?'

I shook my head again.

'Was it something your father did?'

I craned my head to make sure he wasn't watching from the doorway and sat back. 'We should leave him, Mum – listen to what Adam wants us to do.'

Her neck moved as she swallowed. 'We…can't.'

I leant forward to her and whispered, 'He got you that necklace. It doesn't matter if we don't have any money. That necklace was 12.4 million dollars, Mum. We don't need anything more than that. Secure. Once Adam gets us out, we'll be safe.'

She clapped a hand over my mouth and pulled me closer to her body. 'Ssshhh. No. No. It's not even about money.'

I pulled away from her but could still feel her smooth, lotion-tasting hand over my mouth and I grimaced at the sickly taste. 'Is it true then?'

'What?'

'There are people out there who want to hurt us just to hurt him.'

Her eyes widened. 'Where did you hear that?' she hissed.

'Adam is protecting us.'

'I don't trust him,' she hissed. 'Why do you trust him so much?'

I shook my head. 'It doesn't matter, does it. All that matters is that, yeah, we're fucked without Dad. We're fucked with him and we're fucked without him.'

She flinched as I swore. My mind was made up. I'd have to tell him that I knew. I needed the leverage if I was ever going to be safe from him. Mum may be bought, and beaten into submission, but I would never be that weak.

When I walked out of the school building the following week, my father was parked in the queue of luxury cars. He waved out of the window of his BMW and called out for me.

My heart thumped and my legs quivered. I'd be alone with him in the car. It was my chance to tell him them I knew what he'd done – and he would have to be a bit nicer to me because I'd tell Mum – not that I ever would. She would go insane and break if she knew the truth. She was weak.

I took a deep breath and sat in the passenger seat, the door closing itself softly beside me with a click. What was I going to ask for? Freedom? An allowance? Emancipation? It had to be something smaller than that, or I'd run the risk of him smashing his car just to stop me from getting my way.

'Where's Adam?' I asked, and my voice cracked.

'Running something out of town for me.'

'Where's Mum?' Leaving her alone didn't happen. I pictured her, beaten and bloody on the floor somewhere in the house.

'Getting a massage in town. I'm picking her up her later. Once Adam gets home to look after you.'

'What would happen if you left me alone?' I asked.

He pulled into traffic and swallowed. 'Well, I would worry about you. We left you home alone that one time when your mum broke her arm because she tripped on your toy - she fell down the stairs; remember? When we got home, you were a mess, and you had a DKA from the stress.'

DKA was diabetic ketoacidosis. It was how I had been diagnosed as a diabetic, actually. My blood sugar went so high that it started to shut down my organs. I had hidden under the bed, crying so hard that I was sick. After he'd gone to take a step and rolled his ankle on a toy I had left out. He'd come into my room and screamed at me, shaking me until he was spitting in my face and the veins in his forehead popped. He'd blamed me for being a mess. I'd apologised over and over.

'I'm taking your mother to the hospital – because of you, her arm is broken. I hope you're happy! I can't even look at you right now!' he'd screamed and left me alone in the room, locking the door, only to have him having to return to the ER four hours later with me, still crying. 'Never leave me alone again, Daddy.'

Back in the car, I looked at him sideways. He stared ahead at the road. The shadows from the trees roved over his face, mottling and revealing, hiding and shining. He said quietly, 'I would worry about you too much if we left you home alone, you know.'

'I don't remember that day very much,' I lied.

'You were pretty sick,' he mumbled. 'I don't want you to get that sick again.'

My throat was tight as I replied, 'I manage my diabetes now.'

'I know you do, honey,' he said.

'So, you could leave me home alone, if you wanted to,' I whispered.

'That's not going to happen, baby.' He tightened his grip on the steering wheel. We didn't speak until we pulled into the circle drive of the house. I hadn't even got to tell him what I'd needed to, and I started breathing faster at the thought of losing my chance.

I undid my seatbelt so slowly it caught his attention and made him stop. 'What is it?' he asked.

'Are you going to leave Mum?'

He stared at me. 'Where did you get that idea?'

'What does 'riche bite' mean in French?' I asked.

He laughed. 'I don't speak French; where did you even hear that?'

'I heard someone say it about you.' I stared down at my hands and whispered, 'I saw you.'

He shrugged. 'You saw me what?' I looked up and noticed that he wasn't blinking.

'You know…with Tempany.' His mouth opened and I said, 'You won't do anything to me anymore, will you?' My hands trembled but I continued, 'You can blame me for breaking Mum's arm that day, but I saw everything, just the way I saw everything happen with Tempany. Maybe I'll tell Mum. Maybe I'll just tell the cops about everything you do. Think about that the next time you want to hit me.' I got out the car and slammed the door.

He leapt out of the car and rushed to me and grabbed my wrist, tightly. I pushed him away but he grabbed me again. 'Don't even *think* about telling on me, Riley,' he spat.

I tugged away but he held on. 'Let me go you psycho!'

'You didn't see anything! You can't go blaming people for things they haven't done.'

'Let me go!' I shouted in his face.

He let me go but glared at me. 'You didn't see anything.'

I paused, thinking exactly of what I had seen. I'd seen him break my mother's arm and the way he'd blamed me. I'd seen him cheat on her. I'd seen the way he'd strangled her then given her a necklace to shut her up. I thought of her crying that she couldn't do anything right and my anger burst out of me before I could stop it.

'I've seen everything you have done!' I slapped him in the face as hard as I could. While he reeled back in shock, I bolted. I opened the front door with the code and barrelled up the staircase, aiming for the bathroom where I could lock myself in until Adam came home, but Dad caught up to me at the top of the stairs. He grabbed onto my waist and dove downwards, hitting the wall with a painful thud, and I fell with a loud cry that surprised even me. He pinned me by his elbow against the wall and pushed all his weight on top of me and put his hands over my mouth, his veins pulsating and my breath hard to find. I screamed through hands, even though I knew nobody could hear.

'Riley, just stop! I'm not going to hurt you.'

He loosened his hand enough so I could lift my chin and grab a mouthful of air.

'I don't know why you're so upset. You hit me. Come on, Riley! Don't scream.' He raised his hand but made a fist. I flinched. He snapped. 'Don't be stupid.'

I panted but felt my heart rate slowing. 'Don't call me stupid.'

'I just want you to say that I never touched Tempany.'

'You never touched her,' I wheezed.

'Say you didn't see anything.'

'I didn't see anything.'

'Good. And you don't know anything.'

'What are you talking about?'

His fist flattened and he stroked my cheek, ignoring the way I cowered from his touch. 'Good. See. Easy.'

'I'll tell Mum on you!' I snapped.

He tapped my cheek. 'You're a good girl; I know you won't because it would destroy your mother. You love your mother, Riley. Don't you?'

He stood up and rolled his shoulders back with a crunch. 'Go do your homework.' He went downstairs, rubbing his shoulder and shaking his head. I pulled myself to my feet and staggered into my bedroom, slamming the door behind me. My mouth pulsated and throbbed with the metallic taste of my blood. My knee gave a jagged sting and I studied the wound. My back hurt. The burning in my nose and my eyes, and the tickling sensation of two tears running down my cheek hurt more.

I leant into my mirror and studied my lip, noticing I'd bitten it when Dad had held me down.

I was crying and I wanted to slap myself as hard as I'd slapped him. Only weak girls cried. If he thought I wouldn't tell somebody, he would be wrong. The question was…who?

If I told Mum, she would break. Dad was right. He'd hurt her too badly. If I told Adam, he would be hurt and he'd hate my dad, and probably quit, leaving me alone with him. If I told the police at the local police station, they would blow everything and I'd end up in foster care to be raped or taken advantage of. Yet if I told Tempany…

I started to smile and wipe my tears. If I told Tempany, she would stop coming around and maybe eventually break up with Adam, leaving him to focus on me. I smirked and pulled out my homework. Yeah. I'd make sure she knew that I knew, and just maybe – maybe – I'd finally have some power around that house.

Tempany was at our house the next Friday morning, helping Adam with something. I was in my bedroom, getting dressed and ready for school. I tied it into a messy ponytail with lumps on my head. I stood in the doorway and waited for Adam to go into the bathroom, and while she waited outside, I strode up to her with longer steps than my short legs were accustomed to.

'I know what you're doing with my dad,' I hissed.

She smiled at me, but didn't blink, giving her eyes a serene yet ghastly expression.

'Does Adam know that you're a cheater?'

'I don't know what you're talking about,' she said evenly.

I grit my teeth. 'You, my dad, having sex last week.'

I saw her swallow and waited, wondering what she could possibly say to answer me. She glanced at the bathroom, then whispered, 'I needed something. He gave it to me. It didn't mean anything.'

'It would mean something to Adam, wouldn't it?'

'Shut your mouth,' she snapped. 'What do you want, Riley? Hm?

Not such a sweet, innocent kid worth saving like he says you are, are you. Hm? There's something seriously damaged in you. What are you going to do? Blackmail me? Try. You'll lose everything you have here and I'll have the last word, trust me.' She snapped her fingernails in my face and smirked. 'You won't say anything because if Adam leaves you, you're alone…alone with your dad, and you'd be fucked.'

I took a step back as though she'd hit me. She pushed past me. 'Tell Adam I'm downstairs waiting for him.' I watched her go and shifted from toe to heel. Would I wait for Adam and tell him or go after Tempany and make her listen? The toilet flushed so I scurried to the stairs to get on with my day.

Mum came out of her bedroom and smiled weakly at me. I nodded and rushed downstairs, hoping she hadn't heard me with Tempany.

At the breakfast table, my father's vein popped each time he looked at me, and Tempany refused to look at me. Adam kissed her on the cheek and then put his arm around her and she looked up at me with a narrow mouth and the blood in my forehead squeezed as hard as a migraine would. Mum was quiet, staring down at her avocado toast instead of eating it. Adam smiled at me sideways so my dad didn't see. I pushed my muesli aside and muttered, 'I just want to go to school.'

Adam grabbed his car key and said, 'Sure thing.'

Tempany stood to follow us but I snapped, 'You don't need to come Tempany. Just stay here.'

She looked at Adam, then looked at Dad, who shifted his weight and stood up. 'I'll drive you, Riley.'

'I don't want you to drive me,' I said to the floor. 'I want Adam to take me.'

'Adam is busy. He and Tempany have to get to the ferry before it leaves.'

'I don't care. I want Adam.'

The room had fallen silent apart from the coffee machine gurgling and hissing away as it shut itself off after its morning run. Adam's brow crinkled as he looked from him to me, wanting to say something, but knew not to.

Mum whispered, 'Riley, just go with your father. It's not worth the fight.'

Dad's lip curled as he said, 'It's not a fight. It's just how it is. She doesn't have a choice in who takes her.'

'I'm walking.' I turned around and strode out before he could stop me. I marched along the road, my hair messy in the wind and my blazer unbuttoned, collapsing off my shoulders. I half-walked, half-ran onto the main road where cars blitzed past me and trucks screamed by. I focused on my feet, one step in front of the other on the grey pavement that had cracks in places and was made up of small shiny pebbles that looked like crushed shells on the bottom of the bay. I was walking on water.

The rolling, clacketing sound of a skateboard caught my attention and made my heart lurch as it approached from behind. I jumped back and a boy from my school stopped his skateboard and laughed at me. 'You good? Didn't mean to scare you.'

'I'm fine.'

'You're Riley, right?'

I nodded and kept walking, looking behind him for any sign of my father or Adam.

'Whoa, where's the fire?' the boy asked, having to trot alongside me, carrying his board.

'Got to get to school or I'll be late,' I gasped.

'Who cares if we're late?' he grinned. 'The school's not going anywhere.'

I paused and tilted my head to get a better study of him. He was around my age, square jaw, short nose, big lips, bushy eyebrows, messy brown hair, greasy forehead, big blue eyes, pale, small ears, and a freckle on his left cheek. He was vaguely familiar in the way that he looked similar to Adam; I only knew he was from school because of his uniform. I asked, 'How did you know my name?'

'I've seen you around.'

I began thinking of places he possibly could have seen me around since I didn't go anywhere that people knew my name except for school, and we were in different classes. But where else could he have heard my name? I pushed suspicious thoughts aside and asked, 'What's your name?'

'Cody Marshall.'

I stopped walking completely and my hair prickled on my skin. Marshall was Adam's last name. Cody shifted his skateboard from under one arm to the other. 'You okay? You look like you sucked a lemon,' he laughed.

I started walking again, faster to get to school. If I got to school, I was safe. Again, Cody had to trot to keep up with me.

'Hey, Riley, slow down.'

'You don't have to walk with me.'

'No, but wouldn't it be nice.'

'No.' I left him behind as I started to run, peeking sideways and behind me all the while, looking out for anyone who looked at me funny.

When I walked out of school at 3:10, I scanned the carpark for Adam's car or my dad's car. I waited until the cars pulled away and then realised that I was on my own again. I ducked back into the school atrium and chewed on my nails. Looked like I was walking again. I'd finally had the freedom, but something gnawed in my gut that made me nauseous. The rush to school had been panicked and now my legs hurt. I'd never walked or run that far in my life. Now I'd have to dash through town again, being watched and dodging men that may want to snatch me. My eyes watered as I ran my teeth along my nails and I jumped when Cody walked up to me.

'Hey, we meet again.'

'Cody, hi.'

He gestured to the car park. 'Waiting to be picked up?'

I shook my head.

'Want to walk together?'

I pursed my lips. At least I wouldn't be alone. I nodded, and we started walking side by side. We spoke about school. Well, Cody spoke; I stayed quiet. He told me about his favourite subjects. They were pretty much all of them. He was doing well in all his classes, even though he wagged school sometimes.

'Wagged?'

'Yeah, wagged. Played mickey. Truant.'

'What does that mean?' I asked.

'It means I don't go to school but my dad thinks I do.'

I laughed. 'No, really.'

'Yeah.'

I stopped and stared at him. 'Well, what do you do then? Where do you go? What happens if you get caught?'

He laughed and slyly said, 'I never get caught. I just go to the skate park, you know. Nobody ever sees me.'

The skate park was across the road from Ben's Bar. I bit my lip to stop myself from accusing him of seeing me and Adam at the bar. That was why he knew my name. He was a stalker. My dad was right, I realised with an irregular heart thump. I saw in my mind Cody grabbed me from behind. I screamed until his forearm pressed to my neck and I couldn't breathe. He dragged me into the shrubs and straddled me, raising a knife before plunging it into my chest. Cody was a liar. I couldn't trust him.

'I live down here,' I said quickly and went to walk down another street.

'No, you don't,' he replied with a quizzical look. 'Are you feeling okay, Riley?'

'How do you know where I live?' I snapped.

He sighed. 'My name is Cody Marshall. I figured you'd get that I know who you are because of Adam.'

'You could be lying,' I said. 'How do I know you're not one of the people my dad says will hurt me? Strangle me and stab me over there in the shrubs.'

His mouth puckered and his eyes widened. 'What the heck are you talking about?'

'There are people out there who will hurt me.'

He dropped his skateboard; it clattered on the concrete and he bent to pick it up. I took the opportunity to run off on him, pumping my arms as hard as I could and the concrete reverberated through my body and made my chin thud with each step and my school satchel slap me in the caboose.

I ran into the gates and into the house, and gasped for air. My mother was waiting at the door, her eyeliner smudged as though she'd been crying. I coughed and gasped. I doubled over and dropped my bag. 'Oh my god, that was close.'

'Riley, darling. What happened?' She put her hand on my arm.

I panted, 'I ran home from school. I was with this boy, but it was so weird. I started to think about what Dad says about people hurting me and I freaked. I ran. Oh my god. That was so scary.'

'Go to the bathroom and wash your face.'

I nodded and staggered up the stairs with dead legs and went into the bathroom. Mum followed behind me, not speaking. As I walked in, she came in with me, and locked the door, then snapped it with a screwdriver. I looked her up and down and laughed awkwardly. 'Mum, what are you doing?'

She started running the water in the bathtub and didn't answer me. I stood by the door and touched the lock. The lock was sheared off and on the floor. I moved it with my foot and pushed it across the marble floor and it made a chinking sound that was barely audible over the running water. 'The lock's broken,' I said quietly.

Mum said, 'I know, darling.' She held up the screwdriver then tossed it into the bathtub with a scraping 'plud'. She climbed in after it and brought her knees to her chest.

'Mum, your clothes are on.'

She put her head on her knees and shivered. 'Darling, I'm sorry about this.' She lifted a container of Dad's pills and tipped them into her mouth, grimacing as she swallowed.

I pressed my back against the door, as far away as I could from her. 'It's fine,' I lied. I was breathing slower now, but my lungs were still straining. We stayed in the bathroom for an eternity. I sank down to sit against the door and felt my head throbbing. The fluttering in my stomach was turning into nausea.

'Mum,' I said. Her eyes were closed but she mumbled at me so I knew she was semi-awake. 'Why are we in here?' The bathroom tap dripped at me but she didn't respond. I groaned and checked my app. I had to look twice. My blood sugar was at 7.

'Mum,' I said with a yelp. 'I'm high.' I winced. 'And I need to pee.'

She ignored me. I waited until I couldn't wait anymore then had to go use the toilet, trying to avoid looking at her in the bathtub, soaking in the water. Her skin was going pale, and she was covered in goosebumps. Her head lolled back suddenly and she jerked herself awake as I stood up and pulled my pants up shyly.

She mumbled, 'I'm sorry, doll.' She closed her eyes again. 'I can't do this to us anymore. We'll be free of him, soon.'

This was wrong. This is not what a mother does. I went to the door and tried pulling on it for the thousandth time. It was well and truly stuck.

The nausea took over and I bent over the toilet and dry-reached. The acid burning my throat.

My mind raced in my throbbing head. I was sick. Really sick.

I was feeling the same way I felt that day Mum broke her arm and Dad blamed me for Mum breaking her arm. Back then, I had hidden under the bed weakly the same way I'd stood in the bathroom with bewilderment.

I gasped for breath and the bathroom's clinical white tiles all started to blur and shine like a flashlight.

# 6 ADAM

Becoming a criminal opened everything up for me. A beautiful girlfriend, a stunning car, and my own place. Crime did pay, except for that annoying niggling feeling that I was unworthy of anything good. I was waiting for the end to come, even if I didn't know what the ending would be. Something had to break.

The day selling gear with Tempany went smoothly. Rachelle called at two in the afternoon to tell me she was picking Riley up from school with the boss so I didn't have to hurry back. I had been stressing out we wouldn't make it back in time. We had one more deal to make so I breathed a sigh of relief. The extra time gave us the chance to go and fuck in a back alley of Geelong before we got to the ferry at 3:45. The deals in Geelong were always easy. They were the rich buyers from Lorne and Torquay, getting their month supply. They needed something to fuel their surf sessions, trips to Hawaii and hikes up Mount Everest. Money rolled in. Tempany was an asset. The women seemed to buy more when she gave them a warm smile and spoke in her French accent. She seduced women as easily as men, charmed by her ease and praise. They bought twice as much product than they had intended, just to please her.

I dropped Tempany home then I went back to the Flynn house, my second home. It was half past five and the sun was low in the sky, giving the gum trees the glow that a fire approaching would give them. I walked into the house and found it quiet. The boss's office door was closed. I didn't knock. I went upstairs and ducked my head into Riley's room. It was empty.

'Hello?' I called. I went down to the bathroom and knocked on the door. 'Anyone in here?'

'Adam,' Riley's voice came through the door, hoarse and tired.

I leant in closer to the door. 'You okay?'

'No, I'm stuck in here. Get me out.'

I tried the door handle but it was locked. 'Can you unlock it?'

'It's broken.'

How could it be broken? Everything in the house was top of the range. I tried pushing on it.

'Adam, I'm sick.'

'Sick?' I shouted. 'Sick how? What do you mean?'

'Sick,' her voice got hoarser and her breathing was getting heavier. I could hear her sobbing.

'Where's your dad?'

'I don't know.'

'Your mum?'

'She's in here with me. She broke the lock.'

'She's in there with you? What do you mean?' Nothing made sense.

'Adam,' came Riley's weak voice. 'Please just get me...out.'

There was a loud crashing sound and a thud that had me pushing even harder on the door and groaning with all my strength. 'Riley!' I shouted. 'Riley!'

I took a running leap at the door and rebounded down to the floor in a heap. I got up in a sweat and bolted down the stairs to the boss's office and knocked. There was no answer. I opened the door to check the cameras. I walked in and found the boss asleep in his office chair, a glass of whiskey beside him. I glanced at it and noticed it had a gluggy consistency. I shook him but he didn't wake up. I bent in to listen to him breathing. What the fuck was going on here?

'Fuck this!' and grabbed the pistol from his top drawer and checked that it was loaded. I'd blow the shit out of the door and get her out. I could have tried something less violent, but my mind wasn't clear. All I was thinking about was getting her out and getting her safe. I sprinted up the stairs but tripped on the last step, grating my knee against the wooden edge. I staggered to the bathroom, oozing blood through my jeans. I held the gun up high with a pounding chest.

'Riley!'

There was still no answer, but I hesitated. What if I shot her through the door? I'd have to be more accurate than I usually was with the gun. I steadied my breathing, aimed the pistol at the lock of the bathroom, angling it inwards to the doorframe.

'One, two, three,' I counted myself in then jammed my finger on the trigger and my eyes shut. The bullet slammed into the lock and made a loud chinking sound. It bounced back and cut into the opposite wall. I tapped my body down, checking to make sure it hadn't hit me. I was fine, except for the throbbing knee. Fuck, it didn't work! All the movies were bullshit.

'Riley, are you okay?'

No response.

I ran out to the garage and got a ladder, propping it up on the wall outside the bathroom window. With a hammer, I smashed the window. Riley was on the floor, her skin a grey-ish tinge and her breathing rapid. I bent down to shake her. She didn't respond. She only continued panting like a dog that had been left in a hot car. My eyes went to Rachelle. She was fully-clothed, asleep in the bath. I stared down at her, wondering what the fuck she had done.

I bent down, wincing as I put too much weight on my right knee. I reached into the bath and shook her. She roused and looked at me with her eyes half-closed. 'Go away. I know what you are.'

'Go away?' I pointed down to Riley. 'What did you do?'

'I'm saving us both,' she whispered and closed her eyes.

I slapped her across the face and she sat up, the water spilling over the ledge and soaking my feet. 'What did you do?'

She shook her head and said, 'Leave us alone to die.'

My entire body shook and my arms twitched before I jumped into the bath with her, screaming. 'You can't let her die!'

I shook Rachelle violently so the back of her head smacked against the bath and she sank under the water. 'You fucking bitch; you're killing your child!'

I jumped out of the bath and went to Riley. She was still breathing, but sounded awful. I looked up at the window and sobbed. I'd have to get her out that way. I spread all the towels in the bathroom over the ledge and heaved Riley up, luckily, she was a lightweight. I hauled her to the window and lifted her to the window. I looked down at the garage. If she fell to there, she'd be okay, but it would hurt. I sobbed, 'Sorry, Riley. I've got to get you out.' I pushed her and she fell onto the garage roof with a thud and a small whimper.

I climbed down the ladder and moved it over to the garage so I could get her down. My legs shook as I climbed back up and met her on the roof of the garage. I grit my teeth and lifted her over my shoulders, carefully climbing down the ladder. I almost fell backwards when I tried to put her down on the driveway. Her hair fanned out, mussed from her loose ponytail and I tried to smooth it for her. I loaded her into the backseat called Triple Zero from the car, speeding to the hospital.

# 7 ACKERMAN

Husbands are the ones who do it. I put down the phone and tapped my pen against my notepad. The husband reported Rachelle Flynn missing. Dominic Flynn. His wife had disappeared in the early evening of Friday the 26th of August. She had been at home, alone. His daughter was in the hospital, complications from her type 1 diabetes. He'd returned home to find her gone. It was my first week being in the Victoria Police Missing Persons Squad. I had been a General Duties officer for two years, then in Highway Patrol for six. I had a lot to prove. I was determined to save people. Hunt people down. Make things right.

I approached the house of the missing woman and squinted up at a narrow window above the garage on the left. The window was boarded with cardboard and tape. I made a mental note of it and went inside.

Dominic Flynn stood in the foyer of his mansion, showing me a photograph of his missing wife. A stunner. Blonde, curls, spray tan, teeth that were straight and glowed from behind the lipstick in the photo, but looking closer, the smile was mostly a grimace. Dominic Flynn watched the way I studied her photo and said, 'Well, Senior Constable Ackerman, what next?'

I handed him the photograph back. 'She's never taken off before?'
'No,' he replied firmly.

'Nine times of ten, people that go missing tend to have just gone off on their own,' I said, following protocol to reassure him.

He rolled his eyes at me and pinched his fingers to his thumb and snapped them downwards in a pointed motion. 'Not Rachelle. She wouldn't have gone off by herself. She has nowhere to go. She doesn't know anybody else, mate.'

I nodded and replied, 'Okay.' Woman like that, nowhere to go, nowhere to be, no friends or extended family? It sounded off. 'Mind if we take a look around?'

Flynn glanced around behind me at my partner, Senior Constable Zoe Burke, and his eyes fell on Burke's burgeoning pregnant belly. He then nodded with his eyes down. Burke refused to go on light duties until she was ready, so her belly often caught concerned glances from the public. She slipped on her gloves and I did the same.

Burke followed Flynn into the main living area of the house and complimented him on the view of the water, which shone in the Saturday morning sunshine. I left them speaking about the details of the house and made my way up the stairs. There was a chip at the top step that caught my attention. I squatted and peered at it, touching the splintered wood. There was a little discolouration that appeared like it could have been blood. I scraped a bit off and bagged it as evidence.

I turned left of the stairs. A master bedroom, looking out at the bay. An extravagant diamond, pearl, gold, and sapphire necklace was a centre-piece on the dresser. Odd that such an expensive-looking and obviously prized necklace would be left behind if she had run off. I went into the ensuite and collected her toothbrush and hairbrush. All DNA evidence if she rocked up in a not-so-fortunate condition. Next door to the master bedroom was a spare bedroom, with a neatly made double bed with a blue doona. There was a phone charger plugged in and the drawers were filled with male clothes. Who stayed in here? Mr. Flynn? Had the marriage been on the rocks? Maybe they had a son?

Or a friend that stayed the night.

I made my way down the hallway, opposite the stairs was the daughter's bedroom. A swing hung from the ceiling with pink fluffy cushions. The room was impeccably neat. I looked briefly through the drawers then under the bed. Something small and metallic caught my eye on the rug. I reached in and grabbed it. A small razor. I bagged it, then stopped. Was this evidence or just a coping mechanism for the girl? The grimacing missing blonde in the photograph came into my mind and I thought of the daughter in hospital. I put the bag in my evidence collection. It could be something.

Coming out of the bedroom, and going left down the hall, I noticed a bit of wall that had a hole in it. I looked inside it with my torch. It was empty. I followed the line from the hole to the bathroom door, which had scuff marks and the door handle was damaged. I investigated the doorframe and drew a line in the air from the door to the wall with my finger. 'Bullet ricochet?' I mumbled to myself. What on earth had happened here? I tried to open the door, but it was jammed. I mentally tried to configure the layout of the house. Was this where the broken window was?

I took some photos and headed downstairs to re-join Mr. Flynn and Burke. Flynn was telling Burke his movements. He'd been working late and then his daughter had taken ill. He had taken her to the hospital and stayed the night there with her. When he'd returned in the morning, his wife was gone.

'Have you told your daughter that she's missing?' Burke asked.

'Not yet,' he replied. His forehead creased so the three permanent lines on his forehead all crunched together. His hands always moved, as though he didn't know what to do with them. It was normal behaviour though, not a red flag. A lot of people didn't know what to do with their hands. Not me. I always stood at attention. Feet hip-width apart, knees straight, back straight and hands at my sides. I let them dangle. I liked the feeling of the blood pulsing to my fingertips. It reminded me how lucky I was to have hands.

'Was there anyone else here in the house?' I asked.

He looked to me slowly, as though full of recollections. His eyes finally rested on mine and he said, 'No.'

Burke gestured to the camera in the corner of the room. 'Do they work?'

'No. They're there mostly for show. They don't actually operate.'

'Thanks for your time, Mr. Flynn,' said Burke. 'We'll check her phone records and bank activity and see where that takes us. In the meantime, try to have someone here, even when you're at the hospital with your daughter, so if Rachelle does come home, there's someone to sight her and be here for her.'

'How long until she's not considered missing anymore?'

Burke and I exchanged glances. What an odd question.

'I mean,' he scoffed to correct himself. 'When do I need to worry?'

Burke sighed. 'It depends on Rachelle. If this is unusual for her to be gone,'

'It is,' Flynn interjected.

'Then if we can't find a trace of movement, I'd say we can worry.'

'Thanks officers.'

'Please call us if anything comes up.' Burke handed him both our cards and we left out the front door, our mouths firmly closed until we were out of ear shot in the car.

'Reckon she's all right?' I asked.

'Oh, hell no,' she blurted. 'Something happened to her, for sure.' She adjusted her seatbelt to accommodate the bump and smoothed her brown hair.

'Like the husband for a suspect?'

'It's always the husband.' She sniffed and added, 'Well, mostly. He could be innocent.'

'But you don't think so?' I said, starting the car and backing out of the driveway.

'He's got a cupboard in his office that he doesn't have a key for. He says he doesn't have a key for. Be good to get in there and see what he's hiding.'

'The broken window,' I added. 'Seemed off, and looks like somebody's fired a gun at the lock and it's ricocheted into the opposite wall.' I reached behind me and pulled out the evidence bag of the razor blade. 'Also, this was under the girl's bed.'

Burke took the bag and turned it over, squinting at it as I drove back to the station on the highway. 'Not a happy girl.'

'Doesn't seem that way,' I said. 'I wonder if Rachelle Flynn was not happy, too.'

'If they're not happy, what's something they have in common? Oh, the husband.'

It appeared grim. Women often took off without a word from their husbands, but not often without their kids.

'I wonder if the girl knew the mother was leaving – that's if she left,' Burke said, as though she'd read my mind. It was only our first week working together but we just gelled together as though we'd worked together for years. It gave me a positive sense of my choice to change from Highway Patrol. She only had three more weeks left until she was forced onto maternity leave. It was her first child with her husband. They hadn't taken a peek at what sex the baby was, but I hoped it was a girl if it was going to be anything like her mother. Warm and approachable, but a walking lie detector.

'I'd like to go talk to the girl as soon as possible,' she said, slipping the evidence bag back. 'She might know where her mother would go, or if something happened leading up to the disappearance.'

I nodded and knew that something must have happened in that house. Nobody fires a gun inside the house without something being seriously wrong.

At the ward desk of the hospital, Burke mentioned that we needed to speak to Riley Flynn, fifteen-year-old female, treatment for complications due to diabetes, brought in last night by her father. The nurse behind the desk shook her head, 'No, no – she is here, yes, but she wasn't brought in by the father. He only turned up this morning, stressed to the gills and was screaming at us for not contacting him sooner. Bonehead. Absolute bonehead. We tried calling him several times and it always went straight to Message Bank.'

Burke and I exchanged looks.

'Who brought her in?' I asked. 'Was it her mother?'

'No, young bloke. Early twenties, maybe mid-twenties if he had a baby face. Brought her into emergency.'

'How long did he stay around?' Burke asked.

The nurse shook her head with a resigned expression. 'No idea, sorry. We were just focused on getting her stabilised.'

'Thank you,' Burke said.

'Any time; no doubt you want the facts, straight as they come, am I right?' she said with a wink. She came around to the other side of the desk with her clipboard and stethoscope. 'I'll take you to her room.'

The girl was sitting up, propped up by the bed and had an IV in her arm. She looked glumly out of her window, her light brown hair like an oily curtain over her face.

'Miss Flynn,' said the nurse. She looked up with a small smile, then her smile fell when she saw Burke and me.

'You're here because of my dad?' she asked.

Burke introduced herself and me. She leant away from us at the mention of our titles. 'Police.'

Burke pulled a chair closer to her bed and sat down, groaning slightly as she made herself comfortable. 'Yes, Riley, police.'

'I don't know anything.'

I grinned. 'You don't even know what we're here for.'

She chewed on her nails and replied, 'That's what I said. I don't know anything.'

'Has your dad been in since he visited you this morning?' Burke asked.

'No. He came in for maybe half an hour, screamed at the nurses then left.'

'Does he scream a lot?' I asked. She stared back at me but didn't speak.

Burke explained, 'Well, your dad called us.'

'What?' Her head snapped around to Burke and her nostrils flared. 'Why on earth would he call you?'

'About your mum.'

She snorted. 'What about her?'

Burke and I looked at each other. The disdain in Riley's words didn't match the expression on her face. The dull winter sunshine coming through the window didn't quite catch the way Riley looked down with teary eyes, but I did.

'Riley, there's no easy way to say this, but your dad is concerned about your mum because he can't locate her,' Burke said slowly. Riley's eyes went from her lap, to Burke's hands on the clipboard before meeting Burke's eyes.

'Does that mean she's missing?' she croaked.

Burke nodded and immediately added, 'But we're looking for her.'

'That's why we're here,' I said.

Riley looked up at me and asked, 'Do you think I know where she is?'

'Do you?'

She reached for her IV and said, 'Ouch,' as it caught on the blanket. She spent a moment fixing it, then looked back at Burke and sighed. 'Can you ask the nurses for me when I can go home? I'm feeling much better now.'

# 8 RILEY

The day I got back from the hospital, I dove into the ocean, feet-first off the pier, gasping with its shocking cold that made my limbs inactive and dull. My dad stood at the beach calling my name but I kept going out further. Out, out, out until I couldn't touch the sandy bottom anymore, and my hands slapped the surface and my legs throbbed from the cold. I took a deep breath and swam down, down, down to where it was peacock blue and I could have just drowned.

My mother was missing. She'd done what she'd done to me, then disappeared. Dad reported her missing, like he wasn't responsible. He pretended to be a loving father, a loving husband. I surfaced with a warmth radiating through my body like fire. I glared back at him on the beach, a lonely figure in black dress shoes, having to step through the seaweed deposited by the tide to pick his way back up to his silent dead house on top of the hill. Have your silence, old man. I don't need you. I have the sea.

I stayed out in the water, wading and wallowing, for an hour. I didn't feel the cold anymore. I swam out past where the pier was and submerged myself to look at the rippled, sandy bottom. I tugged myself along the bottom of the bay, inch by inch, swivelling my body so it was belly-up to get a glimpse of the surface from below, picturing how the world must have looked for my mother while she let me die. How I must have looked from above, fizzling at the edges of the clear water.

My ears started cricking so I shot back up to the surface of the water, head throbbing and lungs igniting. Paddling at the surface, my teeth began chattering as a cold wind stroked its cool waves over my hair. I floated there, studying the papaya sky and how the horizon was beginning to melt into a fiery haze. The clouds were rolling in, sending arrows of light plunging into the sea and the sun was a tiger orb sinking lower. It was too beautiful; it made my chest hurt.

Word got around town that my mum had disappeared. Everyone acted like they knew her but most were surprised to hear that her name was Rachelle. She'd just been "the wife." Vacuous rich woman, nothing to offer except her youth and good looks. Now she was older, those good looks were fading so he must have asked for a divorce. She must have cleared off with that toy boy that hangs out at the house.

All these things I heard while at school from the army of bitches, burying my head in a book so they wouldn't see me. Did they even know that she was my mother? I was walking out of English class when the teacher, Mr. Estranger stopped me. He propped one butt cheek on a table and leant on it, placing his hands in his lap. 'Let me know if you need anything,' he said quietly, needlessly so because the room was void except the distant chatter in the hall outside.

I looked up at the high ceiling and said, 'You mean because I've just been in hospital, right?'

'Yes, and also…'

I shook my head. 'Don't worry about my mother, Mr. Estranger. She's fine. Haven't you heard? She cleared off with that toy boy that hangs out at the house.' His bulbous eyes searched mine so added, 'I'm fine. Thanks for checking on me.'

Adam picked me up, looking around the school yard as he always did, but this time with a cricked neck as though he'd been shuddering too much. 'You looking for your brother?' I asked.

He turned in his seat to face me. 'What did you say?'

'You looking for your brother,' I repeated slowly as though he couldn't understand English. 'Cody.'

'You've met Cody?' he asked.

I nodded and didn't say anything about how he had approached me in the street and walked home, and I'd freaked out about him.

'When?'

I shrugged. The day I nearly died thanks to my mother.

Adam whistled through his teeth. 'You, kiddo…you can keep a secret, can't you.'

If he only knew all the secrets I kept.

# 9 ACKERMAN

The station on Tuesday afternoon was abuzz with the tip from a woman about Rachelle Flynn. She had called in and informed us that she had been beaten often in the relationship. She refused to leave her identity.

'That woman was slapped, shaken and strangled by her husband. She told me herself when we met over coffee. The husband was forcing her to get liposuction because he thought she was fat – she was a size 14 for Christ's sake. Not even fat. She had bruises all over her body from that man's hands. She could never do anything right by him. Every little thing she did that he didn't like, he'd lose it at her. Saw it myself. With my own eyes. If you check her medical records, you'll see that she broke her arm a couple of years ago. That was him.' She'd hung up quickly.

Burke rubbed her hands together. 'Always the husband.'

We arrived at the Flynn house by 4:28, and informed Mr. Flynn that we would like to interview him regarding his wife's disappearance. He leant against the doorframe, as though he had been expecting this development.

'I don't have to, though, do I.'

'No, sir. We are not arresting you, just have some questions.'

'You can ask me here.'

'We'd rather it be on the record.'

He sucked on his teeth for a minute, mulling it over. 'Let me just organise someone to look after my daughter. Wait here.'

He closed the door and we stood silently, looking at our shoes. When Mr. Flynn opened the door, he was putting on a black leather jacket and said, 'Okay, let's go.'

'We can wait until someone arrives for your daughter, Mr. Flynn,' said Burke, gesturing at the door. He continued to our parked in the driveway and said, 'No need. It's done.'

I peered inside the house and noticed a guy in his early twenties looking back at me with wide eyes. Before the girl came and closed the door, I made a note to myself: short, slim build, brown hair, Caucasian.

In the quiet of the interview room, we sat around a rectangular table. Burke faced Flynn and I sat to his side. I leant back but kept my eyes trained on him. Burke took a moment to neaten her notes; the notebook on the table in front of her, the missing person's report to the right, and a cup of water to the left.

'Would you like a drink of water, Mr. Flynn?' she asked to be courteous. He shook his head and crossed his arms, jutting his chin up at the same time. Waiting. 'All right, we'll get started,' she said, the polite smile disappeared from her face. 'We wanted you to come in and explain your relationship with your wife. In your own words.'

I leant forward, bringing my elbows to rest on my knees to observe.

Mr. Flynn pouted his mouth and widened his eyes. 'Well…we're just a regular married couple.'

'Uh huh,' Burke noted.

We both waited for him to continue but were met with a long silence before Flynn finally added, 'Don't know what else I can say.'

'You work, sir?' she asked.

'Yes, I do. I sell fine jewellery.'

Burke's hand scrawled.

'What about your wife? Does she work?' she asked.

'No. Traditional roles mean a lot to me.' He shrugged. 'I believe in looking after and caring for my woman.'

'Uh huh,' Burke said again, writing and circling what she had written. 'Does your wife have any friends?' she asked, looking up with a curious head tilt. 'Someone that she can talk to, have coffee with…that kind of thing.'

Flynn shifted his weight in his seat and shook his head, bringing his hand to his mouth to nibble on the edge of his thumbnail. 'No…no. She, uh,' he crossed his arms again. 'She has trouble making friends. Always had trouble with that. She's too shy. Doesn't put herself out there.'

'Is it possible she has a friend and you didn't know?' I asked.

He looked to me with a pinched expression. 'What are you trying to say? That she keeps secrets from me?'

I shrugged.

'No,' he replied with a sigh. 'We're not that kind of couple.'

'How long have you been married?' Burke asked.

'Fourteen years and nine months,' he answered quickly. 'We had to delay our wedding a while because she ended up getting pregnant with our daughter Riley.' He scratched at his moustache, peppered with grey hairs amongst the brown. 'She didn't want to be rotund in the photos.' He shook his head, eyes glazing as he was in the memory. 'Seems silly when she was doing such a miraculous thing.' He looked across at Burke and smiled, his eyes shining. 'You must be so excited about your upcoming motherhood.'

Burke chuckled and rubbed her bump. 'Well, yes, of course.'

'You just have the one child, Mr. Flynn?' I interrupted.

'My wife, she, uh…had a difficult time after Riley was born. Trying to lose weight for the wedding. Bit of post-natal depression. It was just…a lot. We decided not to go down the path for a second time.' He levelled his eyes with mine and added, 'Besides, my daughter is perfect so we didn't feel the need to have a second, anyway.'

'So, no children from a previous marriage?' I confirmed.

'No.'

'I thought I saw a young man at your house this afternoon,' I said with a raised eyebrow. 'I thought he may have been a relation.'

Mr. Flynn cleared his throat. 'No, he's just an associate, family friend.'

'Which is it?' Burke asked.

Mr. Flynn paused. 'Both. He works for me, but I've taken him under my wing quite a bit. I mentor him. He's like a son to me.'

Burke scrawled in her notebook and I sighed.

'Are you aware that we've been to the hospital and spoken to nurses, Mr. Flynn?' I asked. He took a moment but he slowly nodded. 'So, you're aware that we know you did not in fact drop your daughter off at the hospital?'

We were silent. Flynn sat, still as a meditating monk and Burke stopped with her pen raised above the paper, waiting for him to speak.

I added, 'You and your wife were the only ones that were at home when she went missing. There's a gunshot in your hallway wall and your bathroom window was broken. Your alibi doesn't make sense with everything else.'

'Alibi?' he choked. 'Am I under investigation?' He stood in a rush. 'Am I a suspect?'

'Just following every possible lead that comes our way,' I replied. 'Including how your daughter took ill just before your wife went missing.'

'What has my daughter being ill have to do with my wife being missing?' he thundered, the skin on his face mottling and a vein pulsing under his right eye. I looked at his balling fists and I saw what Rachelle

Flynn most likely saw quite often, as her "friend" had stated. A man who could snap when challenged. A man who could possibly make someone disappear.

I stood up and stepped beside Burke. 'You're free to go, Mr. Flynn.' He strode to the door and I added, 'For now.'

He glared at me and I gestured to the door as I stood up. 'I'll show you out.'

'Don't bother,' he mumbled and stormed out of the room.

Burke folded her notebook and looked up at me. 'Doesn't really sound like what that tip said.' She blew a strand of hair off her pointy nose. 'He sure got angry about it though.'

'We'll find out who the other guy is,' I said. 'He's obviously around them quite a lot. He may have some answers.'

# 10 ADAM

I stood on the pier biting my nails and waited for Riley to notice me waiting for her. When she did, she swam over. I told her, 'The police have released your dad,' and handed her a towel as she pulled herself up onto the pier.

Riley wrung her hair out so hard she yanked strands out. 'They're idiots.'

My eyes went to her neck. She was wearing the expensive necklace the boss had given to his wife before she went missing. I asked, 'Should you be swimming with that necklace on? It's really expensive.'

'It's fine,' she said.

We walked to the house, not speaking, Riley following me, gingerly stepping with her bare feet on the metal platform and up the tea-tree path to the house. Once she was in the house, I told her, 'I've got to go pick him up. Stay here at the house and don't go anywhere.'

Riley rubbed at the dry skin on her lips and didn't look at me so I repeated, 'Stay…here.'

Once she nodded, I left, my hands trembled on the steering wheel and drove to the police station. Outside the station, a grey-brick building with flags flapping wildly in the cold front that was looming, sending icy shards of rain pelting down in the distance and roared across into town. Rain freckled the windscreen so I turned on the wipers. With each screeching swipe, I thought *I am a bad person, I'm not a bad person, I am a bad person, I'm not a bad person* like a schoolgirl who plucks petals from a daisy.

The boss interrupted my thoughts as he opened the passenger side door and slammed it so hard behind him that the car rocked sickeningly like the boat. I reached for a cigarette to quell the nausea and lit it.

The boss glanced in the back seat. 'Where's Riley?' He cleared his throat. I stole a glance at his face and noticed the pinch between his eyes and red splotches on his neck. It looked like he had cried, but everything I knew about the man told me he wouldn't cry, not even for the wife he called his beloved treasure. Yet there he was with a puffy under eye and a raspy voice. He had a face like he'd run headlong into a wall of onions.

'At home,' I replied quietly.

'You shouldn't leave her alone.'

I looked down at my lap. 'Did they…find her?'

He shook his head. 'Not yet.'

'But they've cleared you.'

'For now.' He scoffed.

'You didn't do anything,' I whispered.

'I didn't not do anything,' his voice cracked. 'I wasn't exactly a good husband to her.'

'But you were drugged. Full on roofied.' I watched the rain getting heavier, just as the pit of my stomach was. The sky turned white with sleet and hail, pinging onto the car. My knee ached where I had dug it into the edge of the top step and my hand went to it automatically to rub it.

The boss cleared his throat. 'They think I killed her.'

I blinked. We'd gone from she was missing to she was dead awfully fast. I sucked on the cigarette and said, 'They think she's missing, not that she's dead.'

He leant back in his seat, bumping the back of his head repeatedly to self-soothe. 'They'll be watching every move we make, especially me.' He locked eyes with me. 'Don't move anything. Tell Tempany not to sell. Don't…move…a thing.'

I nodded, taking the cigarette to my mouth again.

He added, 'I'll have to take Riley out of school. I can't let her be out and about in case she says something. Complete lockdown, all right?'

I nodded again and pulled out into traffic.

# 11 RILEY

As I lay in bed, I touched my neck and realised with a start that Mum's necklace was gone. I hadn't felt it since I was swimming. I gasped, thinking I had lost it in the water, but then remembered Adam had asked about it. It must not have dropped in the water. Unless it came off on the pier? Or on the path? Either way, I had lost it and its value. Oh, no. Security gone.

My bedroom door opened and Dad stepped in. I pretended to be asleep, despite my thumping high heart rate. Dad sat on the edge of my bed and touched my arm and hair. My hair was still wet so I faked a sleepy grunt to make it a bit more convincing that I was asleep. He sighed and stroked my sweaty forehead, which he hadn't done since I was little. I had not expected such softness. I grit my teeth to stop the tears of longing and nostalgia from springing from my eyes. How could both my parents let me down so much? I hated both of them.

'Good night, honey. I love you.' He moved in to kiss my forehead but I rolled away from him. I wouldn't be able to bear a kiss from him.

After he got up and left, I rushed to make sure the door was closed all the way, listening with my ear pressed it as he retreated downstairs. Once his footsteps were gone completely, I breathed a sigh of relief. Hopefully he didn't notice the necklace was missing.

I opened my eyes in the morning and listened. I was still not used to the quiet. Usually, Mum was getting ready, Dad clumped around with his heavy footfalls. Now when I woke up in the morning, I was met with the hum and tinny buzz of tinnitus that rang ever so slightly whenever it was quiet. I replayed the day with Mum in the bathroom in my head and twitched as though I was drowning.

'Riley, you up? Get your arse out of bed!' Dad called through the door.

I rolled my eyes and sat up, sunlight hitting my face. It was sure going to be a beautiful day after the crazy cold cacophony of a storm last night. A tingling, sharp pain reverberated through the left side of my head. Great, I already had a headache.

As we moved around each other in the kitchen, me getting the yoghurt and berries, he getting the coffee and the milk with the machine chugging along like a train, we avoided eye contact. Adam walked in, rubbing his eyes then stretching his arms up. His tee-shirt lifted and revealed the soft brown hair on his lower abdomen. Dad caught me looking and lightly slapped my shoulder. 'What are you doing?'

I lowered my eyes and replied, 'Nothing.'

We settled around the table and I waited for my fifteen-minute timer to go down, the numbers flashing on the phone in front of me. Once it went off with a high-pitched beep, I started eating. Dad cleared his throat. 'Riley, I'm taking you to school today to meet with your principal after I drop you off.'

I stopped with my hand midway to my mouth. 'What for?'

'With everything that's going on…the school has to stay…updated.'

'It's fine. I'm fine. They're fine.'

Adam snorted and sniffed loudly, rubbing his nose. He caught the glare of my father and apologised, pulling his jacket sleeves down, closer to his fingers and slumped atop the kitchen stool. I frowned at him and Dad leant closer to him to look at his eyes.

'Are you fucking juiced?' he hissed.

Adam shook his head.

'Then what the fuck is wrong with you?'

Adam sat up straighter and glanced at me with a sigh. 'Sorry. Been a long night.'

'Been a long night with your fuck buddy, taking my bloody product,' he snapped in a lowered voice.

I rolled my eyes and shouted, 'It's not a secret. Stop trying to act like it's all a big mystery. I know what you do, Dad.'

He and Adam gaped at me. I pushed my yoghurt away, making the ceramic bowl spin noisily across the marble benchtop. 'Get off his fucking back about it and take me to school, already.' I got up and grabbed my bag, striding to the door, muttering under my breath, 'Jesus Fucking Christ.'

Dad drove me to school with his lips pursed firmly together and his knuckles white on the steering wheel. We parked and I slammed the door and hurried into the building, leaving him to stalk slowly behind me, parting ways to go to the administration office and me to the lockers.

I unpacked my school bag that was full of books that teachers had insisted I take home in case I wanted to take work home. It would help me keep up during this "tough time". I didn't need them at all.

I walked into English class. There was a note pinned to the bulletin board that Mr. Estranger was absent and no casual relief teacher had been available. Go to the gym and join in with the boys' P.E class with Mr. Bacon. He was a new teacher who was too doe-eyed to say no to the administration. P.E with the boys? Great…not. Why was school hard just for the sake of being hard? I wished I was still in primary school. The one I'd gone to was little, on top of a hill. The building encompassed with gum trees that peppered the yard with gumnuts. I yearned for the happy, ever excited and bouncy primary school teachers that wore overalls with wacky prints or book-themed earrings.

We used to spend the day colouring, drawing or playing Simon Says if a teacher was away. Lumping us together with other classes was common at high school. It wasn't that I disliked P.E. It usually got my mind off things. I appreciated the exercise because it helped me swim better and faster. But today, I didn't feel up to playing Dodgeball or doing impromptu beep tests.

When the bell rung, the girls and I swarmed into the gym where the boys were already bouncing basketballs. Mr. Bacon blew his whistle and the boys stopped and went silent, staring at us. The sun disappeared behind a cloud and the gymnasium beams and tin roof creaked as they expanded. Somebody shifted their weight and made a loud screeching sound with their rubber shoe.

Mr. Bacon began directing us into groups like an air traffic controller mixed with a race caller. 'You in that group, you over there. Oi! I said you over there! Listen up!'

I met eyes with Cody, bouncing a basketball from his left hand to his right hand. We nodded at each other and while Mr. Bacon organised teenagers into groups, becoming more flustered. His voice became more and more laced with false bravado as teenagers began speaking over him, Cody and I slipped out into the gym foyer, filled with trophies and sashes. I told him my dad was at school, meeting with the principal.

'About your mum?'

I shrugged. 'I don't know. It can't be good, though.'

'Want to get out of here?' he asked.

I hesitated. If Dad caught me, he'd kill me.

Cody made to the door. 'Because I'm heading out. You can come too if you want.'

I let my heart thump uncomfortably filling my ears and cheeks with too much blood, glanced back at the gym where Mr. Bacon was struggling to control the loud laughter and occasional swears. Go back to that chaos or escape somewhere quiet with Cody? It would not have been a hard choice without the threat of what Dad would do if he found out.

'The bus leaves in two minutes, Riley,' Cody called. 'Better make a decision.'

I rushed after him out into the cloudy carpark and out of the school gates.


The bus let us off in main street of town, opposite a grassy knoll that backed up onto the white sand. We crossed the highway and the knoll by the beach. The beach was void of people, save for one lonely Asian man sitting at the picnic table. The clouds overhead threatened rain, winter at its best. Cody stared at the small pier and headed to it as if remembering something. I followed him. Our shoes made the wood creak and echo; the beat ricocheted up and down the entire pier, and the slats bounced under our feet. It was run-down; the bolts rusted and the wood rotting. A photographer's dream with its rickety palings and barnacled pillars. Sea gulls flapped overhead, disturbed by us walking down their perch.

Cody sat at the very end and I sat beside him, dangling my legs over the edge. Cody stared down at the green water at the tiny silver fish darting about, their images retracted by the light.

'I can't see the bottom.' He smiled at the green surface anyway.

'No,' I replied. I leant over a little more. 'No, I can't either.'

'I can't swim you know,' admitted Cody.

There was something about sitting on the edge of a precipice, dangling your feet above a bottomless sea that opened a person up, I guess. I wondered if it would affect me in the same way, but all I could reply was, 'Oh.' I felt an icy shard pierce the space between my collar and the back of my neck and looked up at the sky, expecting rain to pour down on us at any second.

'Do you think your mum's okay?' he asked.

I shrugged. The day in the bathroom replaying again in my mind.

Wherever she was, she was probably better off than she had ever been. I stared at the water and whispered, 'I don't know anything. I didn't see anything. I really, really didn't. I have a lot of questions for her,' I said, feeling my lip curling with disgust. 'Why she did what she did.'

'Me too.'

I looked at him. He explained, 'I mean, I have those questions for Adam. Why he had to leave me.'

I nodded.

'He used to bring me here.' He smiled to himself. 'I'd forgotten it existed until we got here and I saw it. When things would go wrong, he'd bring me here. Dad and the nanny were fighting, I was failing a class, if I fell off my bike,' he laughed at the absurdity of the contrasting problems. 'He's been gone for such a long time that I forgot to come down here…and *appreciate* him, and his presence in my life.'

'Mmm,' I murmured, looking back down at the water. I couldn't really share how I appreciated his brother too when he'd left Cody to come look after me instead.

Cody said, 'It's the little things that make you who you are, you know,' he caught my eye and raised his bushy eyebrows to make a point before we both looked down at the small fish under the pier. 'Not the big things.'

We spent the day wandering around the beach. The two of us loitered at the rock pools on the other side of the headland. We immersed our lungs in the stench of the low-tide and poked at a blue-ringed octopus with a stick, both of us squealing as it raged with its rings. We stepped from rock to rock, crouching until our muscles ached.

Cody and I sat together on the pier again to eat our lunch, dropping pinches of bread to the fish. Two pelicans swooped in and hedged their bets on us to get some, too but were unlucky so gave us the side-eye of disdain. If only life could be this simple, I wished. One day, I could be free to live my life, free of my dad and the issues that he caused. It could just be and Adam, or me and Cody. I only needed to wait it out and see it played.

My stomach shuddered when it was time to go back to school, leaving on the 2:30 bus to make it in time before the bell went. On the bus, picking at my chapped lips, staring into space with the thoughts orbiting around my head. Had my father noticed I was gone? I didn't think so. Adam would have found me by now if my dad realised that I had gone missing. Missing like my mother. Wouldn't that be ironic?

# 12 ADAM

I stood on the pier beside the boss's yacht. The gentle slapping of the water against the posts made my head pound. I blinked with each pulse and my hands twitched at my side. The pier swayed with its soft rhythm and I was sea sick.

I knelt and purged into the water, nothing but bile. I should have eaten something after the binge last night, but my stomach was full with the knot that cut me inside.

My bile dissolved with the aquamarine water then forced myself to stagger back to the house. I'd have to tell the boss I was sick and I needed to go home.

A glint of jewellery caught my eye on the track between steps. A necklace, diamonds with a big blue stone and gold trimming with a pearl. Rachelle's. Riley had been wearing it last time I saw it. I picked it up, brushed the sand from the stone and felt the granules scratching the stone. I put it my pocket and continued back to the house.

Inside, I found the boss hunched over his mobile phone, hand gripping the side of his head as though he felt as shit as I did with a pounding on the side of the head.

'Boss,' I said. He looked up. 'I reckon I caught a bug. I think I should probably go home.'

'Yeah, sure,' he sighed.

As I turned to leave, the boss asked, 'You've been off a bit, lately, Adam…Don't you think?'

I swallowed to quell the rise of nausea in my gut. If he knew anything at all beyond the realm of his drug dealing and addiction to sleeping pills, I was in deep shit. If he knew I was taking too much cocaine, I'd lose my job. If he knew what his wife had done to his child, and that I knew it – keeping it a secret from him – I was a goner.

I shrugged. 'Guess it's just stress.'

He nodded, looking down at his hands, and murmured, 'Yeah, that I can understand.'

'How are you doing?' I asked.

'I'm…worried about Riley,' he replied.

'She's okay.'

He took a deep breath and said, 'I mean, I'm worried that she knows something about her mother that we don't.'

I said, 'I don't think she does; she was in the hospital when Rachelle disappeared. She'll be okay.'

The boss shook his head and rubbed his cheek like he was pawing at an invisible insect the way I had. 'I've got to sort out this mess.'

I bit my cheek as his shoulders slumped. 'It's not…your mess. Just leave it alone.'

The boss nodded and balled his fist, tapping it into his palm. 'I just worry that somebody took her from me, to hurt me.'

I said firmly, 'She'll turn up. Everyone does in the end.' Everything would be fine – as long as I was above the surface.

.

# 13 ACKERMAN

A surfer skipped amongst the rocks to make the long paddle out into Cat Bay. Seagulls dived and squawked, fighting over a clump of seaweed. The surfer made deep strokes, hands cupping through seaweed as he went over to investigate what he thought was a seal carcass. He yanked on the seaweed and discovered a clump of blonde hair.

With a scream, he back paddled so fast that he fell off his board and scraped his back along the sharp rocks. He rushed back to shore, eager to not be shark bait. Eager to be as far away from the body as he could. He vomited up his green smoothie. He flagged down the park ranger who was driving down the road.

The report came to me later that morning. The woman they had found was blonde, had been in the water for around three days. She had a significant head wound. Was this my missing person?

Burke had an appointment with an obstetrician so a probationary constable named Emanuel, E for short, joined me. We made our way to the island and met with the island officers. They stood by the body, now on the beach. Locals stood atop the cliff to get a glimpse of the body. The local officers had wrapped her in a tarp. The media trained their cameras on our every step.

I squatted beside the body, trying not to inhale the stench of salty gas. I lifted the tarp carefully so that I could glimpse at the face of the woman. I lowered it again and looked down at the beach, awash with pebbles and shells, quelling the urge to swear.

'Is it her?' E asked from behind me, his back to the bay and the tide slapping at his heels.

I swallowed. 'I think so, but I can't say officially.'

The paramedics stepped forward to collect the body once I nodded it was fine for them to do so. They did everything silently, sombre, respectful. I met the park ranger, a young bloke by the name of Johnno. He pointed out the surfer that had discovered the body. He was sitting nearby the ambulance, comforted by a female friend. Johnno then pointed to the general area where the body was discovered in a clump of seaweed. It was strewn nearby the tarp. I told E to bag up the seaweed as evidence which he started immediately. As the paramedics took the body to the hospital for the Verification of Death, I approached the surfer.

'You all right, mate?'

He nodded at me, green in the face and trembling. His friend tightened her grip on his arm. 'I thought she was a bloody seal,' he croaked and laughed uncomfortably. 'What a bloody idiot I am.'

'You're not an idiot. You did the right thing going to check. You'll be giving her family a lot of closure.' Dominic Flynn's face flashed in my mind and the cold daughter. Closure for something they may or may not need closure for, but closure all the same.

He sighed. 'Do you know how she died for sure?'

I shook my head.

'Shit,' he said and burst into tears. 'What a fucking way to die. Dead in the seaweed like that. Fuck me.' His girlfriend pulled him into a hug.

I handed her my card. 'I'm Senior Constable Ackerman. If you need anyone to talk to, I'm always available. I'll make sure you get the help you need.'

She thanked me and frowned at the card. 'You're in Missing Persons.'

'That's right.'

'Was she a missing person?'

'I can't say. The body will need to be identified, then examined. If you have any questions, you can call and ask.'

'Thanks.'

'Any time,' I said and walked back up the cliff with E. I glanced back at him, still sobbing in the arms of his friend. People always overlook the people that find the bodies. It always becomes about THE BODY and their grieving family, but nobody ever thinks of the poor sons of bitches who chance across their bodies. First responders, fellow victims, some random young bloke going for his morning surf. Nobody ever asks about the person who finds the body.

By the time I arrived back at the station, Burke had returned from her appointment. She was sitting in the corner, at her desk, eating a souvlaki, garlic sauce dripping on the napkins. Her mouth was full when I walked in with E and the seaweed. She stood and said with her mouth full, 'Wozzit-her?'

I suppressed a gag at the sight of the chewed meat in her mouth and replied quietly, 'I think it was. Blonde, around 44.'

Burke forced her food down with a grimace. 'Which hospital did the coroner send her to?'

'Frankston.' I sighed. 'I guess this means we'll need Flynn to do an identification.'

Burke nodded. 'Yep. Want me to do the announcement?'

I shook my head. 'No, I'll do it.' I shook hands with E, 'Thanks for your help, today, man. I know it's not a pleasant thing to do.'

'Any time, mate,' he smiled weakly and went onto his paperwork duties.

Burke finished her lunch and wiped her hands on her pants. 'Let's go now.'

We arrived at the Flynn house at 4:02. He had just picked his daughter up from school. We parked in the street and watched the daughter get out of the car in a huff and go inside. Mr. Flynn stayed in his car, and remained there until we approached on foot. I knocked on the driver's side window and he jolted upright, clutching at his seatbelt, looking at me with watery eyes.

'Mr. Flynn – we, um...' I began but my voice failed. I cleared my throat as he opened the car door. 'Could you step outside with us, please?'

'Yes?' He stepped out of the car and tried to make it look like I hadn't just caught him crying in his car. He leant against the bonnet of his car.

Burke said, 'Something has come up, Mr. Flynn. I'm afraid that we may have found your wife.'

'Found my wife?' His face was emotionless.

'Yes.'

'Where?'

'Cat Bay – Phillip Island,' I answered.

'Why couldn't you bring her home?'

Burke and I exchanged glances.

'We need to accompany you to the morgue, Mr. Flynn, for a positive identification of the body,' Burke said with her voice lowered.

'I'm sorry?'

Burke repeated herself.

'What – what body?'

'Your wife's.'

I understood how he felt. His wife didn't *have* a body. His wife was now *a* body. It made no sense whatsoever when you hear it about your loved one. I'd felt the same way when my parents had been killed. It was genuine confusion.

'What do you want me to do?' he asked again.

Burke explained we would drive him to the morgue and he what was required of him.

'But I have Riley...' he mumbled.

'Is there someone who can mind Riley while we do this?' Burke asked.

Flynn snapped, 'No. She's coming with me.'

Burke and I exchanged glances before she said quietly, 'All due respect, it may be a little too much for her to handle; it is her mother, after all.'

'What about me?'

Burke stared at him, expectantly. Waiting.

'I refuse to go with you.'

'Mr. Flynn,' I sighed with exasperation.

'I'll come down but only if I can bring my own car and I can bring my daughter. I'm not leaving her by herself.'

'We can't legally let you drive home,' I explained. 'If you drive there, you're not going to be allowed to drive home yourself. I don't know if you've ever had to see a body before, Mr. Flynn, but this may be quite difficult for you to deal with.'

His jaw set and he glared at me. 'I know what I can deal with, you little prick.'

I went to reprimand him but Burke interrupted, 'Fine. Follow us then,' and led me back out the driveway.

# 14 RILEY

I sat on my swing in my bedroom and swung forward and back, using my toes as an anchor. The day with Cody had been the best day I'd had in a long, long time. Not since spending the day with Adam on the beach chasing seagulls had my heart felt so light. I watched the sky darken in the window. The afternoon sun was dull and overtaken by murky clouds as the temperature dropped.

Dad came to the door and leant against it with a heavy breath. 'I need you to come with me.'

'Where?' I asked.

He swallowed hard. 'I have to run an errand. Just come for a drive.'

'Where's Adam? Can't he look after me?'

'He's sick.'

I nodded with a sigh, and followed him back downstairs, pulling on a grey woollen jumper. There was a police car at the bottom of the drive but I didn't say anything. Dad drove with stiff arms. He checked his rear vision mirror, indicated, braked, and accelerated softly. His face was set and there were no fluid motions. He was stiff. Robotic. The police car led his path, the red and blue lights a beacon.

'Why are you following the police?' I asked.

'Just running an errand.'

'Dad, just tell me what's going on,' I demanded.

He spun the radio volume dial to the right. I sat back in my seat. I glared at my reflection in the window, which was getting clearer as it got darker. We stopped at a red traffic light but the police car cruised through.

Dad cursed quietly and drummed his fingers on the steering wheel. 'Can't they see I got caught back here? They want me to bloody follow them but then leave me sitting here. I won't know where to go for Christ's sake!' His bottom lip dropped. He swore again and then punched the steering wheel and made the horn beep. The calmness had evaporated.

'Calm down,' I said.

'Don't tell me to calm down, Riley; I swear to mother fucking GOD!'

'What the hell is wrong with you?' I snapped.

The light went green and he punched his foot to the floor, causing the car to veer sideways twice before going straight, leaving me clutching to the bar.

'This can't be bloody happening,' Dad snarled at the windscreen. He was coming more and more apart with each wheel revolution. His hands trembled.

'Just tell me where we're going.' He didn't even acknowledge me so I shouted, 'Tell me what the fuck is happening, you arse hole!'

His eye twitched. He pulled the car into the emergency lane and turned the engine off. He bowed his head and hunched over the steering wheel. My heart began to beat in my throat.

Trying to get his attention, I decided to use his name. I asked, 'What's going on, Dom? Answer me.'

He finally answered me, but not with his voice. He laid into me, punching me repeatedly with fierce anger that I'd never seen before and slammed my face into the dashboard. I yelped with each blow, and pulled away, hitting my back against the car door. I screamed and tried to cover my face and head from him. Punch after punch, he continued until I managed to undo my seatbelt with one hand and open the car door. I fell out of the car onto the bitumen road, coughing. I sobbed and spat out a mouthful of blood. My body was so knuckled that I couldn't find the strength to climb to my feet.

Dad got out of the car, and screamed at me, 'Don't disrespect me, Riley! Do not call me DOM. I am your father.' He grabbed me by my armpits and dragged me back into the car. To escape the pain, I let him buckle me back in. He slammed the door before my foot was completely inside the car and I yowled like a wounded cat. He muttered something too quietly for me to hear and got back into the driver seat. He slammed his own door, started the car and sped off.

I stared at him through the blur of tears wondering why I deserved such a severe beating. Blood tickled my face as it travelled from the side of my forehead, dripping down into my hands. I didn't dare ask him any more questions.

We drove through town with the moon rising, making the wet road glow. We arrived at the hospital an hour away from home and I grew more mystified. Dad parked the car and turned it off. He drew in a deep breath before he reached for the glove box, making me reel backwards from him. He pulled out a first-aid kit and opened it. The next thing he retrieved was a small box of peroxide.

He looked me in the eye, with the same calm expression he had worn earlier. I looked down at my hands. He pulled tissues from a packet, tipped the peroxide onto the wad of tissues. He handed me the damp clump of tissues.

'You need to clean yourself up…' Dad looked down at his bloody knuckles and admitted, 'I don't want anyone to ask any questions.'

My lip trembled.

He sniffed. 'You need to stay with me to be safe.'

I dabbed at my face, mainly my forehead and lip. Dad watched every move and it scared me almost as much as the assault. I shakily brushed the tissues of peroxide over my stinging palms until he whispered, 'That's enough.'

He took the tissues from me, put them back into the kit and tucked it all safely away again in the glove box.

My teeth started to chatter. 'Why are we here?'

He didn't answer but glanced out the window and said softly, 'I don't know if I can go in there, Riley.'

I searched his face before whispering, 'Do you have to?'

He yelled suddenly, making me shrink against the door again. 'She is my wife!' He put his hands on his head and blinked tears away. He added with a tearful croak, 'She was my wife.'

My heart was beating so hard that it seemed to lurch out of rhythm. 'What?'

'I can't...' he mumbled. 'I don't think I can do it. You can do it for me.'

'Do what?' I gasped.

'Let's just go in.' He opened the door and I followed him, completely lost and confused. His words didn't make sense. I walked at his side, holding onto his hand with my stinging hand, being the good daughter.

We went down to the basement level. I'd seen enough television to know what that meant. I staggered, leaning my body back. Dad pulled me along, gripping my hand tight enough to turn my fingertips blue.

The was a hum of the air travelling through the tunnels above our heads. We were quiet, except for the occasional squeak of my shoe on the reflective, smooth floor. We went into a room with a glass wall that gazed into a sterile room. I lost my breath and fell back against the opposite wall when I noticed the body. There was a body on a table in the centre of that sterile room. It was covered and a person stood nearby, ready to uncover it.

Dad stepped to the glass and nodded. 'I'm ready.'

I slammed my eyes closed as soon as I saw her face, but it stayed with me. It morphed into how she had sat in the bath, hugging her legs, waiting for me to die.

The police officer closest to me, the woman, wrapped her arm around me and led me out back into the corridor. She held my cheeks between her cool hands and I opened my eyes reluctantly to look at her. 'I am so sorry.'

She went blurry through my tears.

'Riley?' Dad came out of the room with the other police officer, a man. The woman officer stepped away from me. Dad asked if I was okay. I shook my head.

The two police officers looked pointedly at each other.

'I want to go home,' I whispered.

'We can take you both home,' the male police officer said. 'We can't let you drive.'

'I'll get someone to drive us. Thank you.'

The police officers nodded in unison. The man looked at me. 'Can I give you my card if you need to chat?'

I glanced at Dad. He didn't say anything so I reached out and took his card. We left the basement floor. Once the police were behind us, Dad wrestled the card out of my fingers and stuck it in his pocket.

Outside the hospital, Dad called Adam. 'I know you're sick, but my wife is fucking dead. I just had to identify her God damned body. Just get to Frankston Hospital and pick us up. They won't let me drive...I don't care about your car; just catch a bus and you can drive my car...Yes, I'll let you drive it. Just stop gushing like a whore and get here!'

I hugged my body against the cool evening air, teeth chattering. The overhead lights of the parking lot sheared in different directions, making me squint.

So...she *was* dead. It was official. She'd abandoned me with this monster. At least I would stop wondering where she was and what had happened afterwards. She was here at the hospital.

I glanced back behind us at the two police officers, waiting for us to get a ride, watching but trying to act casual. Arms crossed, legs hip-width apart, assertive confidence and assurance that they always got their way. I rubbed my fingers together where Dad had snatched the card from me. I remembered the name. It was Senior Constable Johan Ackerman, Missing Persons Investigation Squad. I wish I knew the name of the woman. She seemed to really care. She'd be a good mother, unlike mine.

I stood beside my father and waited for Adam to arrive. Adam. The man my mother didn't trust but I trusted with my life. My breath caught in my throat and I had to force myself to swallow. I trusted Adam. No matter what.

# 15 ACKERMAN

The father's hands were red and darkening to a purple. The girl's face was marked, red and swollen; a scratch ran down from her forehead to her cheek. I couldn't believe he had taken her into the viewing room to identify his wife. She seemed like a smart enough kid to know what she was about to be faced with; she'd practically been dragged into the room, despite Burke offering to wait outside with her. He hadn't listened. I watched his face as Rachelle's face was uncovered. A swallow, a blink. A look down with a nod. Burke had got her out the door as rapidly as she could. I stayed with Mr. Flynn and he signed the paperwork the medical examiner needed.

Yes, it was Rachelle Flynn. Yes, she would have a post-mortem. Yes, she was an organ donor. The coroner would be deciding everything from there on for an inquest. Burke and I would return the belongings and even make the call to the funeral parlour for him if he wanted.

We exited the room and I gave the girl my card. I still wanted to interview her. She was the last person to see her mother alive. The investigation would be going to someone else now that Rachelle was deceased. Curiosity – or a gut feeling, police instinct – made me want to look deeper. Why had Rachelle even gone missing in the first place?

Once they were picked up and had left earshot, Burke and I spoke at the same time. 'Did you see the marks on her face?'

Burke crossed her arms and shook her head. 'Something stinks there, for sure.'

'He had marks on his fist.' I started walking to the car and Burke followed me, having to waddle slightly for the first few steps. 'She was the last person who saw Rachelle alive, so is it all right if I go do a follow-up tomorrow?'

'You can do that, and I'm going to make a mandatory report.' She got into the car with some difficulty. 'Make CPS aware. I think we're looking at a case of abuse.'

'There's definitely reason to think he's a suspect then?'

She sighed. 'See what the post-mortem rules as cause of death then the coroner can decide what happens next.'

The muscles in my neck tightened and I asked, 'Do you get used to not finding the answers? I want to follow it through.'

She placed a hand on the centre console and replied, 'Mate, just finding the body is closure enough. If you want to see it to the end, you may have to look at working in homicide.'

I chewed on the inside of my mouth as I drove us back to the station. There was a heaviness in my forehead that stretched across to the back of my neck. She had a point. I'd joined Missing Persons to help people and find them, bring them back home. My first official case had resulted in a DOA. It was not as satisfying to hand over the pockets of DNA and evidence to the coronial inquest as I had hoped.

# 16 ADAM

I took the boss and the kid home and followed them inside. Riley checked her blood sugar and made herself dinner. The boss went and showered. Everything seemed so…normal. My head shattered with the thought of Rachelle being dead. I watched Riley eating and wanted to scream WHAT THE FUCK IS WRONG WITH YOU? YOUR MOTHER IS DEAD but I stayed quiet, my head still thumping from the migraine from earlier in the day. We didn't speak at all until the boss came out of the shower, wearing grey hoodie and sweatpants, with brown hair slicked back.

'Thanks for the ride, Adam,' he said. He opened the refrigerator and drank from the bottle of juice. 'You can crash here tonight if you want; I'll take you home in the morning.'

'What about school?' Riley asked.

'You want to go to school?' He glared at her. 'Riley, take the day off. Your mother is dead.'

'You keeping me away from school wouldn't have anything to do with what you just did to my face, does it?' she said coolly.

'What did happen to your face?' I asked.

The boss waved his hand. 'I had just been told the love of my life was dead on a table at the morgue. You misbehaved. I overreacted. I

93

apologised then and I'm apologising now. Can we move on?'

'I'm going to school,' she hissed, pushing the stool back and going upstairs. 'I'm going to bed. Leave me alone.'

We watched her stomp up the stairs and heard the slam of her bedroom door. The boss shook his head and looked at me expectantly. 'What can I even do with her? She's been so sullen since Rachelle went missing.' He bit his lip and tucked his chin in as he realised that Rachelle hadn't just gone missing. She had died. 'I mean...'

'I know, boss,' I said. I took the necklace from my pocket and handed it to him. 'I want to give this to you. Riley was wearing it.'

'You took it off her?'

I hesitated. 'No...should I have?'

'How did you get it then?'

'I found it on the path to the beach.' I pointed outside like he could see where I had retrieved it, even though it was like black chalk outside. 'Thought I better give it back to you.'

He flexed his jaw. 'So, she took it from her mother then fucking lost it. Perfect.'

'Boss,' I said to stop him going upstairs. 'It's harder than you think to lose your mum.'

He looked at me and paused. 'That's right; your mother died.'

I nodded.

'So, you can speak to Riley for me.'

'I can be there for her.'

He snorted. 'Yeah, be there for her and don't take your fucking eyes off her.'

I nodded slowly. 'I'm here if she needs me.'

'Good chat,' he said, slapping me on the back. 'Thanks again, Adam. Really appreciate you.'

Before I turned in for the night, I knocked on Riley's door and let myself in. She was sitting up in bed, reading a book.

'Hey.'

'Hey,' she replied, not looking up.

I sat down on her bed and took the book from her. The book's red cover and the piercing eyes between the ribbons of red made me read the title. *Without Conscience* by Robert D Hare. A study into psychopathy. I put it face-down on the bedspread to keep the eyes from glaring out at me more. 'You shouldn't be reading stuff like this,' I mumbled, shaking my head. 'You should be reading John Green books or Harry Potter or shit like that.'

'Oh right. I forgot. I'm just a kid.'

'Well...yeah,' I replied.

'Hell of a way to be growing up then,' she whispered, still not looking up at me. I lifted her face to see what her father had done.

'Shit, Riley...I'm sorry. I should have been here.'

'Where were you?' she asked.

'I was sick...had to go home.'

'Can't you stay here? I don't want to be alone with him.'

The scratch going from her forehead to her cheek was raised and her lip was split. Her hands were scraped and a bruise on her eye was emerging. My job was to keep the kid safe at all costs. I began to wonder if the boss wanted me to keep her safe or keep her quiet. I wrapped her into a hug and waited for her to cry, but she didn't. She stayed as quiet as the book face-down on her bedspread.

# 17 RILEY

The quietness still unnerved me, like being alone in a cavernous hole until a spider crept up behind you with its hairy legs. Waking up to that quiet made me shudder. I sat at the dresser with my legs folded in a cross-legged position. The reflection showed me what my father had done to my face. Mum had taught me how to adapt bruises on our skin so it would be passable to go out into society. Dad could try to stop me going to school if it couldn't be covered. It hurt to smile, so I frowned, but it hurt more to frown, so I smiled anyway.

I dabbed with the concealer and caked on the foundation, layer by layer. Adding eye makeup made me itch. I puckered my lips and applied the lipstick as well, making myself look like the clown I was. I tied my hair back in a ponytail, over-tightened it. The hair tie snapped and flung across the room. I stared down at it for a moment then lifted my chin at my reflection in the mirror.

'You've got this,' I whispered to myself. 'This is where your life begins.'

Stepping out of my bedroom, I lingered near the bathroom. The door had been replaced with a tacky aqua coloured door that still needed to be painted white to match the walls. The hole in the wall opposite the door had been plastered over with a white smear, a grey lead pencil mark noted PATCH HERE PLEASE. Dad – always the control freak, even when covering up what he had done.

He'd pay for what he'd done to my mother and go down for it. I'd find the necklace that should have been mine all along, be with Adam, or Cody, and be free of him. I wouldn't have to wake up to the quiet of the house with the spider anymore. I'd be waking up with a peaceful quiet, the quiet of security, safety. No man would hit me ever again. Adam would protect me and keep me from being hurt by monsters in my house. I wouldn't go out the way she did.

# 18 ACKERMAN

I rapped on the Flynn's front door with my knuckles and pressed the doorbell on the intercom. A loud buzzing sound resonated throughout the house that it was even shrill outside where Burke and I stood. The door opened and the guy I'd made eyes with the day before stood in the doorway. He had messy brown hair, a square-ish jaw and big eyes that looked me up and down. He had dirt under his nicotine-stained fingernails.

'G'day,' said Burke. I looked behind him at the foyer and swept with my eyes up the stairs where the girl was coming down, carrying a school bag and a lot of makeup to hide the hideous facial wounds.

'Hi,' said the man, too brightly.

'Senior Constable Burke and Senior Constable Ackerman; we're returning some of his wife's belongings to Dominic Flynn.'

The man flicked his head back to clear his forehead of a tendril of hair. I scrutinized him as he forced a smile. 'Sure. I'll get him.'

'May we come in?' asked Burke.

'Um,' he said, glancing behind him and then answered, 'Sure.'

Dominic Flynn appeared, rolling up his sleeves on his dress shirt as though getting ready to get into some hard manual labour. He shook our hands and said to his friend, 'You can take Riley to school now.

Take my car.' A muscle in his jaw ticked and I smiled politely as the man and Riley passed us and exited the house. Riley gave me one glance over the shoulder so I held my hand up in a wave. She didn't smile or wave back, just turned back and got into the BMW that was parked in the driveway.

Flynn led us into the kitchen where we sat at the large kitchen table. He stood while we sat.

'Mr. Flynn, how are you holding up?' asked Burke.

He clasped his hands together and said, with a shake in his voice, 'Well, it hasn't really sunken in yet to be honest, officers.'

'That's understandable.'

'Um,' he scratched his head. 'I'm a little curious why you are here.'

Burke produced the bag of his wife's belongings we had picked up from the medical examiner. Clothes. Wedding ring. Bobby pins. Her wet socks that had run blue from the jeans she had been wearing that had even stained her skin a mottled cornflower blue.

'We're very sorry for your loss.'

'Oh,' Flynn mumbled and took the bag, eyes fluttering. He coughed to disguise, or plant, a sob. 'Thank you.' He covered his mouth.

We sat in silence while he regained his stern expression and rolled back his broad shoulders, nodding. 'Thanks for bringing these by.'

'Sir, we also have an update on the provisional cause of death,' Burke said.

Flynn's hand fell from his mouth. 'Didn't she just…drown?'

'With all due respect Mr. Flynn, your wife drowned under quite suspicious circumstances,' I said with a quiet voice. 'We just want to let you know that the case is still open and we need to clear your name.'

'Clear my name?' Flynn scoffed. 'Clear my name of what? She ran away and must have fallen in the water. What has that got to do with my name?'

'Sir,' began Burke.

'No!' Flynn interjected. 'She drowned. I had nothing to do with it. How many times do I have to tell that to you people?'

'How did she get into the water? Why did she go into the water?' Burke said calmly, glancing at the notepad she was holding in her lap.

Flynn shrugged. 'I wasn't there.'

'So how do you know she drowned?' I said, leaning back and crossing my arms.

Flynn opened his mouth to answer but no sound came out. He hung his head and answered with resignation, 'I don't know.' He gave a flippant wave. 'It's all so fuzzy.'

'Why do you think she ran off in the first place?' I asked.

Flynn shook his head. 'I guess she was running off on me. Wives are allowed to do that, mate.'

'Were there any other witnesses? Anybody here around the time she disappeared?' Burke clicked her pen impatiently.

'No.'

'Your young friend...your daughter...'

'No.'

Burke looked at me with an irritated raise of the eyebrow so I stood up. 'Are you sure about that sir?' I said with a glaring squint. I channelled my inner Clint Eastwood and silently said *come on, make my day, punk.*

'No. They weren't here.' Flynn rolled his shoulders and braced his jaw. 'I already told you that I had to take Riley to the hospital.'

'And we've already told you that we know you didn't take Riley to the hospital.'

'Your wife had a significant head wound. How do you think she got that, sir?' Burke asked.

He looked at the floor for a moment before asking, 'Maybe she tripped?'

'Tripped?' I uttered.

He shrugged. 'Isn't this your job to find out?'

'You think she may have tripped, hit her head and fell into the water and drowned?' Burke said, writing notes.

'I don't know,' he groaned. 'I wasn't there!'

'We have one more thing to chat to you about, Mr. Flynn,' said Burke, closing the notepad. Flynn almost let out a breath of relief. 'Handling grief after a tragedy like this is very difficult. We'd like to keep an eye on you, and your family, to make sure that you cope all right. If you ever find yourself waking up at night,' she produced a card from her pocket. 'Please, don't hesitate to give me a call. This kind of thing can be really tough, especially for children, like your daughter.'

Flynn took the card and said, 'Thanks. I'll keep it by the phone.'

As we stood to leave, he held up a palm for us to stop. We waited. He jiggled his leg a few times before he spoke again. 'I do have something I need you to do for me. Wait here.'

He went upstairs. We waited. When he returned, he held the necklace from the master bedroom in both his hands. He held it out to Burke and she took it carefully, eyes running over the glinting stones.

'This was my wife's. I bought it for her as a gift.'

'Extravagant gift,' Burke uttered.

'Yes,' he agreed. He stuck his hands in his pocket and rocked back on his heels. 'I like to provide for my family.' My mind went to the marks on Riley's face, not the jewellery. He added, 'I would like her to be buried with it. It meant so much to her. I…can't keep it.'

'Why not?' I asked.

He made eye contact with me and replied as though I was stupid, 'It hurts too much.'

Burke nodded. 'We'll drop it by the funeral parlour right now.'

He thanked us and we left. As I drove to the funeral parlour, Burke studied the necklace and shook her head. 'This has got to be worth a lot of money.'

'No doubt,' I said.

'Seems strange that he would just be happy to have it buried with her.'

'How did he make all his money?' I asked.

'As a jeweller?'

'Yeah. I don't think they earn that much, do they?'

Burke rubbed her bump, looking out the window at the other mansions. 'It sure seems like they do.'

'His hands are so dirty – surely there's something about him.'

Burke shrugged. 'Well, that's for the coroner to determine. Whether it's a homicide or not…then it'll go over to homicide. All we need to do is declare her no longer a missing person.'

I sighed through my nostrils. 'I know, I know.'

Burke rifled through her lunchbox and produced a sandwich. She had insatiable hunger; I learnt very early on in our partnership to not comment on how much she ate. She took a bite of her sandwich and said with her mouth full, 'It's really none of our business now, except reporting the daughter to CPS.'

'I want to talk to the girl. The daughter.'

'Potential witness?'

'Witness,' I declared. Burke raised an eyebrow but I could see a faint smile of approval emerging from behind her sandwich.

I added, 'He lied about taking her to hospital so I think she saw something. I *know* she saw something.'

'Right,' Burke said, taking another bite and pausing to chew. 'We interview the girl and we need his supervision or approval – we interview the young guy that took her to the hospital and we need nothing. I think we're better off finding out who he is – have you caught a name?'

I shook my head. 'It was her mother, not his. We'll get a better emotional response from the girl.'

Burke waggled her finger at me, the smile on her face spreading to lift her swollen cheeks. 'You be careful, young man – at this rate, you'll make a fine homicide detective.'

I smiled, my face going hot.

# 19 CODY

I lingered on the basketball court. I had a free period and I was supposed to be studying, but I was sick of always doing well and having perfect marks without even trying. Was I even intelligent if I couldn't see that I was heading down the exact same path my dad wanted me to? I admired Adam for getting away. I'd get away too, somehow.

I glanced up when Riley Flynn walked out of the classroom and my stomach did small loops. I could talk to her again.

She sat on a low post-and-rail fence by the staff carpark, looking like the typical teenage loser with a furtive look back at the classroom where she had come from. She pulled out a crinkled cigarette that she lit with her head drawn downwards. I walked up behind her and sat next to her. She butted the cigarette quickly under her shoe and looked up with alarm. Her skin was plastered with makeup, but it didn't quite hide the swollen lip and forehead.

'Are you okay?' I asked with a gasp.

'You scared me. I thought you were a teacher,' she sighed.

'Sorry.'

'It's okay,' she replied and stared at the ground.

I paused. 'I saw the news this morning.' Riley Flynn's mother had been found, dead in the water.

'So?' Riley retorted.

'Kind of surprised you're here today, is all.' I shunted the basketball in my hands, anchored to the pimple grip exterior.

'I'm fine,' she said.

'Really?'

'Yep.'

'Are you sure?' I looked more closely at the swollen parts of her face and thought I could see a split lip and a bruise coming up on her forehead under a scratch.

'I'm fine, Cody. What do you want?' She glared at me.

'Have you spoken to Adam yet?' I felt awful about asking about my brother but she wasn't opening up about herself.

'Cody,' she groaned.

'No, no. I get it.' I scuffed my school shoes on the concrete and hugged the basketball to my chest. 'But I was wondering, maybe, since you're upset, I could, you know…' I shrugged and avoided her interrogating eyes.

'What?'

'Maybe I could come over while he's there and give solace to you.'

'Solace?' she snorted and started walking away, shaking her head. 'I don't need solace from you, Cody, or anybody. I'm all right.'

I followed behind her. 'Your mum just died, Riley.'

She looked at the ground as she muttered, 'I've got to find my necklace.'

She continued walking away, leaving me rooted to the spot. I stared after her, thinking she cares that her mum is dead…surely. She wasn't stopping so I called after her, 'Riley!' I was loud enough but she kept walking. Out of the gate and down the shady street, ignoring me. There was the distinct scent of pollen coming through and the air felt sickishly sweet. Stifling, stealing my breath from me before I'd even fully-inhaled.

I sprinted after her. I ran with flat feet and pumping fists; I'd never be an Olympic sprinter. I could make it as a pizza delivery boy.

Wouldn't that be my dad's dream? One son a runaway miscreant, mixed up with crime and one a pimply flat-footed pizza delivery boy.

I reached Riley's side, my shoes clomping on the pavement and my breathing ragged. I puffed, 'I was calling you.'

'I was ignoring you,' she replied with a thin mouth without meeting my eyes, but she did slow her pace.

'So where are we going?' I asked. I wanted to quiz her on the strange evasiveness of what was a very important deal. Losing your mother to a drowning accident was a tragedy. Surely, she cared and wanted to talk about it. Even if she didn't, shouldn't she cry or be morose or confused? Yet Riley walked with confidence and purpose, nothing I could pinpoint on her face as an emotion.

Riley muttered, 'I'm going to go see someone.'

'Who?' I matched my pace to hers and we walked into the main street of the town centre.

She didn't answer for a while but eventually stopped and sighed. 'Someone who can give me something I need.'

'Right…and what do you need, Riley?'

'Information.'

Her blue eyes glazed and I was stumped for words for a moment before I replied finally with a swallow, 'Where?'

'She lives above the Vietnamese restaurant,' she said, gesturing upwards at the dank, flat window of the unit above the restaurant. It had stained and cracking render with red brick showing through in spots.

'Who does?' I asked.

She led me by my hand, which I worried was clammy after almost giving myself an asthma attack. We went up a creaking, carpeted staircase to a room with an open door, brown beads hung down from the doorframe. Inside, there were two bean bags, a futon and a pile of thick boots that all seemed to be of different topics. There was a woman sitting on the futon. She didn't get up to greet us. She looked up with glazed eyes as we walked in.

'What are you doing here?' she asked in a thick French accent.

Riley's hand dropped from mine and I closed my fingers gently on my empty palm. I shifted my feet on the grimy carpet that was flecked with dirt and crumbs. The smell of smoke and something I couldn't put my finger on was smothering. I wanted to leave, run out of there.

Riley crossed her arms and clammed up like a stubborn baby refusing its greens; the corners of her mouth tilted downwards towards her chin. She stared at the floor.

The French woman turned her attention to me and asked, 'Why are you here?'

I swallowed hard to unstick my throat. 'Riley's mum died.'

The woman's eyes sharpened and she said, 'I know. What does that have to do with me?'

'I don't know,' I stammered and nudged Riley.

Riley replied, barely louder than a murmur. 'I can tell the police I didn't see anything, Tempany.'

Tempany finally stood up. 'I don't believe you. You see a lot of things. You saw me with your dad and you'll squeal and they'll come looking for me to blame.'

I gaped at them.

'I didn't see anything,' Riley replied. 'Can we leave it at that?'

Tempany's eyes narrowed at Riley and she asked, 'Did you see him do something to your mum?'

I stared at Riley. It hadn't ever even occurred to me that Riley may have seen what had happened to her mum. Maybe that was why she was acting weird. I leant back, urging my legs to move, yet they wouldn't. I stayed there between the two of them both glaring at each other.

Riley snapped, 'It doesn't matter if you believe me or not. I'm telling you: I didn't see anything.'

'Then why are you here?' Tempany asked.

'Were you there?' she asked. 'When she went into the sea?'

Tempany shook her head and moved towards Riley and pulled her into a hug and she said, 'I'm sorry that she died.'

Riley was silent, her throat probably as sticky as mine. I guess Tempany just had that effect on people in general, but I wanted to hear her voice. When we left the unit, there was a fluttering in my veins and a stir in my groin that made my face burn. I took one last glance up at the window above the restaurant. Neon letters glared short vowel words I didn't understand and reflected on the glass. Behind the glass, Tempany's face scowled down at us.

# 20 ADAM

I texted rapidly. My thumb ached and I made typos, but I texted like he'd told me to. Iacopetta. I texted that the police had rocked up as I was taking the kid to school. They returned Rachelle's things. I texted as quickly as I could before the boss caught me. The house was silent aside from the nearby hum of the waves lapping at the shore in time with the refrigerator running.

I jumped when the boss walked in. I shoved my phone in my pocket. He glanced around. 'Did you actually take Riley to school?'

I shrugged. 'I thought that's what I was supposed to do.'

The boss's voice went up in pitch as he snapped, 'I told you I wanted her pulled out of school.' I blinked at him, my heart galloping. The boss took a deep breath and took a drink of water before he sighed, 'I thought you'd just drive her around for a while. I swear Riley will be the bloody death of me.'

'She probably just wanted to go to school to be with her friends,' I said.

'She doesn't have any friends, Adam!' he shouted. 'I've made sure she stays safe, away from people.'

I said with my mouth turned downwards into my chest, 'She has a friend.'

He looked at me and with his teeth so close together I could hear them scraping, 'She can't have friends.'

'She's got me, boss.'

'Get out and pick her up,' he snapped.

I stood and felt my phone in my pocket before I walked out, my face prickling, off to pick up Riley and pull her away from the only taste of the outside world she had away from her bomb of a dad.

I walked into the school administration office.

'How's it going? I need to pick up Riley Flynn for a doctor's appointment.'

A buxom woman with red hair and a wrinkled neck curled her lip at me. 'Who are you? We need authorisation.'

I rolled my eyes. 'If you check her file, you'll see I have authorisation from her father Dominic. My name's Adam Marshall.'

She click-clacked on the computer with her long fingernails, before picking up the phone to call the classroom. A bewildered look on her face made my breath stop.

'I'm sorry, sir, but she's not in class at the moment.'

My mind went to those the boss worried about, lurking in the shadows, waiting to jump on Riley. The office lady, red-in-the-face, called out for Riley on the speakers and I paced the creaking floorboards of the office.

'She wouldn't have left the school grounds,' the lady said, bringing her hand to her mouth to chew on neatly painted red nails. The principal emerged and we explained we couldn't find Riley.

'I'll go find her,' I said after fifteen minutes.

'Shall I call the police?' The office lady squeaked at the principal.

'No!' I cried.

The principal and office lady both did a double-take at me, so I took a deep breath and said, 'Not yet. I'm sure she's fine. I'll see if I can find her and…then if I can't, you can call them.'

'We have a duty of care, sir,' began the principal.

'Yeah, no fucking shit – but unless you want to be sued for child endangerment, you'll shut up and let me go find her,' I snapped and strode away.

I made tracks from the school, trying to do the maths in my head. School had started two hours ago, so she couldn't have been further than that away. I drove up the route she could have taken at a walk, and drove up and down each street. I had to find her. If she'd been kidnapped, the boss would kill me. I was hurtling around a corner when I spotted Riley walking briskly down the street with who else but own brother. I braked hard, and shouted from my open window, 'Riley!'

They both halted and looked at me with wide eyes. Riley's hair was mucked up and her face flushed. Cody dropped his basketball and it bounced away. I leant over and opened the car from the inside passenger seat, 'Get in.' They both obeyed and Riley slammed the door. 'Where have you been?' I asked as I floored the accelerator to avoid cutting off the oncoming car behind us.

'Us? What about you?' Cody snapped.

Riley smacked his shoulder and took a deep breath, letting it flow from her lips until her neck blushed. 'School.'

'Really.' I glanced at Cody.

'Yeah,' said Cody.

I watched Cody from the side of my eye as I drove. 'You're so lucky you weren't killed.' They were both silent. 'Your dad would be so worried about you know,' I added.

'Oh, fuck that, Adam; you know he's not,' Cody screeched.

'Okay.' I tightened my grip on the steering wheel. 'I meant Riley's dad.'

'So did I,' he snapped.

So, he knew. He knew about Riley's dad and her face. I had no way of defending him when his handiwork was there, buried under all that cakey makeup. I pulled up at the school. I got out of the car and pulled Cody out, quickly locking Riley in, where she banged at the windows shouting at me. I led Cody to the administration by his collar and scowled at the principal as she walked out of her office.

'Found her…and another one.'

'I hope you fucking die for what you're letting that arsehole do to her,' Cody whispered to me.

I tousled his hair and said to the office lady and the principal, 'Problem solved.' I looked pointedly at Cody and added, 'I'm a problem solver. I will fix it; trust me,' and walked back to the car where Riley was waiting.

I slammed the door and said, 'Riley, what the fuck.'

'I'm sorry.'

I scoffed, 'Sorry? I thought someone had grabbed you and something bad had happened.'

'I said I'm sorry. Why are you even here?' she snapped. 'You promised you'd get me away with all your connections, but now my mother's dead and you're still chewing fat with my father. What more do you need to do before you can take me out of here?'

I sighed. 'You don't understand.'

She was silent the entire drive home and she was out of the car before I had even turned the car off. She ran inside, up the stairs and was returning wearing a short wetsuit by the time I got inside.

'Where are you going?' I asked. She ignored me and walked to the door. I followed a few paces behind her. 'Riley!'

'Leave me alone, Adam.'

'Riley,' I groaned. 'Just calm down.'

She opened the door and paused before she shook her head. 'No. You don't tell me what to do.' She marched off down to the beach, leaving me standing at the door with a phone buzzing a hole into my thigh and a headache pulsing in my forehead.

I answered the phone with a short, 'What?'

I went down to the water slowly. I gave Riley some time. She couldn't dive into the cold water fast enough. She always swam for hours. She would dive and dive, and dig through the sand at the bottom for something. I watched her in the shallows, combing through the piles of deposited sand and grabbing gulps before diving back down. Was she looking for something? As she went out deeper, I followed her along the pier and squatted at its edge, waiting.

As she surfaced, gasping for a breath, she spotted me and reluctantly said, 'Hey.'

'What are you doing?'

'Swimming.'

'Where did you go today?' I asked.

'School.'

'No, you weren't at school,' I replied.

'Yeah, I was…for a while.'

'Tempany called me and told me you showed up there saying you didn't see anything and asking if she was there,' I said. 'Cut the bullshit, kiddo.'

Riley treaded at the surface before spitting out a mouthful of water. 'You doomed Mum and me the second you brought her around.'

How on earth had I doomed her? I was protecting her. Tempany was my girlfriend. She was entitled to visit where I worked from time to time since I spent so much time there. Hell, I even had my own room I had to stay in sometimes just to keep her safe. She didn't understand. I scratched at my head, searching for the words to explain. I sighed, 'You're too young to understand, kiddo.'

'I am not too young,' she argued, splashing the water in my direction, resembling a toddler-ish stamp of the foot.

'You can't just walk out of school when we think you're there, safe, Riley,' I said, looking down at the blurry outline of her legs below the surface. 'Don't do it again.' I stood up and walked away. Riley followed, swimming alongside the pier.

She called, 'I can't help it that nobody is doing anything.' I kept walking. 'I'm not going to let him get away with what he did!'

I stopped and looked down at her. 'What?'

'He killed her!'

'How do you know that? You didn't see anything.'

'I saw him do it.'

'Did you?' I said with flat voice.

'Don't patronise me. I'm not lying. I saw *everything*.' She glared at me. 'I can tell the police I know he did it!' she cried.

'No, you didn't see anything, Riley,' I said, screwing up my nose and gesticulating wildly. 'You weren't even there. You were at the hospital when she disappeared. You didn't see anything!'

'I'm still going to tell the police it was him.'

'You'd be lying,' I replied. 'You know you didn't see anything. *I know* you didn't see anything.'

'But he's a bad man, Adam,' she replied with a whimper.

I sighed and went to the ledge, holding out my hand to her. She took it and I lifted her up. She dripped all over me and her skin rose up in goose bumps. I said, 'Be patient. He just lost his wife.'

'I just lost my mother and I'm supposed to love him anyway?' she coughed.

'He didn't do anything to her, Riley,' I told her. 'I found you and I saved you. Whatever she was trying to do...she achieved her part of it.'

I had to look away as the tears that hadn't come yet from Riley were coming. Her face screwed up and her neck was covered in red blotches. Her lip trembled and I looked away. I couldn't see her cry.

'But he hurt us,' she said with a swallow.

I stared at the horizon and croaked, 'I know, and I'm sorry, Riley.'

I went to put my arm around her but she shrugged and dislodged me, walking off. 'Whatever.'

It was hard, all right. All right, all right, I was wrong. I woke up with dread sinking into my skin, like radiation; it burnt. It seared until I lit a cigarette and sucked it down to quench a hunger that roared beneath my ribcage. I stared out the window as the sun rose, orange and impressive now that spring was on our doorstep. The magpies started their engines if I dared to walk below the towering gum in the front yard. I would light another cigarette as I dodged the magpie and got in my car. Burning rubber speeding onto the highway – some mornings I didn't bother looking. Three, two, one, go. Do I live or do I die?

I began to operate mechanically. Arrive at work. Text Iacopetta. Hide the phone. Wander to the boat. Wait for the call from the boss to say it was safe to sell again. Hide my eyes from the CCTV cameras around the house and finally get to go to Tempany, snort the cocaine. Set all my anger aside, lock it inside like pearls in a clam as I swallowed the gear and fucked my girl.

It was hard. I was not a clown. I knew how it worked. Life didn't just go on when somebody suddenly turned up dead. Job description: keep the kid safe. First and most important. Second, collect the money. The gear wasn't as important as the kid. At least all along I knew that.

Taking Riley to school was no longer on my to-do list. She lingered in the kitchen, ready to go on the off-chance her father would change his mind and allow her back out in the real world. My throat shuddered at the thought of what the boss would have done if he knew she had been skipping school. Or that she was hanging out in a drug addict's hovel and with a teenage boy, no less. Cody was another issue; he had figured out where I was and had latched onto Riley to get to me. That put him in danger, but I didn't know how to tell him to stay away without sounding like a hypocrite, so I shut up.

'Sorry, kiddo; full lockdown,' I said with a tut.

Riley grunted and threw her school bag down. 'Why do you even listen to him?'

'He pays me.'

She rolled her eyes. 'What am I going to do then?'

I shrugged; my mind blank. All she could ever do was study or swim. Now all she had was swim. I glanced outside at the grey weather and at the swaying palm trees that reached over the fence from the neighbour's property. They spanked the edge of the downpipes at night and made eerie scratching sounds on the glass. They'd scared the shit out of me when I had first stayed the night four years ago. They were even larger now, and that morning they were practically doing the Mexican Wave it was so windy.

'I don't think you can even swim today,' I mumbled.

She sighed. 'Where is he?'

'Who?'

'Dom,' she spat.

I blinked at her. 'Funeral parlour. For your mum. Organising some things.'

'Can we at least go to Ben's?' she asked.

I looked at the time on my watch. I didn't know how long the boss would be gone, but I did like her idea of going to the bar. As early as it was, I wouldn't say no to a drink. I nodded and grabbed the car key. 'Let's go.'


Sitting in the booth at Ben's, Jess gave us our drinks and leant against the edge of the seat back with one hip. 'Heard the news about your boss's wife.' She whistled. 'Shit eh.'

I chugged the whiskey, ignoring Riley and Jess's surprised faces and

glances at each other. My throat burned and I grimaced, 'Yeah, fuckin'
rough.'

'Know what happened to her?' Jess asked.

I shrugged but Riley said, 'Murdered.'

Jess's eyes went wide and she stood straight. 'Shit, no.'

I shook my head but Riley nodded, and added, 'Shit, yes.'

'Riley, don't swear,' I snapped.

She glowered at me and took a sip of her diet lemonade. I folded a
napkin at the table into eighths and said to Jess, 'She drowned after
hitting her head. That's what the police say.'

Jess crossed her arms in front of her. 'Sounds gnarly.'

Riley shook her head. 'That's not what happened.'

'You weren't there!' I snapped.

Riley swallowed and looked down. I took a deep breath and said,
'All we can do is go by what the police are saying. She wasn't murdered.
She drowned...after hitting her head.'

Jess nodded with a grim smile. 'All we can do.'

Riley stayed silent and pushed her lemonade away with a pout.

'Anyway, got to get back to it,' sighed Jess. 'Talk soon, guys.'

'Thanks, Jess,' I said. I unfolded the napkin and traced the crease
lines with my index finger, the sensation of it rubbing against my skin
with a stunted bump, bump, bump.

'Riley, you've got to accept this. The police say it was an accident.'

'You weren't in that room with us the whole time, Adam,' she
hissed. 'There could be gaps.'

'I know what she was trying to do,' I said, not looking at her. 'I can't
understand how that must have felt.'

'What do you mean?' she asked with a flick of the head.

I looked up at her. Her eyes bored into mine. *I know what she wanted
to do*, I rehearsed in my mind. *I know what she almost did. I know she was
trying to kill you.* Instead, I shook my head and muttered, 'Nothing. Let's
go before your dad gets back.'

# 21 RILEY

I put on my black dress for Mum's funeral and carefully crafted my hair to cover the bruise on my forehead. Tested out how I might look with bangs. My face was the wrong shape. I looked dirty and old.

I walked into Adam's room; he had stayed the night. He put one cigarette out and lit another, his room awash with the swirling haze that I could barely see through. I coughed pointedly to announce my arrival and he looked up and buried a packet of white powder under his pillow before shoving his phone in his pocket.

'Yeah,' he said with a jittery voice.

'I'm ready. Are you?' I glanced around the room and my eyes stung from the smoke. I opened the window. 'My dad would be mad if you set the house on fire, you know.'

He faked a laugh. I sat on the bed, close enough that I could slide my hand under his pillow to grab the drugs he thought he had hidden in time. He reached around me to grab his shirt. 'Get out so I can get dressed, will you,' he ordered.

'I don't want to,' I teased.

'Get out of here before your dad sees you on my bed and thinks something's gone on here,' he explained and pushed me until I lost my balance and had to stand up. Adam searched his bedside drawers for more cigarettes and clutched them in his lap. He smoked the cigarette he had while leaning his head against the wall. Adam sighed and stashed his lighter in his pocket alongside his phone. I walked out of the room and went downstairs to eat breakfast.

Outside, the sea churned and the clouds moved across the sky. The water darkened from turquoise to a navy blue, and was roughened with foaming white breakers. Dad's boat was moored at the pier but it very rarely left. A tool of possession, not purpose. I felt like I was that boat, bobbing in the rough waters: a rich man's asset and not a loved one.

I shivered as I waited for my fifteen-minute timer to end, and wrapped a cardigan around my shoulders to keep the chill of early spring off my skin. It began to rain, pounding on the windows and the palm trees lashed. I jumped as my timer went off. Dad came into the kitchen as I was making my breakfast. He approached me and hugged me, causing me to freeze and curl my lip.

'We've got a big day ahead, baby,' he uttered. I stepped away and nodded.

He made his own breakfast and we both looked up as Adam came in. He halted, hesitating when he saw my father, tapping his pocket where his phone was. Adam rubbed at his eyes, red and teary.

'You look as though you had a rough night, Adam.' Dad opened the newspaper, slowly turning the page to avoid ripping it. 'I'm assuming you're hung over.'

'You would be right,' Adam sighed. He reached for a coffee mug and turned on the coffee machine.

'The funeral starts at ten, but Riley and I need to be there by nine.'

Adam nodded. 'I'll be fine to drive you.'

'I need you there, son,' Dad murmured without looking at him. I stared at him. *Son?* He wanted to call Adam his child so desperately and why? My eyes flicked from Adam to my dad. I could feel the hurt surging up through my chest until I couldn't take it anymore and I exclaimed, 'As if either of you even care about Mum.'

Dad and Adam both looked at me and I glared at them. Dad

croaked, 'Riley, how could you say that?'

'How can I say that?' I sputtered. 'Seriously?'

Dad rubbed his eye and moaned, 'Don't do this to me, baby.'

'I don't want you there,' I snapped. 'I don't want you to come. You don't deserve to be there.' My voice trembled.

Adam shifted and cleared his throat but Dad held up a hand. 'You don't get to decide who does and does not come. You don't get a say in this.'

'Of course, I don't!' I snapped. 'I don't get a say in anything!'

I stood up and threw my yoghurt on the floor. 'You broke her arm that day, not me! It's just okay for you to do whatever you like to her and then you get a say but I don't. Wow. Way to go, DOM!'

Dad's eyes were watering as he rumbled, 'Don't push me, Riley.'

'I don't care,' I muttered bitterly. 'I hate you.' I shoved him.

He shoved me back hard and I gasped as I hit the hard, unwelcoming ceramic tile floor. I screwed up my eyes as pangs shot up my back. He knelt down on my leg and I cried out. Dad took both my cheeks with his hands and shook me.

'I didn't kill her,' he spat as he moved his hands down to choke me. I clawed at his face and uttered an angry scream.

Adam sprang to his feet and cried out, 'Boss, no!' He grabbed his coffee mug and, with an angry wail, threw it hard against the floor beside Dad and me. It smashed, making him flinch and let me go. I climbed shakily to my feet, rubbing at my neck, trying to catch my breath.

'Enough,' Adam demanded.

Dad stood, panting and wheezing through his tears. He pointed at the mess on the floor and bellowed, 'Clean that up!' He stormed out of the room, choking on his tears. Adam knelt and picked up the shards of the cup. He glanced up at me and said quietly, 'You shouldn't make him so mad. I can't always protect you.'

'I don't care; I've had enough,' I sobbed.

Adam reached into his denims and pulled out a gun without

expression. He held it out to me. 'Here.'

I gasped, 'What?'

He jiggled the gun at me so I slowly took it from him. 'For when I can't always keep you safe.' I nodded and stood in stunned silence at the weight of the gun.

The drive to the funeral parlour was silent. Adam drove while my dad sat in the front passenger seat, sipping from a flask, with his eyes hidden behind reflective sunglasses. Adam had beads of sweat dripping down his ear line even though it was a grey, rainy day. My eyebrows drooped into my eyes with the despair of having to sit through a funeral when I knew my father had caused her death. If he hadn't abused her the way he did, she would not have made such a desperate attempt to flee his grasp. She wouldn't have done what she'd done to me, trying to keep me safe from him. Even if my mother had intended her death to be a suicide, I would never forgive my father. I could, however, forgive Adam, for trying to keep me safe.

When Adam parked the car, I got out and slammed the door, enjoying the way it made my father flinch. *Soft-close doors take that, you son of a bitch.* I couldn't help but smirk as I stalked into the parlour, dimly lit and drowning in the stench of lilies. The funeral director greeted us but I looked around at the open yet claustrophobic space of the foyer. Lilies lined the walls with armchairs and a statue stood in the centre of the room with a book for people to sign. I stepped forward and studied the candelabras coming from the wall. Such an ostentatious and pretentious place for candles to be in the twenty-first century. Adam lingered, biting his nails and looked furtively around. Dad spoke to the funeral director and I glanced at him and thought, *what a dick* because he wouldn't even take off his sunglasses.

My footsteps creaked on the dark beige floorboards and I stumbled on the steel grey rug – Adam caught my elbow before I stacked it completely.

Dad came over and explained that we could have a viewing if we wanted. Adam shook his head no and I hesitated. See my dead mother? See a dead body? My fingers and toes curled at the thought of it. Dad went into the room at the back of the foyer and closed the door behind himself, leaving Adam and I standing with our hands folded in front of us, waiting.

'You going to go in and say goodbye to your mum?' Adam whispered.

Every thought I had screamed no, I don't want to see a dead body, let alone my dead mother, but I was interested, too. How did she look? Would there be something in her face that offered something of an apology to me? Would she be at peace? So, I nodded and committed myself to going in after my father. I would see my dead mother and see if there were more answers in her flesh than there was when I was dying under her drugged-out gaze.

Dad came out of the viewing room, squeezing the top of his nose and knocking his sunglasses up onto his forehead. Adam looked up and as he opened his mouth to speak, I slipped into the viewing room and shut the door behind me. The room was dark with the cool, dimmed lights directed at the casket. The flowers towered around the casket like an amphitheatre of death. I loitered by the door before working up the courage to get a closer look at my mother. She was propped up in a bed of soft lining of the casket. Her eyes were closed and her hair was straighter than I had ever seen it. She wore a black dress and her hands were folded neatly over her abdomen.

'Hi,' I whispered and studied the make-up on her face that made her look as though she was merely asleep. Soft, relaxed lips and her head resting upon the silk pillow inside the casket. My eyes went to her neck and I gasped. The necklace. It was on her neck. How did it get here? I thought I lost it.

My father choked her and got her this necklace as an apology as a bribe to stay quiet. Dad had choked me twice and had given me nothing. I bit down so hard that my ears hurt. How was that fair that she got to keep it even when she died? It was going to be burnt up with her in the cremation. I couldn't let that happen.

I glanced around before reaching in and undoing the necklace. Her skin was cold as if she'd been refrigerated and my fingers trembled with the disgust of touching the deadness. I tucked the necklace into my underwear and left the room, rolling my shoulders and working up some tears. If I wasn't crying when I walked out, people would begin to say there was something seriously wrong with me like I was beginning to think there was.

As I re-entered the foyer, Dad hugged me ostentatiously and I flinched. The necklace was grazing a very sensitive part so I had to place my legs slightly apart as I walked out, but when he hugged me, they were scissored together and I wished I had brought a handbag or something that could have worn the prickly prize instead.

The woman my father called Tetka Jana arrived from Sydney in a flourish of black lace and heavy perfume that left me breathless. I hadn't seen her since I was little. She squeezed me into her boulder-sized boobs and hugged me saying, 'Oh child, child, child.' She pushed me away so I was at arms-length and shook her head. 'You must be devastated.'

My eyes searched hers for the pain of losing a loved one that she hadn't seen in ten years. All I saw were eyes searching mine, so I settled on mirroring her expression back at her. That must be better than the nothingness or mild irritation I felt. I nodded and was bear-hugged again and swayed side-to-side like she was soothing a baby. Adam sniggered and then was accosted by Jana's granddaughter Bibi asking him who he was. He had to explain that he worked for my dad and what dad did only to have Bibi engage in the conversation and reveal she was an investigative journalist in Sydney. His face went pale as he nodded, feigning interest.

Dad roved, speaking to his family that he hadn't seen in a decade. Family he hadn't even spoken to as far as I knew. Family that looked at the photographs of my mother and said, 'Tragedy; what a tragedy…' and not knowing how their beloved Dominic treated her, treated me and how it had all been because of him that she was dead. I couldn't be sure my eye started twitching because of the frustration or the necklace in my underwear.

The funeral director finally started the funeral so we could make our way to our seats in the main room. The casket was now closed. I breathed a sigh of relief that Dad hadn't gone back in to see her again and he hadn't boasted of the necklace to anyone who may have been confused and replied, 'What necklace?'

I sat down, carefully and placed my hands in my lap. The room was filling slowly with people I did not recognise. I eyeballed the doorway and recognised a man and a woman, wearing plain clothes, but they were the police officers. They stood at the back with their hands folded the way I folded mine. Respectful, yet out of place, not belonging. Adam stood the same way, an outsider, with eyes on my father. My eyes went to Tatka Jana and Bibi. I could not end up with them if my dad was arrested. I'd rather go to foster care.

I snapped my head away from them and watched Dad on the podium and test, test, test the microphone. His broad shoulders were shifting up into his ears.

'Thank you all for coming,' he said with a nod to the crowd. He met the eyes of the police officers in the back and he fell silent for an awkward pause, filled with people clearing their throats and coughing, all gazing upwards at him. He finally choked out, 'It would have meant a lot to Rachelle to know she had so much support.' I had to suppress a snort.

'Life…is short.' He grasped the edges of the lectern and wiped the sweat off his forehead. 'I've been blessed in my life with the ability to work hard and provide for my family. Safety,' he nodded each noun as though he was ticking them off; 'Security, wealth and prosperity.' I interlaced my fingers to keep them from shaking. 'I lost my father a long time ago, when I was a boy. It destroyed me for the longest time.'

His eyes met mine. 'Now I have to see my darling daughter suffer the same horrendous experience that I had when I was twelve years old.' *Sure, Dad, make it about yourself.* It was enough to make me roll my eyes and his brows creased enough for me to know that he'd noticed.

He blinked back tears and continued. 'Rachelle was a gift from the universe for me. She came into my life at a very low point and held me together with strings, like I was a marionette.' He chuckled. 'I made some really terrible mistakes early in our relationship but she never called me on them. Ever.'

He gazed at me, biting his lip. 'I guess that's something she should have done.' His fingers gripped and ungripped the lectern. 'If there's a particular way that I want you to remember Rachelle in…it's in her undying faith and loyalty to me, her husband…but also to our daughter, Riley…and please keep us in thoughts and prayers. Thank you.'

He stepped down off the podium and sat beside me, reaching for my hands and wrenched them, attempting to be supportive. All he managed to do was crush my fingers and tear a cuticle. Even in his efforts to be friendly, he hurt me.

We hosted the wake at our house. I wandered around with glazed eyes, holding a cheese board filled with cured meats and gherkins. Dad drank with his long-missed family. My mother's family did not exist. She married Dad young after running away from some boarding school in Perth. She found out by official letter that her parents had died in a plane crash in 2016. I had never met them. She had wanted to go to the funeral but it was too public, Dad said.

Shared with hundreds of other people, televised…he couldn't risk her being seen. So, she'd watched it on the television instead. I had sat with her as she curled up on the sofa in a foetal position with tears running down her face. Rachelle Flynn nee Mackesy had never felt so low. That is until the day she decided to try to kill me before killing herself.

Adam pinched the sleeve of my dress and whispered, 'Hey kiddo.'

I smiled weakly at him.

'How's your neck?'

The dress was high-necked and was rubbing but I said, 'It's fine.'

'Where'd you put it?' he asked, leaning his mouth in closer to me.

I thought of the necklace that I'd hurriedly shoved into my wardrobe as soon as we arrived back, telling my father that I was going to the bathroom to freshen up, but Adam did not know about the necklace, so I hesitated.

'What I gave you,' he hissed.

'Oh!' I had forgotten that he had given me the gun in the first place. 'It's in my bedside drawer.'

'Make sure you put it somewhere he won't find it,' he replied, looking around to check where Dad was. 'If he ever hurts you badly enough, you should be able to protect yourself.'

'Isn't that your job?' I asked with a straight face. 'Keep me safe.'

He placed his palms on his forehead and surveyed the room. 'I can't have eyes everywhere, Riley.' He flung his hands outwards, palms up. 'I mean, I'm trying.' He searched his pockets for his cigarette pack and lighter. 'I do my best, but I...'

'You worry it's not good enough.'

He nodded, lit his cigarette and took the cheese board from my hands. 'You look whacked. Take a break, kiddo.'

I nodded and walked outside with slumped shoulders. I sat on the patio with my arms crossed to ward against the chilly afternoon air. It had been less than five minutes before Dad came and sat down next to me, making me shudder. I wiped the hair away from my face.

'You're missing her,' he said as he hovered his hand over my back but didn't place it upon me. It lingered in the air, the gap between almost repelling me as an opposite attractive magnetic force. I gulped and bit my lip, waiting.

'It's okay, Riley. I'm still here for you. I'll look after you.'

I balked and my skin went hot. My forehead thumped and I could taste a lump in my throat. 'I don't want you to say you're here for me and you'll look after me. It's all a lie.'

He gave an exasperated sigh and I watched the vein in his neck pulse. 'You're wrong, Riley. You couldn't look after yourself if your life depended on it because you're too weak and pathetic.'

'Oh yeah?' I jumped to my feet. 'I hate you because I know what you've done. She's dead because of you.'

His mouth dropped open.

I continued, 'I will never forgive you.'

He stared at his hands.

I shook my head and looked down at him. 'You're the pathetic one.'

As I turned to leave, he called out, 'Riley, I'm trying to make things right with you.' I stopped. 'I know I fucked up, baby…and not just with your mother. Can't we…at least be civil to each other? We're both grieving.'

I paused and with a shrug of my shoulder, said in a flat voice, 'Are we?'

I left him alone on the patio and retreated to my bedroom.

# 22 CODY

Riley wasn't at school the next day, or the following. It was five-to-nine and she hadn't shown up again. My stomach churned with the thought that she had disappeared just as my brother had. My breath shortened and ached. Everyone left me. I stood by the History classroom door, scuffing my shoes on the lino floor and smoothing out my tee shirt. I went by the lockers, moving quickly, hoping to see her there loading up her books for the day but there was nobody standing beside her locker.

I scratched at my head which I hadn't washed all week. I blew a breath of air through my lips and looked from the corridor to the history classroom – No Riley – to the door where I could go find her. If I went to her house, she may be there. Why wasn't she at school? Was she finally taking some time off to grieve her mum? But three days in a row? That was weird.

I hitched my schoolbag up on my shoulder and slipped out the door with my head down against the rain. It wasn't a bad walk on a sunny day, but it was hideous in the rain. I got to her house and knocked on the door, rang the doorbell and peered through the windows. My eyes cornered in on the security camera looking at me. I waved at it and waited. There was still no response.

127

I sighed and stuffed my damp blazer in my bag and thought where I could go next to look for her. Tempany clearly had some answers so I could go there. I put one foot in front of the other and ignored the miserable rain, headed to the bus stop to get to the main part of town.

It took me an hour and a half to get into town by the time I had to wait for the next bus and then walk the eight blocks to the Vietnamese restaurant because I was an idiot and got off a stop too early. I couldn't find the restaurant at first and had to double back around the same block for three separate circuits, but I found the narrow alleyway and climbed the stairs, kicking aside litter.

I knocked on the door. The brown painted wood was peeling off and a splinter stabbed my knuckle before setting up camp under my skin. I winced and sucked on it, feeling a little childish when Tempany came to the door.

She looked me up and down with a furrowed brow.

I said, 'Um, hi.'

'Hi,' she said.

'I'm Cody.'

She stared at me blankly.

'Riley's friend,' I offered.

Still nothing.

'I was here the other day.'

'Oh.' Her eyes were quite red, as though she'd been crying. It looked like she had a monster flu, too, because she had what looked like bits of tissue stuck on the side of her nostril. White clumps and a bad sniff.

A man with blonde hair, a wide flat nose and strong shoulders came up behind her and gently pushed her aside. His bulging blue eyes locked onto mine and his brow furrowed. 'Who's this?'

'I'm Cody,' I said.

'Cody, eh?' He had a slight English accent, but not a posh Londoner type. It was more like the sound of a soccer fanatic that grunted his words instead of enunciating them.

'Cody,' murmured Tempany, closing her eyes. An electric tickle ran up my thigh when she murmured my name. Co-deeee. I'd never liked my name so much in my life.

I cleared my throat. 'Can I come in?'

'Sure,' Tempany said and stepped aside, holding onto the wall.

I thanked her and stepped inside and glanced around. There was shopping that hadn't been put away. Open bottles of wine and cheap champagne. Half-full wine glasses lined the yellow bench. The entire room smelled of BO and an odour I'd never smelled before, a mixture of rubber, urine and old gym socks.

'I bet you want a cup of tea, Cody.' The guy walked towards the kettle.

I got a quick glimpse of black mold near the kettle and answered, 'No, thanks.'

'So then…what can we do ya for?' he asked, placing a hand on his hip. He had one painted middle finger, deep red, and a tattoo of a number four over his veins in his wrist.

I turned my eyes to where Tempany was groping the wall and trembling. I turned back to the guy. 'Is she okay?'

He shrugged. 'Yeah. She's just…Tempany.'

'Who are you?' I asked.

'I'm Elias; Tempany's lover.'

I paused. Hadn't Riley mentioned that Tempany was going around with her dad? Or something? I gave Elias a polite nod anyway and said, 'Well, I'm here because I'm worried about my friend. I came here to ask Tempany if she's seen her.'

'Who's your friend?'

'Riley.'

'Why would you come here looking for her?'

'Elias, baby, chill,' Tempany groaned, inching closer to where we stood in the kitchen. 'She's just some kid I know.'

'Shouldn't he be in school?' he called to her then looked back at me and asked me directly, 'Shouldn't you be in school?'

'Yes, and so should my friend.'

'But she's not?'

'She's not,' I said.

'Damn it,' he sighed. 'I don't want to be involved in some missing kid.' He patted down his pocket until he found some car keys. 'Tempany, I'm out of here.' He pecked her gently on the lips and lowered her into the bean bag on the floor by the front door. 'I'll see you soon.'

'You're just going to leave me alone with her?' I asked. 'She looks really sick.'

He narrowed his eyes at me. 'Don't waste your headspace worrying about our kind of people, kid. The second you do…you're in a world of hurt.'

He left, his sneakers squeaking on the steps down to the street, leaving me alone with Tempany, who kept closing her eyes and drifting off before snapping her eyes open again with a bob of the head. I stood there, not sure if I should stay or leave. She looked pretty sick. If I left her alone, she might get worse, but what if she wanted to be alone and I was annoying her by being around? My stomach churned with indecision. Adam would have known what to do.

I eventually asked Tempany, 'Are you okay?'

She came more conscious as time went by and nodded, picking at her nails. I started to sweat so much that I couldn't distinguish between the wet caused by the rain or the sweat from myself.

Tempany fidgeted, moving on the bean bag. 'Oh, I am so sick,' she moaned.

'What's wrong with you?' I asked, taking a step towards her.

She ran her hands through her hair, her fingers catching on knots but she yanked them down anyway and looked up at me from the bottom of her eyes. 'I have a little thing called…' She pinched her fingers together to show *little*. 'Cocaine.'

I took a step back away from her again without meaning to. I'd never met a real drug addict before. Dad had told me Adam got into drugs, but I'd never really believed it. 'So, you're not actually sick?'

'I am sick, but I'm not sick,' she explained. She got to her feet by splaying her spindly legs and rocking back and forward, leaning over to compose herself again. It was almost as if her legs and arms worked independently of her body. Sometimes they were willing and cooperative, and other times they were not. I went to grab her and help her but she veered away from me. She took some deep breaths and stood tall.

I asked quietly, 'If it makes you feel this bad, can't you just quit?'

She smiled. It made her skin warmer and less sweaty-looking. 'Why did you come here, Cody?'

'I don't know where Riley is and I'm worried.'

'Did you try her house?'

I nodded.

Tempany sniffed a noisy, wet sniff and shrugged. 'I don't know.' She looked at me sideways. 'You remind of someone.'

'You have met me before,' I said with a chortle.

'No...you remind me of someone I know. You look a lot like someone I know.'

I shrugged. 'Maybe you know my brother Adam since you know Riley.'

She laughed. 'Adam!' She looked down and scratched at her arm. 'Yeah, you are so much like him.'

I nodded, swallowing a lump of phlegm and my hands trembled at my side. My brother had once been a successful student but he had to work hard at it – so hard that it broke him. I was in all the accelerated programs at school but I didn't want it. None of it. Even if I never cracked a book, I just got it. Dad had a spark in his eye and a greedy thin smile, planting his career onto me. I didn't want to be a doctor any more than Adam had. Was I really like Adam? Heading towards the path of a teenage runaway didn't seem like such a bad path. It seemed to be working out well for Adam, having a nice car and getting to spend time with Riley at the extravagant Flynn house.

The rain got louder outside, smashing against the tin roof, and drowning out the sounds of Tempany's sniffs. She asked, 'Why are you looking for Riley, anyway?'

I shrugged. 'I figured she'd come here to you.'

Tempany narrowed her eyes and her head tilted backwards. She studied my face. 'Did you now?'

I nodded and wrung my hands together to stop them trembling.

She smiled. 'You like me, don't you? That's the reason why you really came here.'

The side of my mouth lifted in a sideways grin. 'I don't really know you.'

She scratched at her ear. 'Didn't we just fuck?'

'No!' I exclaimed.

'Ha…who did I just have sex with then?'

'Elias?' I guessed.

'Oh, Elias…definitely not your brother,' she laughed. 'Or you.' She licked her lips and her eyes laughed hysterically and doubled over.

I grabbed at her before she fell but she pushed me away. 'I'm okay, Cody.'

Tempany stumbled into the kitchen and rummaged around the junk at the cluttered table. She eventually found a cigarette and lit the flame on the stove. She bent over to light the cigarette resting between her lips. Tempany drew in deeply as she stood tall. Clarity returned almost straight away. She opened the window and moaned, 'It's too hot in here.'

It was not. Icy air floated in from the open kitchen window and made my neck collapse as my ear met my shoulder.

I followed Tempany to the table where she smeared a clear spot with her hand. I sat opposite her after she sat down and savoured the cigarette.

'You're a good kid, huh?' she said thoughtfully, tapping the ashes directly onto the table.

I nodded with reluctance. All people ever thought of me was what a good boy – such a good boy compared to that older Marshall boy. That older one that ran away and gave up a decent career to go take drugs. Such a good boy that young Cody is. It made my throat burn with bile constantly being told I was the good one. The chosen one. Even when I was the one wagging school and trying to rebel. Anything I did – it was always GOOD BOY.

I sighed. 'That's what people tell me.'

'Your brother used to be a good kid, too.'

'Used to be?'

She chortled. 'He's not such a good boy anymore.'

I swallowed hard and wanted to ask if Adam was taking cocaine like she was, and if he was still addicted. What did she offer him that made him run away from me?

Tempany's leg bounced under the table and her eyes grilled into mine. She finally said, 'You don't have to be his clone, you know.'

I felt my face burn. 'I'm not worried about being a clone,' I lied.

Still, her eyes fixated on mine. 'You're wondering if he takes drugs with me.'

I stayed quiet. Please say no, I thought. Please say my dad was wrong all these years.

She blew smoke directly into my face and my eyes stung. I looked down and coughed. She sucked on her lips and said, 'It's not really my business. If you know him like I do, you'd know everything he does is a lie.' She plucked a hangnail off and squeezed her finger to let it bleed. 'I'm sorry for whatever he did to you.'

'He didn't do anything to me,' I said in a rush.

She gazed at me again with a pitiful stare. 'He's done something. You're not whole. I can tell.' She ran her hand through her hair, causing the smoke from the cigarette to create a curl that hovered in the air between us for two seconds. 'I can tell these things about people, and besides…you've got this look on your face like you're searching for answers.'

Her eyes softened. 'I guess he lied to you, too.'

I groaned. 'I am just looking for Riley, remember.'

'Why?'

'Riley isn't mourning properly,' I said. 'I'm worried and I want to know why she isn't acting normally.'

'Cody,' she said as she opened a little bag of white powder and tipped it onto the surface of the table. She used the filter of her still-smoking cigarette to mark it into separate lines. She continued, 'Riley's not going to cope well at all. All girls need their mother, especially when they have a dog of a father like she does.'

She licked her lips again and stared hungrily at the cocaine in front of us, then across to me. 'The best thing you can do is just forget about her.' She beckoned to me. 'Come here.'

I stood up and went closer. Tempany moved away from the table and took my hand. Her hands were hot. My own skin tingled at the sensation of being touched by her. She raised her hand to her mouth and softly sucked on my index finger, staring at me the whole time. I shifted, hoping I wouldn't just cum on the spot and make a complete fool of myself. She then took her finger and pressed it down into the cocaine, which was coarser than I thought it would be. It looked soft as baby powder but it was harsher to the touch, like a washing powder.

Tempany sucked the cocaine off my finger and I nearly fell through the floor. She wet her finger with her tongue, pushed it into the powder and held it up. 'Your turn.'

'I've never, I'm not...I don't, um...'

'Prove that you're not such a good boy.'

I closed my eyes and sucked her finger.

# 23 RILEY

After the fight with Dad, I strode down to the beach with weak legs and sat on the sand. The seagulls flew lazy arcs above. It made me think of a day I had almost forgotten about, however, since Mum had drowned, it kept coming back to me, as if I had drowned with her.

A day at the beach on the first family holiday to Tathra that Adam had come along with us on the boat. I was eleven. He'd taken care of me since that day with more care.

Mum had taken my hand and walked me along the beach. It was winter, so the beach was abandoned, save for seagulls and sea mist that rose into the hills of trees. The sandbar shunted the water back from its advances with booming explosions of white. My feet were bare, my toes dug into the wet, cool granules of sand. I had broken away, making a beeline for a flock of birds.

'Riley!' my mother had called but her voice had been drowned by the large waves that crashed nearby. I flapped my arms, circling around the confused birds who made hesitant attempts of escaping my boundless energy. I only glanced back at my mother to see if she was watching with pure love and admiration, but she wasn't watching at all. She was wrapped in the arms of Dad. I tried not to let my disappointment show by going to the water's edge.

The water came in so fast it made me dizzy. One particular wave was bigger than the rest and it sucked the sand right from under my feet. The wall of water knocked me over and I was soon floating out to a spot where my toes couldn't even graze the sand below. I wasn't used to such powerful water. The water I swam in outside my house was a calm bay but this was the South Pacific Ocean.

As the water kidnapped my legs and pulled me from the safety of the sand, I paddled the way I'd learned in swimming class, trying to keep my head above water. But the water moved me along in the opposite direction, out towards the wharf. My legs were heavy and pulled at me like an anchor. I was on fire even though the water was so cold I could barely breathe. I gulped at what I thought was air but was actually the surface of the water. Salt and sand scraped my throat and burned the insides of my nose. I kicked and kicked with my anchor-heavy legs. The water was so deep and I started to wonder *where's Mum? Where's Dad?* I flailed until my strength dissipated but then there were arms grabbing me. I would have panicked, thinking it was a sea monster, but I was too weak to even care if a sea monster ate me right up. *Gobble, gobble.* I wanted to close my eyes and sleep.

'Stay awake, kiddo.' I looked into the eyes of Adam, who had just started working for my dad and had come with us on holiday despite my mother complaining about it out of earshot. He pushed me up onto a big rock out of the water. I shivered so hard that it made me vomit up yellow sea water.

'Are you okay?' he asked, resting on the rock, still in the water being bombarded by the current. His skinny arms wobbled with the effort of holding on. I nodded but my teeth chattered so loudly I thought my head might jitter clean off. Adam grunted as he pulled himself out of the water. He wrapped me in a big hug. At that point, he was like a stranger to me so I vehemently protested being touched by him.

'Don't – d-d-d-don't t-t-t-touch me.'

'Body warmth. I'll get you warm.' I collapsed against him and breathed in at his chest. Something fell from his wallet and he grabbed it, but I saw its shiny interior. I gazed up at him.

'I have to tell you something,' he said after a pause. 'But it has to be our secret.'

I nodded.

'Riley! Riley!' I could hear my mother calling, sounding worried, over Adam's voice as he told me the truth. I was about to shout back, but I couldn't find the energy to speak. I cuddled closer to Adam's wet tee-shirt and closed my eyes.

Now, I felt hot and sweaty despite the cold day. I got up and walked into the water, feeling the icy water numb my toes, then my ankles, then my knees. With a gasp, I submerged myself and allowed my body to float on its back in my funeral dress. I floated and floated. The water danced with me, bouncing and bobbing me. A boat went past and soon the kick back was now rocking me. I opened my eyes at the sky. I was stretched out on my back, letting the water freeze me and the afternoon sun warm my face. Hours. I could stay there for hours. I was sinking.

'Riley!' Someone shouted with a hoarse voice.

I yelped and splashed upright. I looked around and saw Cody, standing on the pier, red in the face and fists balled. He said, 'I've been calling your name for ten minutes! Didn't you hear me?'

I shook my head and spat water out. 'You scared me, you moron.'

He sat down, rolled up his jeans to his knees, and took off his shoes. His feet were pale while his legs were tanned lightly even so early in spring. He dangled his legs over the edge, the awkwardness radiating from his pale feet and long legs.

'Are you coming in?' I teased. I paddled to the pier and grasped the sharp barnacled post, but did not climb up.

Cody winced. 'Doesn't that hurt?'

I studied my scratched-up hand and said, 'No.' I laughed and looked up at him. 'What are you doing here?'

'You haven't been at school.'

'My dad took me out.'

'Why?'

'He doesn't want me talking to anyone,' I said, rolling my eyes. I glanced back at the beach. 'Speaking of, go to the front of the boat. He won't see you. I'll meet you there.'

I ducked under the pier and swam in the dark shadows of the pillars. I swam by the flatheads and the whiting; they speared away. It was a whole different world in the depths just off the shallows. An entire aquamarine city thrived amongst the poles of the pier. I surfaced on the other side of the boat and sat on the edge of the lower platform while Cody leant against a pole, rubbing his nose.

'What are you going to do?' he asked. 'I can come with you to the police or something.'

'No. I don't want the police involved.' I avoided his eyes as I explained, 'They'll ship me off to Sydney to live with my dad's family.' I scraped beads of water from my legs.

'Why is that such a bad thing?' he asked.

I thought of Adam. He had rescued me, holding me as I shivered and vomited. I thought of how he handed me a gun. I thought of how he got me out of that bathroom and taken me straight to the hospital, leaving my mother alone. Afterwards, was blank. I looked down at the metal grate and mumbled, 'I want to stay with people who actually care about me and I can trust.'

There were footsteps marching along the pier. 'Somebody's coming,' said Cody, standing up and craning his neck to see. We both froze in place until Adam came into view, and I breathed a sigh of relief.

'What are you two doing here?' he asked. He wiped his face and squinted at Cody. 'Have you both lost your mind?'

'No,' Cody snapped.

*Yes, it's down there*, I thought. *Just below your feet.*

I watched him thinking. His brain could work so fast sometimes I couldn't keep up. I remained at the edge and waited for him to continue, but he didn't. I began to shiver in the murky shade of the boat.

Cody finally asked, 'Were you there the day she died?'

Adam chewed on his lip. 'I don't want you going to see Tempany for a while.'

'Why not?' Cody asked.

I finally looked up at Cody. Had he gone to see Tempany without me or was Adam talking about the day he came along with me?

'Because I said so,' replied Adam.

'You can't tell me what to do.' Cody crossed his arms.

Adam shrugged. 'I don't want you to get involved, that's all.'

'I'd rather be with her than be with you – at least she wouldn't leave her own brother.'

I clucked as I realised Cody had certainly gone to see Tempany without me. What was it with that woman? Why did she have to take everyone away from me?

'Don't,' Adam tutted.

'Yeah, yeah; you know what, Adam? You're just as much a bastard as Riley's dad is. You just can't see it.' He turned and stormed away, the metal grate clanking loudly with each step and the echo cracked against the boat and the trees.

Adam looked at me and I rolled my eyes. He pointed at me with a curled lip. 'Do not get him involved in this. You know it needs to be secret. I swear to mother-fucking God.'

I flinched. He never spoke to me like that. It made my lips numb and I snapped, 'If you're not going to help bring justice to my mum or tell me what really happened, just stay out of my life!'

'Hey!' He pointed at his chest and bellowed, 'I *saved* your life!'

I could have throttled him I was so furious. Instead, I dove back into the water, the dress splaying up around my ears as I listened to the thumping of my blood in my veins, snaking its way from limb to limb under the surface.

Adam stalked my swimming path under the boat. His hands shook, his breath short as he called my name, following me along the pier. I surfaced and clumped through the sand and made my way back to the house. He tailed me. 'You're not talking to me, huh?' He panted as he had to jog to keep up with me. 'Look…I'm sorry.'

'Don't say sorry. You don't mean it. If you were sorry, you wouldn't be here.'

'Why do you say that?' he asked with a grunt as though I'd wounded him.

I turned to him, the dress heavy and slapping against my icy thighs that were prickling from the salt and the cold. 'He needs to be held accountable for what he did to her,' I hissed. 'Until you can at least believe me when I tell you I can say that he killed her, don't try to stop me speaking to Cody.'

I left him standing on the beach and trekked my way back to the house.

I went to bed early that night, wanting to sit and listen to the silence. It was loud in my ears – it hummed and tickled. It made me restless beneath the covers. Everything had become so messy.

Cody kept jumping into my head. He was hanging around with Tempany and that could mean two things. Sex or cocaine. What if he was on it? What if nothing he said was true and he was using me to get access to not just his brother, but to my father and his drugs? What if Tempany was a liar like my father and she was never interested in Adam? What if Adam was covering for my dad and I really had no idea? What if Adam wasn't really going to help me? Why did everyone keep lying to me?

There was a gentle rap on the door. I gasped and called out, 'Who's there?'

Dad opened the door slowly, flushing light into the dark room. 'Adam and I are going to set off some fireworks, to celebrate your mother's life. Are you coming down?'

I gestured to the window. 'I can see from here.'

'It's for your mother.'

'So?'

'It'll be good…you know…' He took a deep breath and pinched the bridge of his nose. 'I'd like you to come down and sit on the beach with us, as a family.'

'Adam's not family, Dom,' I mumbled and rolled the other way, expecting him to walk away. Instead, he walked into the room, and pulled the blanket off me. 'Hey!' I screeched.

'No. Get up. I've had enough of your shit. Get up.'

I stood up and glared at him, wanting to throw something really nasty in his face but exhaustion rendered me mute.

'Come on.' He took me by my wrist and led me outside to the beach, where Adam stood on the pier, smoking a cigarette. I forced myself free from my dad's grip and tried to act casual by crossing my arms in front of my chest.

'Adam, please,' said Dad. Adam used his cigarette to light a succession of fireworks. Each one exploding with a shout from my father to my mother. I couldn't quite hear as I clapped my hands over my ears.

'I love you, Rachelle. Never forget you, my world!'

Colour rained across his face and his lips moved as he stared upwards at the display as though they were my mother herself. The fireworks boomed and cascaded and as the last one zipped and pinged up and outwards, he screamed, 'I'M SORRY!'

Then, it was silent. Adam and I stared at him as he began to choke and his shoulders moved up to his ears. He crouched down on one bended knee as though proposing and bowed his head. Loud sobs cracked through the air as loud as the fireworks had. I stepped towards him with trepidation. He reached up and hugged my waist, clutching at me like a child. My hand moved to his shoulder and I clutched him back. He was human for a single moment, a small glimpse while we hugged, leaving Adam on the pier in darkness.

# 24 CODY

I stood at the back gate of the house watching Riley at the end of the pier. I had to tell her what I'd found out. I knew in my gut if I told her about Tempany, she would understand. Adam and Riley's dad set off fireworks and I stood in amongst the ti-trees and the marram grass and waited.

I waited until Adam went home and Riley's dad staggered past me up the stairs until nobody was around but Riley. She loitered at the end of the pier, under the tall light at the end. I stepped out of the shrubs, scratching the itches that I hadn't dared move for. I walked slowly down to the end of the pier to speak with her. She heard my footsteps approaching and looked up with dread. 'Whatever you're going to do...just do it. Get it over with.'

'What makes you think I'm going to do something?' I asked, coming into the light. She let out a sigh of relief when she saw my face.

'Cody, oh my God. You scared me.' Her face relaxed but then her mouth tightened and she looked behind me. 'I thought you went home.'

'No,' I grinned. 'I just waited for you to be alone.'

She raised an eyebrow at me before she asked, 'What do you want, Cody?'

'Just to talk.'

'It's kind of late.'

'Stay.' I lowered my voice and spread my fingers as if calming to a wild animal. 'I have to tell you something.'

The whites of her eyes shone in the dark under the dull orange light above us. She crossed her arms and waited. I asked, 'Do you know what Tempany is into?'

Her arms dropped to her side and she stamped her foot. 'Just tell me, Cody.'

'She's a drug dealer,' I announced.

Riley's hand slapped my chest and pushed me. I stumbled back a few steps.

'Don't say things like that in public. People could hear you!' She leant against a pole and rubbed her eyes and before she snapped, 'What do you mean anyway – Tempany's a drug dealer?'

'She deals cocaine.'

'No, no. You've got it wrong.' She sighed. 'She takes cocaine. She's not a dealing it.'

'Yeah, she does,' I said with a nod. 'I think your dad does, too, doesn't he?' I gestured to the lavish boat moored behind us. 'So, this is why my brother left me, huh.'

She shook her head slowly. 'I'm sorry, Cody. I can't tell you anything.'

I slumped down on the edge of the pier and she came to sit next to me. 'So…that's it. Adam's a drug dealer.'

'He's not a dealer.' Riley grabbed my hand and placed it in her lap. 'It's my dad. He's the drug dealer. He's…not a good person, Cody. But your brother is.'

I looked up into her face. 'Did your mum find out something about your dad?'

She nodded.

'Do you think he killed her?' I whispered.

Her eyes went to the house and she swallowed before she nodded again.

I hissed, 'We have to get you out of here.'

She held up her hand to stop me as I went to get up. 'It's not as simple as that.'

'What do you mean?' I scoffed, sitting back down.

Riley stared off into the water, a black inky liquid that was slapping against the pier, making our bodies sway when we relaxed into it. She bit the edge of her lip and said, 'Adam doesn't want to.'

'What do we do then?' I asked with a tight throat.

'We let my dad think we believe that she fell, or did it herself…and get the proof he did it. Leave the drugs out of it. Adam will sort that out. Then I can get away…' She looked me in the eye as she squeezed my hand, making me smile. 'But for now…be careful when you come here.'

I nodded. She kissed me on the cheek and I waited to feel the thrill I had felt with Tempany but it didn't come. I looked down and swallowed. I guess something was missing.

Walking home in the dark, I hesitated at the corner of my street. A truck nearby on the highway used its airbrakes as it approached the descent of the winding hill that overlooked the bay to the city. A dog barked and birds flapped. I knew Dad would be working all night. An empty house waited for me. I could go home and go to bed, go to school…or I could go to Tempany's and feel that tingling in my groin again and have that exhilaration of the cocaine on my tongue.

I took a deep breath and turned around, heading to the main street of town instead, and this time I did not get lost. I jogged up the stairs and knocked on the door, carefully avoiding getting a splinter again. Tempany opened the door with a bottle of wine in her hand. She drank from the lip and licked it when she saw me.

'Back again, Codeeee.'

I nodded and brushed my hair back off my face. She stepped aside to let me in and closed the door behind me. She smiled warmly, her eyes looking me up and down. 'You look hot.'

I took off my jacket. She stepped to me and swept her hand from my naval to my back, then back to my naval and up to my chest. 'You want something, Codeeee?'

I blushed and shuddered at her touch – or was it her accent? My heart pounded and I nodded while biting my lip. She snickered and led me to the kitchen, sipping from the bottle of wine again. She gestured at the table; three lines of cocaine were ready. I wet my finger and pushed down. She touched my hand. 'Codeeee, let me show you how it's best.' She bent down, her loose tee shirt falling down and I caught a glimpse of a nipple before looking away. She snorted one line and then stood up. 'It hits better this way.'

I tried to do as she said, but it burnt my nose and was stuck at the back of my throat and I spent the next minute trying to swallow it down with wet, ugly inhales and snuffles and coughs. She laughed and drank more wine. 'I probably gave you too much.'

My heart lurched. 'What do you mean too much?' I broke into a sweat. 'Am I going to overdose and die?'

She laughed. 'No. No. You'll be fine. You just might be...' She gently touched my naval again and I doubled over. It was as though she was touching me *down there*. Then I realised with a start that she was. I leant into it and her hand massaged. 'You'll be hard for a long time.' She laughed and stepped away.

I wanted more. I followed her and tried to kiss her but she put her hand on my mouth. 'Cody, you're too good.'

I winced.

'Besides, your brother would kill me.' She laughed. She looked down at my bulging erection and pointed to the bedroom, where a mattress was on the floor with no bed. 'Go whack off in there. I'll wait here.'

My cheeks burnt and I wanted to crawl in a hole and die. She cocked her head to the side and licked the lip of the bottle. I shifted my erection and grunted. Realising, she had a point. I had to do what she said. Without a word, I stepped into the room and started to close the door but she stopped it with her foot. 'I said I'll wait here…but I get to watch.'

The night became a blur. I did things I didn't believe I had done by the next morning. I wanted more, more and more again. I went to bed naked beside her, wondering how on earth I had got there when I had been such a good fucking boy.

# 25 ADAM

It's not like it was hard or anything.

I put my pen down, pausing for a moment to light my second cigarette in the early morning light. All I needed was a shot of whiskey and some poncy bloody hat to fit the stereotype of the writer at work. Strange that I was even contemplating a career in writing when all I had ever wanted to do was fix things that had gone wrong. But was I writing fiction? Nobody really knew the difference between myth and history, did they? If it was collectively agreed upon, it was fact even if it was fiction. Frodo Baggins was a hobbit. Fact. No. It was fiction. My story would be fiction but nobody really knew, did they?

I filled the notebook that I hid in the dresser drawer with words that came to me. It was as if I had someone listening to me while I wrote: He fell hard, pushed too hard, worked too hard until the lines blurred. He won't ever return after this. Good guys don't hurt people this way. Good guys don't slam a woman's head against a bathtub and throw her into the sea to cover up their mistakes. Good guys don't take drugs and good guys don't lie.

My skin crawled. I'd been working on-site for four days. Staying overnight at the Flynn house was normal but not for days at a time. The boss was really locking us down. I began to even feel the itch that

Riley must have felt. I suppose that's when I started putting words down onto the page. It was something that might get rid of the cold sweats that woke me each night and left me gasping and clutching at my chest, trying to erase the memory of Rachelle's face, first defiant, then terrified.

I wrote…*Not all of us are smart or lucky. Not all of us…*

…can look out their bedroom window at the sunrise on a weekday morning and see the alluring blue of the bay and the grey skyline of Melbourne in the distance…or see Riley jumping into the water from the pier. God, she was like a fish lately. One would think she was actually trying to drown and be with her mother. Maybe she would have been happier that way.

I continued writing. Chewed on my lip. Stubbed out another cigarette. When I heard Riley coming upstairs, I went into her bedroom and sat at the edge of her bed while she dried her hair and splashed a vanilla-scented perfume on that reminded me of Rachelle – the way her scent would linger as if she was dancing circles around me. I breathed in deeply. 'Was that your mum's?' I asked.

Riley nodded and began putting on her socks.

'I remember her wearing that…' I said, looking at my hands, folded in my lap.

'When will you stop pretending that he didn't kill her?' she asked without looking at me.

My stomach turned. My voice cracked as I answered, 'He didn't kill her…She fell in the water, Riley.'

She rolled her eyes and left the room, leaving me completely alone with the vanilla scent lingering like a ghost.

I had to get out of that room, out of that house. I told the boss I was going to get groceries and took off in my car, my hands turning the wheel too quickly out of the driveway that I almost ran over a pot plant. It teetered and rocked as I drove away, but it did not fall.

I went to Tempany's unit. I hadn't spent enough time with her since Rachelle had died. Her unit was a mess. I screwed up my nose when I walked in. There were booze bottles everywhere, muddy footprints, fast food packages and it looked like the cupboards had been turned inside out. I found Tempany spread-eagle on her bed, her shirt barely covering her midriff, her underwear was nowhere to be seen. Her eye make-up smudged down her face.

I roused her gently. 'Baby...wake up.'

She rubbed her eyes and snorted as she rose to a seated position. She pulled her shirt down so she wasn't as exposed. 'Hi.'

'Some bender last night?'

'Yeah.'

I pressed my hands to her cheeks to steady her gaze onto mine. 'This has to stop. You're in too far.'

She nodded and kissed my hands. 'Just a little more and I'll be clean.'

I kissed her on the forehead. 'You need food.'

She nodded.

I left the unit to go get the groceries for the boss. The store was abandoned, as expected at seven in the morning, save for a couple of tradies and an elderly woman, hunched over her basket. I collected the usual in a little red basket. Riley ate the same food over and over. It helped her manage her diabetes so I made sure to get the same brands and serving sizes of everything. Then I got some staples for Tempany too, not many, just enough to get her through another couple of days. I conveniently let the receipt be sucked into the air by the wind so I wouldn't be lying too much when I told the boss the receipt was lost.

I swung the door to Tempany's unit open and bit into an apple I'd bought. I needed food, myself. I shut the door behind me and headed to the kitchen. I dropped the bag I was carrying when I saw my brother leaning against the bench, eating out of a cereal box with his hands.

'Hey, Adam,' said Cody with a mouthful.

Tempany greeted me with a kiss on the cheek.

'What are you doing here again?' I asked with gritted teeth.

'Just hanging out,' he said with a big smile with closed lips.

I dug my toes to the ends of my shoes. 'I don't think that's a good idea. You should leave.'

'Adam!' hissed Tempany. 'You're being rude. Let Cody stay.' I hated the way his name sounded in her mouth. Her accent made it too affectionate: Co-deeee.

She slapped at my chest then announced she had to pee.

'Lady-like,' I teased.

She stuck her middle finger as she walked to the bathroom.

I finished my apple and then crossed my arms, staring at Cody. He stared back.

'When did you get here?' I asked.

'Last night.'

'Where were you this morning?' I challenged.

'Bathroom.'

I shook my head at him. 'Cody, do not do this.' He was risking everything. There was a fine line between breaking yourself and breaking others. I was beginning to realise I needed to become the person I had claimed to have become. It was the only way Cody would listen.

He rifled through the cereal box and paused. He licked his lips then looked up at me and said, 'You don't have a say in what I do or don't do.' He stuck his chin out and straightened up, turning from me and carefully packing the box back up and sticking his hands in his pockets before he faced me again. 'I'm not leaving just because you tell me to stay away.'

'You'll leave when I'm throwing you out of here by your ankle off the balcony.'

Cody swallowed and wiped crumbs off his hoodie. 'I'm Tempany's guest. I'm not leaving until she tells me to.'

'I guess I'll make her make you, then,' I snapped.

'You can't control her,' he smirked.

'Really?'

'You can't control Riley and you definitely can't control Tempany.' He laughed.

'Kid, I'm going to hit you,' I said with gritted teeth.

'Promise?' he scoffed.

I glared at him and sat down in one of the chairs; the table was broken on the floor. 'Why are you really here, Cody?' I asked.

'I like Tempany,' he replied with a shrug.

'You want her to fuck you, eh,' I laughed.

He smiled and looked down, fixing his zipper and picking at his teeth before saying with a smirk, 'She already has.'

I glowered at him. He looked at me with a bored expression. He knew. He knew what he was doing – all to get back at me for leaving him.

I roared and lunged at him, pinning him to the floor. There was too much at stake for my little shit wipe of a brother to come in and tear it apart to get back at me for leaving.

'Get off!' he squealed.

'Get the fuck out!' I shouted.

'Get the hell off me!'

'Stay away from Tempany. Stay away from Riley. Stay *the fuck* away from me!'

'Okay, okay; get the hell off me!'

I released him. Tempany re-entered the room and stared down at us. Cody ran out without looking at her. I stood up and got my breath back. Acid rose in my throat and I had to fight the urge to vomit. Why didn't anyone realise I was trying to help?

I turned to Tempany and cried, 'Ya fucked him?!'

She didn't answer.

'He pay for that cocaine he just took with him?' I asked.

'What?'

'He took a bag!'

'No, no. No, he didn't.' She hurried to the cupboards and looked for her stash. I picked up the cereal box. She collapsed down onto her knees.

'Who supplied you with that bag anyway?' I asked, peering inside the box. 'That didn't look like one of Flynn's.' I frowned.

She swallowed and looked out of the corner of her eye at me. The sunlight came through the tattered curtain and pierced her eyes and made her close them. She replied with a sigh, 'I have another supplier other than your boss.'

'Who?' I snapped. 'Is he the supplier of the boss?'

She nodded as she slowly got up, picking up bits of trash from the floor as she climbed to her feet. 'His name is Elias.'

'You fuck him, too?' I croaked.

She slapped the side of my face and made me bite my lip.

'You don't own me, Adam,' she said with a wavering voice. 'I do what I can to survive.'

I rubbed my cheek where she hit me. She kissed the side of my head and said, 'Sorry, baby. I didn't mean to hit you. I'm sorry. I love you.'

I kissed her and squeezed her cheeks with my palms. 'We are so close...don't blow it. You have to stop sabotaging this.'

'I'll have to explain to him...that I don't have the drugs.' She trembled and sank down into the chair. 'You'll have to get them off your brother, or...'

I nodded, and ran out the door after Cody.

# 26 RILEY

I sat cross-legged in my wardrobe with the door closed and held the necklace in my hands. I scowled into the darkness, remembering the cold of the tile that viciously chewed into my cheek as I lay on it. I remembered how she had been in the bathtub and Adam had climbed through the window to get me out. My temple throbbed with the blurriness of the memory.

There was a thud on the balcony outside my bedroom. I sat alert with my heart lurching.

*Knock, knock* at the balcony door. 'Riley,' came a hushed voice. 'It's me. Cody.'

'Cody?' I climbed out of the wardrobe and shut it securely behind me. I opened the door to my room and allowed him inside. 'What are you doing back here?'

'I've got proof.'

'Proof?' I wrinkled my nose. 'How could you have proof of anything? You haven't seen anything.'

'Maybe not proof that your dad killed your mum, but I have proof that Tempany is a drug dealer because you didn't believe me.' He sniffed and lifted his jacket to reveal a packet of white powder shoved down the front of his pants.

I gasped, 'Is that...?'

'I stole it from Tempany's.'

I took a deep breath and asked with a cool voice, 'What were you doing at Tempany's?'

His face went red and he shrugged. 'Just hanging.'

I set my jaw and ran my tongue over my canine teeth to stop myself from snapping at him that he was idiot, hopeless, officially a loser. Hanging with Tempany could only mean that he was using her drugs and being taken advantage of.

He threw the packet of cocaine onto my desk and paced the room. 'So, what should we do? This obviously proves that Adam and Tempany are doing illegal things. They're criminals.'

'Criminals you just screwed over,' I retorted, pulling at my hair.

'What?' He blinked.

I scoffed. 'Do you really think they didn't notice you take that?'

'They don't have a clue.'

I rolled my eyes. 'They're not stupid, Cody. I can't believe you just stole cocaine from a drug dealer. People get killed for doing stuff like that, you moron.'

'Should we take it to the police?' he asked with widening eyes.

I chewed on my lip. 'No, I told you. We have to avoid the police.'

He groaned. 'Riley, they're not doing the right thing! We have to tell the police.'

I snapped at him, 'Are you doing the right thing, Cody?'

He gaped and stepped away from me. 'What do you mean?'

I listed things on my finger. 'Truancy, theft, drug use.'

Cody sat on the edge of my bed and rubbed his thighs. 'Okay, I get it.'

I scanned the backyard from the window as though the answer to what we could do could be found on the crisp grass or hidden inside the clipped hedge.

'You're thinking about doing something really risky, aren't you.' Cody cleared his throat.

'I'm scared,' I admitted. 'Dad always says there are people out there that would kill me or my mum just to get to him.'

'Maybe that's what happened to your mum? Maybe your dad had nothing to do with it.' Cody's eyes went to the packet on my desk.

I shook my head. 'I know...I just know he's in on it.' My lip trembled and I threw my hands up in the air. 'Now you've done this and I'm scared you're going to get hurt, too.'

He gulped. 'I'll be okay.' I paused, my eyes on my bedside drawer. Cody's eyes followed mine. 'What is it?'

I stood and pulled open the drawer. I lifted the underwear up and pulled out the handgun that Adam had given me. It was weightier in my hand than I remembered. Cody's eyes widened and he leapt back. 'Riley!' he gasped. 'What is that? What-what-what are you doing with that? Why? Why?'

I handed it to him with one finger looped in the trigger. It dangled heavily from my index finger and swayed, pointing downwards. I whispered, 'You need to protect yourself.'

He crossed his arms over his chest as though hugging himself. 'Nah, nah...' He went to grab the cocaine but I flicked the gun up and pointed it at him. He dropped the bag.

I said in a level voice, 'If you take that, they'll kill you. Just take this gun...and I'll make sure they get it back.'

'Adam wouldn't...' Cody's voice trailed off.

I gestured to the camera. 'The only reason you're alive right now is because my dad is asleep...and Adam isn't here.'

His Adam's apple bobbed as he swallowed. He took the gun from me with a furtive, trembling hand and he nursed it to his chest like a baby. He looked up at me with wide eyes. 'I don't know how to use it.'

I dug my fingernails into my palms and shrugged. 'You better learn.'

'What are you...what are you going to do that?' Cody asked with a pointed look at the cocaine.

'I'll make sure they get it back,' I repeated. 'I promise.'

'Are you sure?' he asked.

I nodded.

'Okay. I'll go home now.'

'Bye.'

Cody climbed down from the balcony and sprint off down the lawn and down to the beach. I picked up the bag of cocaine. It would have cost a bit. I didn't understand how the pricing worked but I gathered it had paid for the boat at least three times over. Mum had known all about Dad's business, and was even complicit in it. I wondered if that had been why she felt she couldn't leave. Had she worried all these years that if she had left, she knew too much? The old saying that knowledge is power certainly wasn't true for drug dealing. The more you knew, the shorter you lived.

I turned the bag over and hefted it in each hand. So Tempany was not just playing around behind Adam's back – she was also playing around behind my dad's back. Was she the one who my father had been worried about all this time? Coming to take us away to get to him? Had she slid right into his house under his nose...after all this time?

I picked up my phone and texted Adam.

**Where r u.**

Little dots blinked across my screen. Then stopped. I groaned and started looking for a place in my room that I could hide the bag, all the while glancing at the camera hoping Dad really was asleep. He'd taken a sleeping tablet (or six) last night so I expected that he was, but dread still coursed through my body.

Placing the bag in the hem of the curtain, my phone buzzed. Adam had finally responded.

**Sorting out work. Be by soon.**

I texted back: **Tempany is cheating on you.**

No response. I smirked. *Bye Tempany. You're going to stop getting in the way of me and Adam and what I want. I want to get away from my father and nothing is going to stop that happening.*

# 27 ADAM

My head throbbed and my ankles jarred as I pounded the road, running after Cody towards home. Old home. Past home. The home that made me. Split me. Broke me. Or was that the Flynn home? I clutched at my side and gasped for air. I thought I would have seen Cody by now – it was the whole reason I hadn't driven. I thought I would have caught up with him but he had slipped into the morning like stars in a polluted sky.

I stopped to catch my breath at the corner of the road. I had to give up the drugs. Now that Cody had been lured into this sordid realm of the upper class, everything would blow apart. My heart hammered loudly in my ears and it thumped in my throat. I squinted in the early morning sunlight and felt my forehead rip with a headache that had come from nowhere. I needed a fix, but I wanted to hold out. I had to get the gear off Cody before he got himself caught with them. I sucked with desperation at the crisp air and leant on my knees. It was all going wrong. Cody becoming as slippery as me. Monkey see, monkey do – even after I'd been gone for four years.

My phone buzzed. I looked at it. It was a text from Riley. **Where r u.** My throat burned from sucking in the cold air as I typed **You really are a selfish bitch sometimes, you know that? ...God damn it!**

**You could have a little bit of respect! Is that too much to ask?**

I chewed on my lip and ran my tongue along my furry teeth. I sighed. *She's a kid. I look out for her. It's what I do.*

I read back over what I'd written. Yes, it was too much to ask. For Christ's sake. I pressed my finger on the backspace button until my message was deleted. It was the fourth time I'd done that this week. Then I texted, **sorting out work, be by soon**. I was about to slip my phone back into my pocket when it buzzed again.

**Tempany is cheating on you.**

My stomach tightened and my headache pounded with the reminder that Tempany had slept with my brother - my *under-age* brother.

She was messed up; I could forgive her. We could work through this. She was just really struggling at the moment with her addiction – she wasn't thinking right. I lowered my phone. But how did Riley know? I looked towards the beach and thought Cody must have gone to see her. He would have gone along the beach and that was why I hadn't found him…and he hadn't come home – he'd gone to her. Which way would he be coming back?

Tempany texted me. **Have you got the gear back?**

I texted back **yes**, even though I was lying. I would have the gear back in a moment – the second I found Cody.

I strode down the street, still clutching at my side and my phone. A blue car pulled up beside me and two guys pounced onto me without a word. I was shoved to the ground and had a knee jammed into my chest before I could process what was going on. The guys grabbed and twisted my arm up beside me. I bellowed as it made a crunching sound before a pop. 'Get off me!'

I fought back but I couldn't gain traction on the road to propel myself up; my sneakers kept sliding in the chipped gravel. I managed to knee one guy in the groin and he stumbled back, allowing me to try running but as I got to my feet, my head erupted and fell to my chest onto the ground.

'Hey!' screamed a voice. 'Get away from him!' I looked up to see my younger brother springing towards me, snatching a baseball bat from one of the guys. He swung upwards with his face contorted and his teeth bared. I leapt up and rammed my head into the chin of the guy closest to Cody, but the other guy grabbed my arm and he swung me around like a ragdoll and released me into the car door. I landed on my wrist on the asphalt and heard a crack. I nursed it with a wince and stood up with shaky legs, trying to get my walk straight. Cody swung the baseball bat again and the guys got back into their car and took off.

Cody looked at me, breathing hard and his hands were white on the baseball bat. My lip wobbled like a baby's and I inhaled to keep myself from crying from the pain and indignity of having the shit beaten out of me. I fell to the ground and threw up, leaning over as the contents of my stomach emptied onto the ground beside Cody. He supported me and pulled me back to my feet.

'Adam, move.'

I staggered and asked, 'Where are we going?'

'We're getting out of here before somebody sees us.'

I switched off the tap and stepped out of the shower at my old home. The shower dripped as if to summon me back in, under the soothing water.

I stared at my reflection. The mirror seemed to vibrate like a rippling pool as I tried focusing through the clearing steam. My eyes were straining, exhausted, with dark rings below them. I stroked my dirty hair. It was getting too long and the edges were beginning to kink. Blood pulsed from my forehead and trickled down the bridge of my nose before catching in the crease of my cheek and drying before it touched my upper lip. I was lucky to be alive. The guy had only hit me hard enough with the baseball bat to knock me down. Hitting the road had almost knocked me out. It should have delivered a pretty clear message, but I was confused anyway.

I didn't remember arriving back at home with Cody. I only remembered him dragging me up the stairs while I clutched at my head. I had stumbled into the shower, seeing nothing but blood in my eyes. The shower was steaming hot, but I hadn't felt the intense scalding of my skin, turning it bright red. Washing the gash in my forehead, I gagged with disgust as water and blood joined together, circling around the drain.

Now I stood in front of the mirror, getting dressed even though I was wet all over. I wiped away the steam on the mirror and spotted Cody, shell-shocked in the doorway. I whirled around to face him, too fast, and was overwhelmed with dizziness. I cried out as I slipped and hit the back of my head on the sink and slid to the floor, sobbing at the irony.

I touched the back of my head gingerly and tried to ignore the pain in my wrist.

'What was that about, Adam?' Cody asked. 'Why were those guys beating you up?' He took a hesitant step into the bathroom.

'Get back, Cody!' I yelled.

'What was it about?' he demanded.

'Nothing,' I groaned and put my hands over my face.

A moment passed before Cody said, 'Okay,' and walked away. I calmed myself down before following him. I stood in his doorway while he tried to read a book. I leant against the doorframe and our eyes met in the mirror reflection of his dresser. We could have been twins we were so similar, if not just our eyes.

'I'm all right, Cody,' I said quietly. 'I'm sorry.'

'That's okay. What happened to make those guys jump you like that?' he asked.

I shook my head, and answered, 'I don't know anything.'

Cody rubbed at his upper lip and moved the baseball bat from his bed to a spot where it could rest against the wall. 'Your head is still bleeding.'

'I know,' I sighed. I went into his room and tried to sit on the edge of his bed, but fell onto it instead, clutching at my head. 'Man, I stuffed up.'

'Adam, you need to go to the hospital. I can't fix that.'

'I can't. The boss…he'll find out.'

'Dad'll fix it.'

'Dad?' I scoffed. 'He wouldn't touch me to save my life.'

Cody shrugged. 'Too bad then because he's already on his way home. I called him.'

I tried to argue but my lips went numb and my head throbbed. I lowered my head into my hands and winced as I put too much weight on my wrist. Cody patted me on the shoulder. 'You'll be okay.'


When Dad got home, I limped down the stairs and greeted him with my eyes down. He stood in the foyer with a bulky first aid kit in one hand and his phone in the other. He looked at me and shouted, 'Oh my God.'

'It's not a big deal,' I mumbled. Cody lingered behind me. Dad grabbed my wrist and I wailed like a baby seal pup and doubled over. He pushed up my sleeve and inspected it, before slowly moving my fingers.

He announced, 'It's not broken, but it's a nasty sprain. You'll need an ultrasound on that when this swelling goes down.'

I pulled my wrist away from him and held it to my chest. Dad said, beckoning to the kitchen. 'Come sit down and we'll look at your skull. You better hope it's not a skull fracture.'

Cody shoved me into a seat at the table under multiple lights, then leaned on the island bench to watch. Dad pulled on gloves and a face mask. I sat there stock-still as he shone a torch on my forehead and grabbed tweezers to pick out bits of bitumen and my hair that I had missed when I had showered. His mouth went thin and he tutted at me. He looked to Cody. 'Get the dog clippers.'

Cody nodded and collected dog clippers.

'We have a dog?' I asked.

'*I* have a dog,' he said with his nasally voice. 'You left this family.'

'You didn't want me anymore,' I mumbled.

'It's not that I didn't want you.' He gave me a stern look. 'You made your choice to ruin your career by going and taking drugs. You could have really made a difference and helped people,' he sighed. 'You could have saved people.' He shone the torch in my eyes and held them open so I couldn't blink. 'You have signs of a concussion. Your head will be fine but I'm going to stitch it.'

I closed my eyes and saw the thumping headache flash as neon lights behind my eyelids. I said, 'I didn't want to hurt people.'

He was quiet so I opened my eyes to see if he had heard me.

'Have you hurt someone, Adam?' he asked.

I swallowed and shook my head slightly. 'Nah...I just...I mean, as a doctor or a cop...or whatever.'

'I don't hurt people,' he said with a nasal sigh. 'You and your stupid ideas.'

Cody came back with the clippers and Dad shaved a small bald patch at my hairline.

'You understand that I'm only doing this to avoid you dying,' he explained tightly. He carefully weaved stitching thread through the thin section of my head and I gripped the edge of my chair with my good hand and bit down on my tongue. 'I appreciate you trying to make things right with your brother by playing baseball with him, but maybe don't continue.'

I looked at Cody, who shrugged. I cleared my throat and said, 'Loud and clear.'

Dad stuck a large adhesive patch to my head that irritated the corner of my eye. He lowered his facemask and said, 'You'll live.' He cleaned up everything and said, 'I have to get back to the hospital...I don't think it's a wise choice to still be here when I finish at three…unless you're ready to apologise to me and turn your life around.'

'Thanks, Dad,' chirped Cody. Dad strode off and slammed the door behind him, muttering about me under his breath.

Cody turned off all the lights and put things away while I gingerly felt at the wound. We were silent. The hum of the refrigerator burned into the kitchen with the odd drip of the tap.

I stood up and pulled my jacket and walked over to Cody, whose shoulders and elbows went closer to his sides.

'Pour me a drink,' I said. 'We need to talk.'

We sat in the living room drinking shot after shot of Dad's $300 bottle of aged Scotch.

'You reckon you're old enough to hang out with my girl and take my drugs, huh,' I began.

Cody nodded, screwing his face up as he swallowed his sixth shot. 'It's not like you were much older when you left us.'

'I was eighteen.'

'Yeah, and I'm seventeen,' he retorted.

I tapped the shot glass on the coffee table repeatedly. 'You're still too young.'

'You made us think you were lying in a ditch dead,' he snapped. 'Do you know what that does to a person? When they think someone that they love is dead?'

I remained quiet before a moment before I answered, 'I'm not dead.'

'Obviously not,' Cody said, the left side of his mouth curling up in a half-smile, half-smirk.

'So…am I the reason why you've…*attached* yourself to Riley?' I asked.

Cody swallowed another shot and hesitated before he shrugged. 'I saw you with her one time at Ben's Bar. Fighting in the car park. I did what I had to.'

I raised my shot glass. 'Here's to…lying to girls.'

Cody scoffed. 'It wasn't like that.'

'But she thinks you're her friend.'

'Yeah.'

'And you're not.'

Cody flinched. 'Why not?'

'You're using her,' I replied.

He rolled his eyes. 'It's not what I meant.'

'Don't feel bad,' I said, swallowing the Scotch. 'She's using you, too.'

He blinked at me. 'Why are you telling me this?'

'Sick of lying, I guess,' I sighed. I stared down at the Scotch and breathed out a little laugh. 'I'm the liar of the family aren't I. Time to start doing right?'

'What do you do for Riley's father?' Cody asked in a hushed voice.

'Riley's father is an arsehole,' I blurted out. I pinched my eyes closed and groaned. 'Ah, shit. Shouldn't say that.' I took a breath and regurgitated what I had to: 'He cares. He just gets frustrated.'

Cody cocked his head with a drunken swerve and sneered, 'I know that he hits Riley, like, all the time. He's an arsehole, you can say it. Whatever he does, I don't care. He's got you brainwashed or something.'

'Did she tell you that he hits her?' I asked quietly, putting my shot glass down on the coffee table beside the bottle.

'I've seen the bruises.'

'Where?'

'Everywhere, Adam!' he cried. 'She needs to get out of that place.'

I leant back into the sofa and watched Cody take another shot. The kid was annihilating himself. Taking cocaine, drinking, hanging out with Tempany and Riley...He was a goner and he couldn't even see it...just like a real little me.

'Why haven't you gone to the cops?' I asked, studying my empty glass.

'Why haven't *you*?' Cody snapped. 'You obviously know what goes on, and you're right there, man. You're *right there*. Why don't you *do* something?'

I murmured, 'Because I *can't.' It's not in my job description*, I wanted to add.

Cody swallowed another sot and scrubbed at his face with his hands as though trying to cleanse the fuck-up.

I reached for the bottle of Scotch, filled the cup and then downed it. Nothing really made sense; I was drunk and concussed. What did I know about anything, really? I didn't even know why I had just been beaten the fuck up but it made me wonder.

'Cody?'

'What?' he mumbled.

'Where did you take the drugs that you took from Tempany today?' I stared at my glass as I ran my finger along the rim. I waited. I looked over and saw that Cody had passed out asleep. I stood up and staggered to the door, and wandered back to Tempany's.


I knocked quietly. I usually walked right in. It was later in the day by the time I got there with my head stitched up and haphazardly bandaged myself. It was at least one in the afternoon. Tempany opened the door but I swayed in the door way.

'Where's the bag?' she asked. Her eyes went to the wound on my forehead and then to my wrist, but she didn't ask

'I don't know,' I said.

Tempany raised an eyebrow. 'But you got it back from Cody.'

'Cody didn't have it.'

'You said you got it back from him,' she argued.

I leant against the doorframe with a grunt; it was making sense even though everything was blurry. 'Tempany…you messaged me to check if I got the bag off Cody, right before these guys jumped me.'

'Yeah?' I searched her face for any clue that she felt bad but her face remained blank.

'Did you send those guys to get it off me?' I asked.

She whispered, 'Yes.'

I closed my eyes and felt my skin tingle with revolt. I said through gritted teeth, 'They beat the shit out of me!'

She stared blankly at me so I shrugged at her. 'You don't even care.'

Tempany still didn't respond.

'You knew I was with my little brother yet you…sent…those pieces of shit…to beat the shit out of me. Why?'

She said with a level and serene voice, 'It was you or me.'

'What?' I croaked.

Tempany took a deep breath and looked at me with a tilt of the head. 'What do you want me to say, Adam? "All is fair in love and war?" I think you're smart enough to know that everything doesn't revolve around you and your issues.'

My throat caught and the muscles under my tongue dropped. Numbness took over my face as it flushed. The entire time she had known who I was looking for – sacrificing everything for. We could never recover from the lies she told me.

I croaked, 'It's over.' I heard it almost echo as I spoke.

'What's over?' she spat. 'Us? We are not over.'

'We're over.'

'How can you say that?' she hissed. 'After all we've been through.'

'Goodbye,' I murmured and went to turn.

'No! This is not goodbye.' She stepped outside and tried to grab my arm but I dodged her. 'You can't leave me. No!'

'Get the fuck out of my life!' I pushed her and she fell with a loud crash against the wall before stumbling and crashing down the stairs. I gasped and stood at the top to see her stagger up to her feet and glare up at me.

She called, 'You'll never be able to leave me.'

I went down the stairs and tried to pass her. 'I know too much, Adam Marshall. I know the *real* Adam Marshall.'

I shoved her aside then half-walked, half-ran down the street with hot tears in my eyes, ignoring the looks of people I passed. I considered going home and crawling under my bed covers and sleeping for the rest of my life but my phone rang and it was the boss.

'Where the hell are you?' he barked. 'You went to get groceries at seven and now it's 1:30!'

I stopped in the middle of the path and blocked at least four people trying to get past. 'Ah, shit!' I groaned. I had forgotten about the groceries altogether…and my car. I looped back and drove my car to the Flynn house, throwing Riley's spoiled yoghurt out the window onto the promenade.

I went inside with the bags held in one hand. Sunlight poured through the window in the kitchen. The boss turned from where he was sitting at the table to see me walk in. I could smell burnt pancakes and coffee. My stomach flipped over. I wanted food. I put the bag down and rubbed at my eyes and squinted at the light. The headache threatened to blow my brains out.

The boss stood up and looked at me. 'Run into a little trouble, son?'

'Yes, sir, just a little,' I mumbled as I scratched at my adhesive bandage. I took out a cigarette and lit it. I stared at the boss and he stared back before finally asking, 'Well, what happened?'

'I got hit in the face with a baseball bat,' I offered with a smile.

'Who did it?' he asked, going to the sink and grabbing a glass. He filled it with water and looked to me. *Your supplier.* 'Well?' he asked impatiently before passing me the glass. I sipped and grimaced at the boring taste. I replied, 'I didn't see who it was.'

'You didn't piss anyone off that may have bought gear off us?'

'It wasn't because of that,' I said.

'If you didn't see them, how would you know that?' he snapped. I shrugged and sat down at the table. 'Did anybody-?'

I interrupted, 'Nobody saw. I was the only one there. They jumped me from behind. They pinned me to the ground to search me, saw that I had nothing to steal and then…lights out.' I curled my lip. 'I don't remember anything else. Just arseholes.'

'Do you think they knew who you are?' he asked quietly.

I reached across the table for the ashtray and nodded. I looked at the cigarette burning, the smoke willowing about. 'Reckon that's why they tried stealing from me.' From the foyer, I could see Riley coming down the stairs and lingering, trying to listen in. Had she known what was waiting for me when she had texted me? Had she been distracting me? I gently blew out a smoke ring and it wafted off beside the boss's ear.

He pointed at me. 'Right, you are hiding something and I intend to find out what it is.'

I shrugged and inhaled my cigarette. 'Told you everything I know, boss.'

'There are no secrets in this family.'

I whispered, 'Riley doesn't know everything. Isn't she family?'

'She's not part of that part of *the* family,' he hissed.

'Right, and she's disposable too, just like Rachelle was,' I muttered under my smoky breath.

The boss seemed to chew on his tongue for a moment as he wrestled to get his temper under control before finally answering with gnashing teeth, 'Don't you dare start blaming me. It was not me, boy – you know that.'

'Yeah, I know. I was there, remember,' I said. I sighed and butted out the cigarette, recalling when I'd finally managed to rouse him. He'd fallen off the chair.

I'd told him: 'I just took Riley to the hospital. You've been drugged.'

The boss had looked at his glass and sneered at it. 'Fuck.' Then he looked up at me and blinked. 'Riley's in the hospital?'

'She's sick. High blood sugar.'

The boss had got to his feet and staggered to the desk so he had something to hold onto. 'Who the bloody hell drugged me?'

I shrugged and asked, 'Where's Rachelle?'

He'd searched the house and I'd had to explain about the bathroom. His body had darted from room with jerky movements and he'd stacked it against the wall multiple times. His eyes widened and bugged out. He looked at me and asked, 'Why is there dirt smeared on your face?'

I remembered what I'd done when I'd returned home.

My teeth had chattered as I pulled a cigarette out of my pocket. They were squashed but salvageable. The orange glow illuminated my living room and seared her face into my mind. I'd put her over the edge of the yacht into the Bass Strait near the heads of the peninsula.

Getting home, I had stripped off my clothes, balling my pants and shirt together in a knotted clump of material. I threw my cigarette into the sink. I bent over it, watching the smoke curling before it extinguished in the wet base, almost vomiting with a surge of disgust.

I gagged.

Looked at the ball of clothes I'd left on my kitchen table and let all the air escape from my lungs. Wet from the bathroom, soaked in my blood and dusted with cocaine. I marched out into the backyard. I grabbed a spade from the garden shed and started hacking at the ground, beside the row of snapdragons the previous owners had lovingly installed in their immaculate garden. They were dying at the hands of my neglect and now I was murdering them.

As I dug, I sliced a stem and the petals littered the dirt like confetti, as though burying my clothes was a sacrificial ritual. I stared at the buds, gone before they could bloom this upcoming spring. I could taste the dirt and the lingering stench of salt water. My skin started to prickle and I realised with a screech of horror that I was covered in bugs. I ripped off my second shirt that day, reaching for the soggy towel with shards of glass and slapped my bare skin with it to get rid of the bugs but my skin continued to tingle and itch. I rolled on the prickly, damp grass of the backyard, bellowing with tears because I couldn't get them off. I was perched on all-fours, heaving and sobbing when I began retching.

Now, with that memory, I scratched as though I could feel the bugs from the garden again. The boss crossed his arms and sneered. I studied my bloodied cuticle before gnawing at it, trying to look unfazed by the look on his face. He said, 'The police were at the funeral.'

I nodded. 'Normal. Closing their case.'

'Feels as though it's not closed though,' he murmured. He sighed and uncrossed his arms. 'It is the weirdest feeling to wake up in the morning and not have her there. The mornings are quieter now. Never thought I'd miss someone so much.'

I leant back on the chair, resting my arms behind my head and frowned. 'Didn't seem like you were the type to miss someone at all.'

'Of course, I miss her,' he snapped. 'Don't you?'

I fiddled with my fingers for a moment before finally saying, 'Yeah.'

The boss got some Scotch and passed me a tumbler of it. 'To Rachelle,' he said, raising his own glass in cheers. I swallowed hard, still numb around the edges from drinking earlier. I rubbed at my forehead, counted to three and then slammed it down. 'To Rachelle.'

The boss eyed me carefully then put his hand across the table for me to shake. I shook it awkwardly with my bad wrist. 'You're a good man, Adam.' My eyes welled up. 'I know the way it happened…it was…' He searched for the words but I didn't help him. He asked with a gulp, 'Are you good?'

I shook my head and curled up in the chair. 'No.'

I huddled under a blanket on the couch downstairs of the Flynn house that night, watching the moonlight cast shadows on the wall of the living room as my head pounded. I was trying to stay awake with the blue light of the television and the uncomfortable couch preventing me from getting comfortable. The sharp pangs from my sprained wrist were doing an awfully good job at keeping me awake anyway.

I needed to get into touch with Iacopetta now that I finally knew who the supplier was. I tapped into the keyboard on my phone but glanced up when I heard light footsteps descending the stairs as if a ghost was walking. My muscles tensed as Riley sat casually on the edge of the couch and peered down at me with eyes that reflected the blue light.

'Adam, are you okay?'

'Yeah, yeah I'm fine, Riley, just dandy,' I answered in a low voice, staring at the ceiling.

'Was the other guy hurt?' she asked with hope in her voice.

I merely grunted in agreement. 'Riley,' I said. She nodded at me. 'It wasn't right what you did, you know.'

She asked, 'What did I do?'

'You got Cody involved.'

'Did I?'

'He has grand visions of rescuing you,' I mumbled. 'He is convinced that you need him.' I narrowed my eyes at her to see if she reacted but her face stayed calm. What I would give to be the hero in the story, instead of the guy that made everybody fall apart and hate each other. Why did she have to bring my baby brother into it?

'Why are you doing this?' I asked. 'You knew that Cody was over there and you knew that Tempany was cheating on me. You know a lot more than you let on to me.'

She wet her cracked lips with a swipe of her tongue. 'I've been thinking about the day Mum did what she did.'

If Riley had been thinking about what had happened that day, she must have been remembering some things. No doubt she had questions for me, but I couldn't bear the thought of the day so I said, 'I don't want to talk about it right now.'

Her eyes bore into mine and in the blue light, they looked almost yellow.

'Did you mean to tell me that Tempany was cheating on me with

Cody?' I asked.

She twitched. 'With Cody?'

'Yeah.'

She paused. 'I meant with somebody else.'

I sat up and grimaced. 'With who?'

Her eyes went to the second floor where her dad was sleeping, then back to me.

I looked up and it dawned on me what she meant. I shook my head. 'No…no.'

'I caught them,' she said with a straight-face and a mono-tone voice. 'He knows. She knows. They know I know.'

'When?' I whispered.

'Before Mum died,' she whispered. 'I think she found out, and that's why she did what she did.'

My ears went numb and my lips tingled. What sort of idiot was I? I could have easily buckled under this revelation from Riley but I got up and stepped out to the patio in the dark.

The air was so crisp it made me gasp and quiver as I lit a cigarette. Riley stood in the doorway. I couldn't stay in this house. This house where people lied to each other, hit people, strangled each other…killed each other.

I glanced back at Riley and the way she watched me unnerved me. A vacant stare, with cold eyes.

She whispered, 'We can say he did it.'

'I think I'm going to go home.' I cleared my throat, numb.

She stepped out to grab me at my hips – a too intimate action. I stepped away.

'What are you doing?' I hissed.

'You can't leave,' she said. Her face contorted and she grabbed at me again. 'Please.' She gasped, 'Please don't leave me because of what he's done. Don't give up.'

I paused and held up my good hand with my cigarette. I'd got what I needed: a name. Possibly a face if that was who jumped me. Yet I

lingered. Riley was right. I couldn't leave her. I said, 'Not for good –
just…for now.'

She moved in and tried to kiss me and I recoiled. She'd lost her
mind.

I took a deep breath and asked, 'What are you doing, Riley?'

She closed her eyes, grabbing my hands, and whispered, 'I want to
go with you.'

'You can't, kiddo.' I stepped further away. 'No.'

Her eyes flashed open and she screamed, 'I lied for you!'

I glanced upwards at the camera. Surely that woke up the boss.

Riley paced the patio with her arms crossed and her head down, her
bare feet slapping the wood lightly that at any other time other than
midnight would have been almost silent. The light turned on in the
kitchen and the boss came to the open door with sleepy eyes and his
hair mucked up like a cockatoo crest.

'What on earth are you two doing?' he grumbled.

My eyes went to him and imagined him with my girlfriend.
Imagined him *knowing* she was my girlfriend. Imagined him hiding it
from me as he spoke about having no secrets in the family. Memories
of him strangling his wife and child, telling me it was my job to protect
his wife and child, realising I had been doing my job wrong all this
time.

I looked down at my feet and rested my cigarette on my lip, forcing
myself to inhale in so I was at least breathing.

'Riley, leave Adam alone – get to bed,' he barked.

Riley sneered at me. 'You know what? You're a coward, Adam. You
know what happened that day, *what he did*, don't you? And you still just
say nothing.'

'What I did?' The boss's eyes flared.

Riley glared at him and slipped past him and disappeared into the
house.

I faltered and looked up at the boss. He sighed through his nose
and reached out an arm to place over my shoulder. 'You should be

inside, son.' He added, 'I was watching on the camera.' I hoped I was doing the right thing by leaving her there with him.

'I'm really sorry, boss, I hope you didn't get the wrong idea. I made a mistake.'

He said, 'It wasn't a mistake. You stopped.' He sat me down on the couch again and sat on the floor of the living room. He crossed his legs like he was back in primary school, his hairy toes catching my eye.

'Why is she the way she is?' I asked.

He looked at me with his chin up and forward, defiant, yet defeated. 'She learnt it from me.'

I studied his face. Was he really hiding a big secret from me? A secret as big as *I was fucking your girlfriend behind your back*? Or was this something Riley had created? I sat awkwardly on the edge of the couch, unsure of what I could even say or ask.

'Those guys that jumped you...' He stopped himself, and I waited. He continued, 'Would you kill those guys?'

I stared at him in disbelief. 'I...don't think so.' I rubbed roughly at my hair and muttered, 'I don't know...maybe, but I'd have to leave town.'

He leant forward and said, 'Don't you miss your family, Adam?'

I cleared my throat and tried to answer without emotion, 'Sometimes.'

The boss pulled back and reclined on the floor, still looking at me. We sat together in silence that was louder than any argument he'd ever had with his family. We stared at each other thoughtfully. The longer it went on, the longer I worried. 'Have you ever killed someone?' he asked.

I reeled back with a hiss, the searing burn of a question.

He stood and clapped a hand on my chest. 'It's okay, son.' Then he added, 'Don't trust Riley for a second, though. She's a liar.'

'I guess I've got nobody left to trust,' I mumbled.

'Don't you trust me anymore?' he asked.

I swallowed. 'I did trust you.'

The boss eyed me and then asked in a voice quieter than a whisper, 'I didn't kill my wife.'

I nursed my wrist and imagined again the moment he would have cheated on his wife with my girlfriend. He must have read something was running through my mind because one eyebrow peaked higher than the other. Instead of asking me what was really wrong, he gestured to my wrist and asked how it was.

'It's fine,' I answered shortly. I couldn't really complain to him about the constant throbbing and the uncomfortable feeling that it was so wrong, out of place and un-deserved.

I stiffly wriggled my fingers under the stiff bandage to prove that it was fine, but I had to grit my teeth to even move them.

'Good,' the boss sighed. 'I was worried it was broken when I saw you.'

'It's not.'

'You know I'd do anything for you,' he said.

Except not screwing my girlfriend.

I wondered if I could truly do what Riley wanted me to do. Blame it on him. He was a crook, but he wasn't a murderer. He came and sat on the couch beside me and asked, 'What's on your mind?' I fiddled with the thin blanket that I had been using before Riley had woken me up. He added, 'I won't tell anyone whatever it is.'

'I just want to go home,' I burst out.

The boss's lips made a very thin line. 'Not happening.'

'Why not?' I cried, more upset than I wanted to be.

'You're safer here, clearly,' he grumbled.

I shook my head. 'This wasn't anything to do with you, I know it. It's my brother. Riley's got him involved and I'm worried about him.'

'You're a terrible liar, Adam.'

Heat flushed into my cheeks and I thought of all the lies I had already told for him and even to him. He may have been a powerful man, with a lot of money, but he didn't know anything that really mattered. He didn't understand what it was like to leave your family in the hopes of following your dream but getting caught between a murder investigation and the crazy dealings of drugs and laundering money. He didn't understand what it was like to be in charge of something, like sailing that expensive yacht – he only knew how to sit still, get drunk and wasted on sleeping pills then blame his wife for every short coming that he couldn't control. Strangle her when she didn't listen, slam her head into the floor or the wall, or the edge of the bathtub in anger and rage he could barely see through – the walls ran red and the boat stalled.

He didn't know what it was like to speed through your life high on drugs that you had no business getting involved in anyway. He didn't have the perpetual headache that sent you silly and made you suspicious. He didn't know what it was like for his family to think he was dead, but he did maybe know how it felt for his family to want him dead.

The lines were blurring and I rubbed my face and asked, 'What am I supposed to do to keep my brother safe?'

'Just tell him he has to keep his distance – that you don't care about him anymore,' the boss instructed. I began to object but he interrupted me, 'You may be lying when you tell him that but if he thinks you don't care about him, he will cut you off. It's the only way you can keep the people you love safe.'

I studied his face and he smiled weakly. 'If they care, you destroy them.' He swallowed with a frown. I nodded and he stood.

I clutched at the blanket and pulled it up to my chest like a child, as if it would protect me from him if he were to strike me the way he hit the people he claimed he cared for. He left me alone in the dark, thinking over my pure accidental progression of stupid mistakes that had put me there on that couch, too scared to move.

I blinked and the blue light from the television seared into my eyes. I had fallen asleep. I groaned and sat up, my neck tight and my wrist swollen. My eyes ached. I squinted out the window and saw that the sun had barely risen but it felt like I had slept for a week.

I peered around and found my cigarettes, going out to the patio again to smoke with the palm tree that scraped the spout. A crunching and rustling made me jump. Riley was coming up from the water, but she wasn't wet. She did a double-take when she saw me and then walked up to me with her head lowered.

I waited with dread for her to say something to me. I should have just done what my father had told me all along. Gone to the graduation ceremony. I could have been on my way onto being a specialist earning $600 an hour. I could even be a police detective and be putting Riley's father in prison where he deserved to be. I could have made it. I may have even married Tempany – got down on one knee and presented her with a decent ring. I grinned at the potential that I had once had, that I had pissed away to spite my dad.

I sighed, no point fantasising.

'I thought you'd still be asleep,' Riley said without looking at me. She murmured, 'I'm sorry about last night.'

'It is what it is,' I said, lighting my cigarette.

'Is Cody all right?' she asked, still not looking at me.

'You're only asking now?' I snapped.

She sighed and rolled up the sleeves of her jacket, revealing damp hands.

'What were you doing?' I asked.

'Walking,' she said too quickly. She looked up at me at last and said, 'You didn't answer me about Cody.'

'He's fine – why wouldn't he be?' I narrowed my eyes at her.

'Because I know he took your drugs, Adam,' she whispered. 'He came to tell me.'

'Then you texted me to distract me.' I slammed my cigarette down and stomped on it.

She nodded. 'Sorry.'

'Did you know that Tempany sent someone to get the drugs back?' I asked.

She shook her head. 'I'm not surprised.'

'We broke up,' I admitted. 'So, yeah, I'm worried about Cody.'

'She doesn't know where he lives,' Riley said with another shrug. 'He'll be fine.' I saw her eye twitch and she looked down again.

I chewed on my lip, thinking through what we could do. I could go to Tempany, go after those guys before they got to my brother. It was my only chance to protect him, except I'd given the gun to Riley.

'Riley, I've got an idea, but you need to give me back the gun.'

I turned to go inside but stopped when she announced, 'I gave Cody the gun.'

My heart gave a weird thump that stopped me. 'Are you kidding me?'

She shook her head. 'I was worried that he'd need it,' she said with a furrowed brow.

I looked at the time. It was 7:05. He would be getting ready to go to school. I rushed to the door and called back over my shoulder, 'You're coming with me so hurry up!'

I strode into the school building bypassing the office and fought the urge to run out of there screaming. The memories of the stifling pressure and conformist expectations arrived on my shoulders and pummelled me into the floor.

'Show me where he would be,' I said.

Riley moved along quietly after me, her hands at her chest, wringing before she eventually stopped outside a classroom and said, 'He's in here.'

I marched in. Cody was taken aback when he saw Riley in the doorway and me standing in the front of the room, in front of the chalky, ashy blackboard.

The teacher looked across at me with a befuddled expression. 'Yes, can I help you?'

I ignored him and held out my hand to Cody. 'Give it to me.'

'What?' Cody squeaked.

'Don't fuck me around, Cody. Hand it over.'

'Adam, I don't know what you're talking about!' he shouted.

The teacher stepped between my brother and me. 'You need to leave. Please leave my classroom,' he grumbled through his thick moustache.

I stared at the facial hair with revolted fascination before responding, 'This actually can't wait, sir. Cody needs to give me what he took; it's my EpiPen.'

Cody gripped the edges of her desk and stared at me. How long could I stand in the classroom before the teacher gripped me and threw me out? I didn't move and Cody eventually stammered, 'It's in my locker.'

'Very well,' said the teacher impatiently. He opened the door and gestured out the door. Riley stepped away. 'Cody, please go get it and come straight back.'

He nodded and got up. I followed him to the locker. Riley followed with her head down.

Cody snapped, 'I hope this is important because we're about to do a test.'

I shook my head. 'Give me my gun.'

He flinched and looked to Riley, almost sighed. 'It's in my locker. Hold on.' We kept walking. 'Why do you need it? Those guys from yesterday?'

'Tempany,' Riley quipped.

Cody stopped. 'No.'

'Could you please go get it for me, Cody?' I said with my teeth closing on one another. I didn't like the direction this was going.

Cody shook his head. 'I don't want to.'

'Cody!' I scolded.

'I'm not going to shoot her,' I hissed. 'I just need to get information from her about who those guys are.'

'I can tell you who they are. I knew one of them.'

I stepped back without even realising. 'How do you know one of them?'

'I just do,' he said with a defiant snub of the chin. 'I'll only give it to you if you don't take it to Tempany.'

'Okay, yes, fine,' I hissed.

I followed him to his locker. He took the gun carefully from behind some books and handed it to me. I swiftly put it into my waistband and covered it with my leather jacket. I looked at Cody and saw a dark expression on his face. 'Why do you need it right now?' he asked.

'I need it to protect you,' I whispered.

'Protect me from what?' he spat. 'Who saved who yesterday? You're the one who needs protecting.'

I rolled my eyes. 'Come on, Riley. We're going to Tempany's.'

Cody shoved me. 'I knew you were a liar, Adam.'

'Shut up,' I snapped. 'You don't know anything! Stay out of my business.'

'If I stayed out of your business, you'd be dead right now!' he cried.

'Yeah, and whose bloody fault would it have been? Why do you think they were beating the shit out of me, you ignorant little shit?' I yelled. 'They were doing it to get from me what you fucking took from that bitch!'

He tackled me and slammed us both to the floor. He gripped onto my neck and screamed, 'Why should I believe you?' He reached into my pants and tried to snatch the gun off me, fumbled then caught it. He cocked it and pointed it at me.

'What are you doing?' I howled.

Riley dragged Cody off me and slammed him against the open door of his locker, bending it completely off its hinge with an echoing crash. Riley pulled his arms behind his back and screamed, 'Leave him alone!'

The gun fell from Cody's hand and slid across the floor so fast it was like a blur. I slowly sat up, clutching at my wrist, pain radiating across my body. I tried to stand but couldn't.

Teachers came out of their classrooms and into the corridor. Three male teachers rushed over and protectively pulled Cody and Riley away from me. One teacher noticed the gun on the floor near my feet. I tried to pick it up but it was too late. The teacher dived for it and another grabbed me by the collar and pinned my arms, shouting 'Lockdown! Call the police!'

I went limp and let them pin me down. Riley reached out for me but she was dragged away alongside Cody.

# 28 RILEY

I sat in the principal's office, bouncing my foot up and down, waiting for the police to arrive. I picked at my nails and gnawed at them. Cody was in the assistant principal's office.

I wanted to scream at him *do you have any idea what you've done; you've ruined everything*. I couldn't believe he'd put the gun to Adam's head for Tempany. Nobody had seen the way he'd almost killed his brother. I wondered if I would regret my decision to keep that secret for him.

That boy! I could slap him for almost ruining everything. The police were already dealing with Adam and taking him to the police station, now they had to come "chat" with me.

I fretted that they would know about my mother dying, and not listen to me when I figured out how to word what I wanted to say about who killed her, and they'd be *sympathetic* and the fact that I didn't fucking care would come to their attention.

I could hear the principal across the hall, ranting and raving about behaviour, morals and not bringing personal matters to school. I stared down at the timber floorboards and continued to bounce my leg. The door creaked open and I swivelled to see the two officers who had been dealing with my mother's disappearance, Senior Constable Burke and Senior Constable Ackerman. The assistant principal followed them.

Senior Constable Burke sat down in front of me, slowly and cumbersome with her pregnant belly affecting her flexibility. 'Why did you give a gun to your friend, Miss Flynn?'

I shrugged.

'Did you feel like he needed to have it?' Senior Constable Ackerman asked.

I looked up into his eyes and, with all earnest, said, 'I didn't want him to shoot anybody at school, Senior Constable Ackerman.'

'Who does the gun belong to?' he asked, ready with a notepad and pen. He looked at my expectantly and I froze. If I said it was Adam's, it was probably a lie. If I said it was my dad's, they'd figure out he was in crime and I'd be in foster care within the half hour. The police finding out that my father was the killer had to come from Adam's mouth. All I could do was back him up. It was the only way to avoid foster care.

'We'll need a statement from you, Riley,' said Burke. 'Do you know the gun belongs to?'

'No, I do not,' I replied.

'Did you give the gun to Mr. Marshall?' Ackerman verified, tapping the ballpoint of his pen against the notepad.

I glanced to the assistant principal, who was watching attentively, then looked back to the two police officers. 'I gave it to Cody Marshall, yes.'

'Right,' Ackerman muttered, scribbling in the notepad.

'Is there anything happening at home that made you feel like you needed the gun, too, Riley?' Burke asked. 'Given the recent passing of your mother.'

I couldn't see a way I could feint my way around not wanting sympathy for my mother's tragic death and I pursed my lips.

'Yes, Miss Flynn has her problems,' the assistant principal butted in. 'It most likely accounts for this sudden turn of behaviour. We all deal with problems in different ways – it doesn't make us bad people.'

She gave me a small smile.

'That's true,' mumbled Ackerman. 'But there is absolutely no reason to bring a gun to school.'

My eyes went to his thigh, where the same type of gun was gartered neatly at hand height. I said, 'When you go to work, you take a gun. You take a gun without intent to fire that gun, but you take it anyway. You do your job, feeling a little safer with that gun than without it…even if you know you won't use it.'

'Don't get into semantics,' said Burke in a level voice.

Ackerman asked, 'Did you feel Cody was in danger?'

I looked down to the floor again and mumbled, 'Yes.'

'Where did you get the gun?' Ackerman asked.

'I don't remember.'

Ackerman and Burke exchanged frustrated glances but I pretended that I didn't see them.

Burke asked gently, 'Riley, could you tell us why you and Adam Marshall came to the school today?'

I pushed my body further back on the couch and my feet left the floor. I crossed my arms in front of me and snapped, 'Why don't you ask him? He brought me. I don't even go here anymore.'

The police officers looked to the assistant principal who nodded and stammered, 'Her, um, father, withdrew her from classes for the rest of the term. Grief…and whatnot.'

I scratched at my head and sighed. 'What's going to happen to him?'

'He's at the police station and he'll give a statement just like you're doing right now, except you're a witness; he's a suspect.'

I scoffed. 'Cody's the one who did the wrong thing. Talk to him.' I gestured to them and said, 'You're Missing Persons anyway – why are you bothering me? Nobody is missing.'

Burke smiled with a slight chin tuck. 'Well, I like to think we've built a bit of a rapport by now, Riley.' I raised an eyebrow but swallowed hard. She continued, 'I think a couple of friendly, familiar faces are what you really need right now.'

She probably thought I would find that endearing and it would help me break apart and spill my guts like we were two old girlfriends just chatting over coffee, but it made my muscles tense and my pulse quicken. I hid the cracks that threatened to break me open and I stared at her with an unimpressed lazy eyelid.

Ackerman got it. He cleared his throat and said, 'Your father has been called to come and get you.'

I looked to the ceiling and dreaded the impending car ride home with him, no doubt he would lose his temper and beat my head into the dashboard again.

Ackerman said, 'So if there's anything you want to tell us, or let us know…before he gets here…' He made sure to catch my eye. 'Now is the time, kiddo.'

Adam's nickname for me coming from Ackerman's mouth made my heart flutter. I gasped and snapped, 'Don't call me that.'

He held up his hand. 'Sorry.'

'You don't get to call me that,' I mumbled. Burke and Ackerman made small-talk with the assistant principal who would wait with me for my father to arrive. The two officers left and then it was just me and the assistant principal who tried to appease me with hospitality. I ignored her and stared out the window instead.

# 29 ADAM

Senior Constable Ackerman sat diagonally across from where I was handcuffed to the table in the interview room at the police station. It was a narrow room, with pale blue walls and lemon skirting boards that showed off the dust. I wondered if it was the same room that they had interviewed the boss about Rachelle's disappearance. I wondered if he had felt as claustrophobic as I was feeling.

'Where's my brother?' I asked. 'Where's Riley?'

Ackerman ignored me and rifled through one pile of paperwork that was on the table in front of him. He frowned as he gazed at a sheet of paper and then looked at me carefully. He put the papers down and crossed his arms over his chest. 'What's your name?'

'Why?'

'You are giving an official statement in regards to the incident at the college this morning.'

I scoffed. 'The incident?'

'What's your name?' he asked again. 'Name and date of birth, please.'

I couldn't see any way I could deny my identity so I just nodded and told him my full name and date of birth. I wouldn't be lost in the system anymore. I was merely lost in every other way.

'I gotta tell you, mate...I'm not impressed.'

'I didn't do anything wrong,' I said.

'You didn't do anything wrong?' He repeated, shifting in his seat and frowning. 'Wow. That's something I've never heard before.'

'Why don't you tell me what you think I have done then if you're so smart?' I snapped, wincing at the pressure the handcuff placed on my bad wrist.

'You must know we've wanted to speak to you for a while.' I shook my head. He scratched at the stubble on his chin and said, 'I'm investigating the disappearance of Rachelle Flynn.'

'She's not missing – she was found – I didn't have anything to do with it.' I spoke over Senior Constable Ackerman but he continued speaking calmly, '...The hospital reported a young man brought the daughter to the hospital and I'm thinking it was you.'

I froze and stared at him, my heart pounding and my hands sweating.

Ackerman pointed his finger to the table with each word. 'I think you know something happened that day and you're covering your boss's arse.' My mouth fell open and my face tingled as I shrugged. 'Someone is responsible for that woman is disappearing,' he said in almost a whisper.

'I'm not that someone,' I croaked, looking down.

Ackerman sighed and looked away and chewed on his lip before looking back at me. 'I'm meant to be asking you about the gun today.'

'My brother...I...' I took a deep breath that still didn't give me the air I needed. 'Look...' I cleared my throat. 'The gun is mine. It's not registered. I'm sorry, I fucked up.' Ackerman wrote a note and looked at me with expectant eyes. 'My brother has been getting...picked on...at school,' I said.

Ackerman said, 'He didn't seem like the kind of kid to get picked on when I spoke to him before.'

I pretended I hadn't heard him and continued, 'Our mum died when he was a baby. He's just...going through a rough patch.'

He sighed and said, 'I'm sorry that you and your brother lost your mother, Adam. I'm afraid kids feeling like they're alone are common place in this town.'

'I'm not common,' I said before I could stop myself.

'I...didn't say you are,' said Ackerman with a concerned narrowing of his eyes. 'I'm going out on a limb here, but it sounds like you don't blame Riley for stealing your gun.'

'No,' I replied. Yes, she stole it – if you find out that I gave it to her, I'm in even more shit with the boss.

He nodded and said, 'So tell me what happened that made you trespass onto school property to get the gun back.'

I tried shifting in my seat to make the handcuffs dig into my wrist less. It didn't work. 'I asked Riley if she had seen my gun and she said she gave it to Cody. We went straight to the school to get it off him.' I could give him a reasonable recount of what had happened that day but I hoped with desperation that he wouldn't ask for me to tell him what happened the day I had found Riley and taken her to the hospital – I couldn't.

'So, Mr. Marshall, you are admitting to possessing, holding and carrying an unregistered handgun.'

'Yes.'

Ackerman scribbled notes on his pages and then clapped his pile of paperwork together on the table. 'You will be held on remand until a judge can look at your case. You're going to jail.'

I gobbed stupidly as he led me into a nearly abandoned hallway. There were ten desks all over the stations. The door was to the right, and the sergeant's office was at the back, concealed by a frosted glass door. Ackerman parked me on a wooden bench in the hallway and went to the sergeant's office with the paperwork. I looked to the left and saw Cody sitting there in handcuffs too.

'Happy now?' I grunted.

'What do you mean?' he asked.

I nodded my head around. 'Look where we are!'

'Relax. Dad will get us out of here on bail,' said Cody with a wet sniff. 'We just have to wait.'

Burke approached with two Styrofoam cups filled with water. She handed one to Cody first then the other to me. We sipped at them. I wasn't thirsty but was grateful to have something else to focus on instead of my impending stint in the clinker. After some time, Ackerman stormed out of the sergeant's office and slammed the door behind him. We looked up at him and he glared at me. He stormed out of the station.

Burke leant against the desk facing opposite us and said, 'There's a man here for you. We have to let you both go on bail.'

I squeezed the Styrofoam cup too hard and it snapped, sending water gushing all over my lap but stayed quiet.

Burke straightened up and unlocked our handcuffs and said, 'Come on. I'll walk you out.'

Cody and I stood and, guided by Burke, made our way through the station to the exit. I expected to see the boss waiting for us in the foyer, but he was nowhere to be seen. My jaw dropped open when I saw who was standing there. Aldo Iacopetta. He was a stout man. He was standing casually in the foyer, wearing a beret, with his hands tucked into his jacket's pockets. He smiled up at me with yellow teeth.

'Hello, boys,' he greeted with a sociable and cheerful tenor. 'Aren't you glad to see your old pal Aldo?' He winked at me.

Cody followed him readily out the door but I hesitated. I watched Burke in the corner of my eye, studying me and I knew I had no choice but to follow Aldo out if I wanted to stay out of police custody. I swallowed hard and followed him.

I dreaded what he would say to my brother. He wasn't a discreet man. Aldo Iacopetta stopped on the front steps of the police station and lit a stinking cigar. He was quiet while I stepped up beside Cody and I put my good arm around my brother's shoulders.

'What are you doing here?' I asked.

'I'm bailing you out,' he answered with a diminutive, casual shrug.

'Who are you?' Cody asked.

'He's nobody,' I said firmly and shook my head. The sun was breaking through the clouds and reflecting off the glass and it hit me right in the left eye so I shielded my eyes.

'Adam, I need you to do what I say, no questions asked.' He admired his burning cigar. 'I don't intend to beat around the bloody bush. I want him done for before you're in too deep of shit.' He looked up at me finished, 'Consider your bail my deposit.'

Iacopetta extinguished the cigar and held out his hand for us to shake. We glanced at each other and shook his hand. He began walking away but called over his shoulder with a chuckle, 'You're a liar and he's a thief – I love your work already!'

Cody and I watched him down the street and get into a waiting taxicab before being driven off.

'Who was that?' Cody asked.

'Don't listen to him,' I said.

'Sounds like you already know him,' Cody muttered. 'How do you know him? What did he mean by "I want him done for"? Who is he talking about?'

'He wants information on my boss,' I slipped, covering my face with my hands.

'Is that guy a drug dealer or a police officer?' Cody asked.

I dropped my hands and looked at him as if for the first time. 'What?' I uttered.

Cody shrugged. 'He wants information. Sounds to me like he's a cop working undercover.'

While my gut sank, I swore to myself. 'We shouldn't have let him bail us out,' I muttered.

'Too late now,' Cody sniffed and looked down the street. 'What were we supposed to do? Say no?'

'We have to be careful,' I said. I began marching down the street and Cody followed. 'He knows too much about me and you're going to be in danger.'

Cody snapped, 'I don't think he's the one we need to worry about. Lest you forget, he's bailed us both out. He's not the jerk who broke your wrist and beat your head in with a frigging baseball bat. If you're going to trust someone, trust him!'

We walked together down the street, heading for the bus stop. I said, 'I didn't want you in this. You need to stay away from me.'

'Oh, do I, Adam?' he sneered, stopping and facing me. 'What about whatever you did to help cover up Riley's mum being murdered?'

'What?'

'I know you saw something and you're walking around with it dragging you down. You are fucking stuck!' With each word, a bit of spittle landed on my cheek, making me flinch. I didn't wipe it away. I looked down at Cody's feet. He groaned and kept walking. 'Forget it. I don't know why I even bother trying to help you. You'll never leave Riley's dad. He's had you brainwashed all these years and you still can't see that he's going to ruin your life. Thought I could talk some sense into you but nope – I guess I'm the idiot. That became clear the second Riley's mum hit the fucking water.'

I grabbed Cody's wrist and twisted it. He reared back and punched me in the face with his other hand. I stumbled back with blood spurting from my nose.

Cody roared, 'What do you think you're doing?' He was breathing heavily.

'I'm sorry.'

'Were you ever going to come back for me?' he heaved with his eyes welling. 'Were you ever going to tell me what happened to you? Was it really just because you got into drugs? Or something else?'

I bent over and pinched my nose to stop the bleeding. The blood spattered on the pavement. I squeezed my eyes shut to keep the tears from showing before I stood back up, composing myself with the skills worthy of a woman. I shrugged.

Cody's lip wobbled and he waved me off. 'Don't bother talking to me anymore, then.'

I watched him walk away. I began to sob but stopped myself. Keeping secrets from the people you love had to be the hardest things I'd ever done, yet I continued to bury myself with the lies. I wandered down to the beach and sat on the sand. I watched a couple kissing at the turquoise shoreline. I never really understood the appeal of the beach. I'd always preferred the calm pool, or the safety of the boat. Water scared me a little. I remembered saving Riley at Tathra and being so frightened I couldn't breathe even with my head above the water. I missed being a hero. Now I was nothing but a monster. A trampled, beaten monster.

I was losing my grip on everything. In too deep, the water was surrounding me.

# 30 CODY

I stood at the door of the Flynns' house and my stomach tightened. I took a deep breath and knocked. The door opened and Riley's father loomed in the doorway, swallowing an entire glass of whiskey.

'What?' he barked. He looked me up and down.

'I'm here to apologise to Riley,' I said, shaking my fist in my hand. It throbbed from where I had just decked Adam in the nose.

'Who are you?'

'I'm Cody Marshall.'

'Marshall?' he scoffed. 'You related to Adam?' His eyes were slightly glazed but then came clearer as he looked at me. 'Shit, you're that brother he was talking about.'

'Yes, sir.'

He scuffed his feet back and made room for me to walk in. 'She's in the kitchen.' He showed me to where Riley was changing her diabetes pod. He leant against the window and stared out at the water as if he wasn't going to listen to every word we said.

'Where's Adam?' she asked as I walked in.

'I left him. He's probably gone home or something.' We glanced at her dad. 'Can you come for a walk?'

193

Riley looked to her dad. He mumbled, 'Stay on the beach. Don't go near the water.' We started moving towards the door and he added, 'I'll be watching.' Riley's mouth narrowed and her eyes went steely as we hurried outside and down the path. Once we hit the sand, Riley turned around and slapped me so hard in the face that I had to feel for all my teeth.

'What the hell is wrong with you?' she asked coolly. 'Didn't you realise you could ruin everything and send me to foster care?'

I rubbed at my jaw and moved it in slow circles. I'd hoped she would listen to me about Adam but those hopes evaporated. I said, 'If you want to side with my brother, you're in a lot of trouble.'

I groaned and felt the back of my mouth to see if her slap had made my gum bleed. I checked my slimy fingers over and saw that it was clear.

'You don't know anything, Cody,' she spat. She kicked at the sand and walked in circles around me, her head jutting out but sitting low on her neck like a stalking cat. 'Let me get this straight for you, Cody. I do not trust people until I know exactly what they want from me. I know what Adam wants. What do you want?'

'I'm trying to help.'

'Well, you're not!' she snarled. 'Adam is trying to help me and you just...' She made a pistol shape with her hand and smacked it to my forehead, then grunted as she turned away and continued to circle me. She walked up the beach and I had to follow her to hear her rambling about how Adam was the only person she could trust anymore to get her away from her father.

'What?

She gave me a piercing look.

'What's wrong with you?' I asked, finally giving up. 'Ever since your mum died, you've been acting really weird.'

'You didn't know me before my mum died,' she snapped.

'Well, I kind of did.' I stayed quiet about how many times I'd watched her interact with my brother at Ben's Bar. She'd dance in front of the fire with Jess and laugh hysterically at Adam's quirky moves with his skinny legs. Jess would pour their drinks and she'd laugh with her about some flaw of Adam's, all in jest but her eyes would shine when she looked up at him – the same way I once looked at him.

Riley glared at me at me with a puffy under-eye but wide pupils. 'Cody, what are you really doing here now? You got what you wanted. You reunited with Adam. You got him arrested. You got him beaten up. What else could you possibly want from me because there has to be something?'

I swallowed and said, 'Tempany sent me to pick up the coke.'

She looked at me blankly, with a non-committal ha and whispered, 'There it is.'

I sniffed and added, 'Tempany wants it.'

Riley's mouth opened as if she was going to say something but she studied my face before replying, 'Tell her I'll bring it by.'

'She wanted me to bring it.'

'Why would you?' she asked, leaning towards me and pursing her lips.

'Because…'

'Because why?' she snapped.

Just give me what I'm asking for. Just stop being so annoying. 'She wants it back.'

Riley crossed her arms, indignant and petulant like a toddler. 'She's not getting it.'

'Riley, come on!' I whined.

'Tell her I'll come by and bring it later. If she doesn't want to see me, she doesn't get her drugs.'

I felt the rejection coursing through my body with icy shivers as I considered my options. I could try forcing her to give me the drugs, but her father was no doubt watching and I'd have to explain why I was tackling his daughter or I could go back to Tempany and beg for her forgiveness and hope she wouldn't have the living shit beaten out of me like she'd obviously had done for Adam. Or I could wait for

Riley to give up its hiding spot.

I glanced at my watch. 4:30. Dad wouldn't be home until 11:00. I could wait. I took a deep breath and said, 'Okay. How about…I meet you at Tempany's.'

'Cody,' she said firmly.

'Or I'll go with you.'

'I think you should leave now.'

I nodded with a glance up at the pathway to the house where her dad was now standing, too far away to hear what we were saying but watching as promised. I said see you later to both of them and jogged up the pathway, covertly ducking into the garage to wait until they were both back inside before I could wait in the scrubs like I had done before. I was starting to realise I had a big problem but I needed the drugs to solve it.

# 31 ACKERMAN

After I had to set the Marshall boys go, I had to take myself for a walk around the block to cool off, punching my hands into fists and splaying out my fingers again and again. Anger gripped me and stiffened my jaw and wired my energy. The sergeant sent me out and I found it difficult to keep my mouth from running so had to bite my tongue so hard that blood dribbled out.

I became a police officer to help people and I went into Missing Persons to do just that. There she was, my first big case, found with a head injury and lungs full of water. Now we had this massive drug dealer case getting in the way and I'd been ordered to keep clear of Flynn until they had enough evidence. Were they serious? Did the sergeant honestly think I could leave that girl in that house with that nut bag?

I stopped outside an office and got in the way of a worker trying to get in with a tray full of coffees. I apologised and stepped back, letting her in and thinking quickly. If Flynn was already a person of interest, there were already eyes on him. However, I could do a welfare check on the girl. Do a drive by to see how it was all going. I could make sure she didn't end up dead in the bay, snagged in seaweed, like her mother.

I marched back to the station and dropped my keys in front of

Burke. 'Come on – we're going to drive-by and check up on Riley Flynn.'

We were outside the Flynn house within ten minutes. We sat there all there afternoon, until it got dark.

'Lights are on,' Burke observed. 'They're home, Ackerman. What are we going to do?'

I craned my neck to judge which rooms had lights on. 'Something has got to come to the surface. A crook like Flynn has a wife that vanishes and nobody's interested? He's drowning in it, he's in that deep.'

'We looked into him. Seems clean,' said Burke.

'Seems.'

Burke grinned and opened a packet of chips. 'The boss is going to furious with you if you keep hounding this guy.'

I laughed dryly. 'I'm either a bloodhound or a Labrador retriever – keeping the blind from jumping off the cliff. Either way – I'll be there.'

We sat and watched the house for a moment until we spotted a figure much like that of the girl, Riley, jogging down the pier.

'What's going on here?' I mumbled.

Burke crunched on a chip and shrugged.

'Should we go up to her?'

'Nup.'

'Why not?' I asked.

'We have no cause.'

'She was involved in a gun being taken to school today. Isn't that enough cause?'

'She's at home now,' she said.

I watched Riley. 'But what do you think she's doing?'

'She's running down a pier,' Burke replied. 'Big deal.'

Riley got onto the yacht and disappeared. Suddenly, I spotted that she was followed by another figure, too short to be that of her father. 'Who's that?' I asked.

Burke frowned; chip suspended on the way to her mouth.

I shook my head. 'Nah, this feels weird to me, Burke.'

'The whole family is bloody weird, Ackerman.' She sighed and said, 'Let's just go. We came. We saw. She's all right.'

I stuck my head out the window and watched, listening. There was a thud and a few yells. The two figures wrestled on the edge of the boat before Riley fell into the water. The second figure sprinted down the pier and disappeared down the beach. Burke and I both stared at her. She didn't resurface. She was a goner, like her mother. My hand moved to the door handle and I jumped out. I bolted down the hill, stumbling over roots and having to catch myself. Burke waddled after me, dusting crumbs off her belly and using her radio to report to the station what was unfolding. I thundered down the pier, reefing off my heavy holster as I prepared to jump in. I took deep gasps of air before I jumped in, fully clothed.

I found Riley below the surface, gripped her by the arms and heaved her to the surface. She screamed. 'Help!'

I shouted, 'It's all right – I'm,' Riley punched me in the mouth and I let her go as I sputtered, 'I'm assisting you!'

'Get away from me!' She paddled a few strokes before she recognised me and stopped and gasped at me. 'What are *you* doing here?'

'Helping you.' I spat blood and water out of my mouth.

Burke helped me out of the shallows and then helped Riley out. She wrung out her tee shirt and asked, 'I mean, why are you here in the first place. It's a bit weird.'

'Routine check,' said Burke with a warm smile. 'Just making sure you're all right after today. It's a pretty tough thing you're going through.' Riley narrowed her eyes at Burke but she continued. 'It's hard to go it alone.'

'I'm not alone.'

Burke and I looked around at the abandoned pier, save the boat which reflected the setting sun and the purple sky of the sunset.

I joked, 'You've got a pretty funny definition of company.'

'My dad's just inside.'

'Your dad huh.' I picked up my holster and put it back on. 'He knows you're out here?'

'Does he know *you're* out here?' she retorted.

'Why don't we go inside and then he can know we mean no harm and we just helped you since you fell off the boat,' Burke suggested.

Riley's eyes were razor sharp as she levelled them at Burke. 'I didn't fall.'

'Why don't you just go inside and he doesn't have to know we were here,' I said.

'You want me to lie to my dad? *Actually lie?* Encouraging me to dishonest to my guardian – seems like kind of a shitty thing for a police officer to do.'

'There's no reason to worry your father, Riley. He's going through a lot, too,' said Burke.

She rolled her eyes. 'You guys love that soppy crap. We're going through something. It's a tough time. It's excusable because we're in mourning.' The way she mocked our sympathy I could see was bothering Burke. Her brow furrowed and her shoulders tensed. I guessed Burke was used to nurture to build rapport and connection. It clearly was not working on this feisty young woman. I decided to take a shot at calming her down in a way that worked well on my brother after our parents had both died.

'Let's go Burke.' I gestured to her to follow me. 'We'll leave Riley here with her father. She's fine and doesn't need pity from us clowns. We'll leave her be.'

Burke muttered, 'Great idea.'

I went to leave but paused. I looked at her bare feet and placed one hand on her slight shoulder, giving it a gentle squeeze, not saying anything more. I didn't even look her in the eye. I just squeezed, and walked away.

As Burke and I walked away, me slapping out my wet shirt, Riley Flynn burst out, 'He's sleeping!' She swallowed hard. We looked at her and she marched towards us, her hands trembling either from the cold or anger, I couldn't tell.

'He takes more and more sleeping pills every day. He's lying to you about that day. He's not who he says he is.' Riley sniffed and wiped her eyes with the back of her hand, covering the side of her face with damp sand. 'My dad has anger issues, and he blames me for my mother being dead because I knew about something and it broke her heart. He keeps knocking himself out to sleep and leaving me all alone. I'm left with only my memory of what she did to me – she did to me – I'm sick of drowning again and again and again –' She burst into tears and sobbed, heaving. 'She didn't want me. Nobody wants me. They don't listen to me!'

I looked to Burke. I had no idea what to say. The kid was so internal that she bordered on cold sociopathy and suddenly she was crying her eyes out and babbling in front of us. Speechless, my discomfort increased when Riley reached for me and hugged me, sobbing into my already soaked shirt. 'Hold me,' she begged.

I put one hand on her back and the other on top of her head. Burke put her hands on the backs of her hips and waited. I took her cue and waited too for Riley's sobs to subside and she blinked up at me. 'I lied…I *am* alone.'

Riley sat in the back of our car, wrapped in a blanket, the sunlight setting upon her face through the tinted window. Burke sat with her, entering information on the computer. I made my way to the front door of the Flynn house and gave it a strong knock. When nobody answered, I stepped inside and made my way to the living room, my wet shoes squeaking on the floor as I called out for Mr. Flynn. He was where Riley had told me he was. He was recumbent on a sofa, clutching a photo frame of his wife to his chest.

I squatted beside him and checked that he was breathing. 'Mr.

Flynn,' I said loudly. He snorted and stirred. I cast my eyes around the room and saw the sleeping pills on the coffee table, along with an empty bottle of Scotch. I tried rousing him again. 'Mr. Flynn, wake up. Mr. Flynn!' I picked up my radio and requested an ambulance. The guy was absolutely out of it. Back in the police car while the paramedics wheeled Dominic Flynn out on a gurney, Riley leant forward to press her hands against the cage to ask, 'Is he dead?'

'No, honey, no.' Burke tried to swivel to face her but her bump got in the way. I shook my head. Riley sat back in the seat and twiddled her fingers, looking at the paramedics. 'Is there some family we can drop you off to?' Burke asked.

'Can you drop me at Adam's?' she asked meekly.

Burke and I exchanged glances. I cleared my throat. 'Yeah...We can do that.' I ignored the quizzical look on Burke's face. I was about to drive off when the paramedics came and waved me down. I got out of the car and went to the ambulance, where Dominic Flynn was coming back to consciousness.

'I'm fine,' he slurred, shrugging off the blood pressure and heart rate monitors.

I crossed my arms and said loudly from the driveway of the house, 'Mr. Flynn, you either go to the hospital or you are arrested for child endangerment.'

'Child endangerment?' He sat upright and was overtaken by dizziness and slumped down again. 'Why child endangerment?' He squinted at me. 'Have you got my kid?'

'Riley is safe with us.'

He wailed and tried to get up but I stepped up and held him down. 'Do you consent to going to hospital?' He grunted through tears at me and I repeated, louder, firmer, 'Do you consent to going to hospital?'

'Yes, I consent,' he whispered. 'But my daughter –'

'She is safe. We're taking her to Adam's.'

Flynn closed his eyes and nodded. I handcuffed him to the gurney just in case and gave the paramedics a nod. The photograph he'd been clutching had dropped onto the ground. I bent to pick it up. The glass had one crack across the front and the photograph inside it shifted up. I turned it over and noticed the back was open. I tried to put it back in place but something was in the way. I opened it up to find a folded-up piece of paper. On the piece of paper in cursive writing was a message in blue ink.

*Now do you believe me?*

We dropped Riley off at Adam Marshall's. He looked furtively around as he opened the door to us before growling, 'Do you have any idea what it looks like to people to have cops at my door?' He looked to the car where Riley sat with a serious expression. He raised one hand in greeting. 'Where's her dad?' he asked.

'Hospital.'

He cleared his throat. 'What happened?'

Burke walked with Riley to Adam's door and said, 'Mr. Marshall, can Riley stay with you until her father is well enough to come home?'

Adam pulled Riley into the house and practically shoved her down the hallway out of view. He whispered, 'Don't come by again,' before shutting the door in our faces.

Burke murmured to the door, 'Not quite right, is it mate,' and I shook my head and walked back to the patrol car. I grunted and wondered about the letter that I had just put in the boot of the car with the frame. Was that evidence? Who wrote it? I closed the car door and I drove away, feeling a clamminess in my neck and chest.

Burke and I went to the hospital to interview Dominic Flynn the next morning. The nurse showed us to his private room and we walked in with a rapid knock. He jerked his head up in our direction from where he had been sitting at the window overlooking the carpark.

'I saw you fuckers arrive,' he grunted. 'Absolutely ridiculous that you put me in hospital just for taking some sleeping tablets.'

'You may be right, sir,' I sighed. 'But I couldn't rouse you and you had a child in your care. I didn't know how many you'd taken.'

Flynn moved to the seat and sat down, his robe opening between his legs and revealing the black hair on his white inner thighs. He rested his head on his hand, elbow on the arm of the chair and shrugged. 'I won't argue that I made an oversight. In case you forgot, I did just lose my wife.'

'Yes, you did.' I put my hands on my hips. 'And she lost her mother.'

Flynn blinked at me. 'Where is she now?'

'Safe,' replied Burke. 'With Adam.'

He nodded and reached for a cup of coffee on his side-table, sipping at it. I produced the note and handed it to him. He didn't have to read it. He saw the handwriting and his face changed from irritation to dread. He rubbed at the top of his ear and whispered, 'You found it?'

'You were holding it when I found you,' I replied. Burke cleared her throat and narrowed her eyes at me. I ignored her scathing expression. 'Do you know whose handwriting this is?'

Flynn scratched at his eyebrow and coughed. 'Rachelle's. It was my wife's letter.' He scrunched the note up in his hand.

'Why would she write that? What is she alluding to?' I asked.

Flynn's breath increased and he dropped his shoulders. 'She had ideas about someone I know, and I didn't believe her.'

'Why would she leave the note for you like that?'

He shook his head. 'I don't know.'

'Is that why you decided to wipe yourself out?' I asked. Flynn crossed his arms and refused to speak. His lips curled. 'When do you think she left the note?' I asked.

Flynn stared back at me before he declared, 'I want you to both leave. Now.'

'Shall we go speak to Riley and Adam about this?' I threatened.

He shrugged. 'What's that going to do?'

'Maybe they know what the letter is about. Maybe your little friend Adam will spill his guts.'

Flynn tore the note into pieces and sprinkled it like confetti on the floor beside our feet. He shook his head. 'It makes no difference if you do. Adam works for me and he listens to me. He'll only tell you what I tell him to.'

Burke tried turning me to leave but I snapped, 'Is that what you think? Adam is your little man? Your confidante? Is that why your daughter wants to go stay with him?'

He turned his lips upward in a smug smile. 'We're family.'

'Do you tell the truth in your family, Mr. Flynn?' I asked.

'Of course.'

'Did Adam tell you that he took a gun to a school? Got himself arrested. Luckily, he was bailed by someone very high up.'

Flynn's jaw tightened.

I shook my head. 'See, this family business? I don't buy it. Anyone that works with you can't stand you. Neither can your kid. That's why she's going to spill her guts about who killed your wife – and I can guarantee, that person will be seeing me as I shove his arse in jail.'

Burke nudged me roughly and Flynn's eyes flashed. 'You're going to come to an unpleasant end one day, Senior Constable Ackerman...and I hope I see it happen.'

'Not if I see it meet you first,' I spat.

Burke hauled me out of the room and was apoplectic, sweeping her arms in wide movements and hissing at me through gritted teeth. Her face was even red and sweating. 'That was incredibly unprofessional; I can't believe you just did that! You could be suspended over that behaviour.'

'He threatened me!' I cried as we stepped into an elevator. 'Did you hear that?'

'You concealed evidence. You were bordering on harassment how long we stayed at the Flynn house yesterday in the first place.' Burke bent back her fingers with each point she made. 'You aggravated him and threatened him! IN A HOSPITAL!'

I slammed my fist against the wall of the elevator and shouted, 'He fucking killed his wife; I know it!'

'You need to calm down.'

'But Burke!'

She grabbed my wrists and looked me in the eye

'You...need...to...be calm.'

I took a deep breath and closed my eyes, counting back from ten with each breath like all those counsellors had taught me as a teenager. Their faces came to my mind as I remembered what it was like to be so angry and hurt about what had happened to my parents in that home invasion robbery. How that criminal had shot them before getting away, leaving my brother and me orphans and in foster care. My anger had been short-lived but it had been intense. My brother had to deal with oppositional defiance disorder well into his teens and had struggled through school as a result – even if all the teachers knew he was a trauma case, it didn't help him cope. I took a last deep breath, unclenching my fists and replied to Burke while opening my eyes, 'I'm calm.'

My anger hadn't been an issue for me in such a long time. Something to do with Dominic Flynn just made me spit with rage. I felt just how Rachelle must have felt. Nobody was believing me. I guess it was because of a gut feeling and you can't charge people on gut feelings

# 32 ADAM

Riley lounged in my living room and ate potato chips after checking her blood sugar. I lingered in the doorway to the kitchen, adrift in my own house. The crunching reverberated down my back and I asked, 'Do you have enough insulin and keto strips?'

She nodded and turned on my television. She gasped. 'Adam, you don't even have Netflix.'

I shook my head. 'I don't have anything, kiddo.'

She tilted her head back and laughed. 'Yeah, I forgot how broke you actually are on your wage.'

I grimaced and wrung my hands. Where did I put my smokes? I dug through the bag on my kitchen bench but stopped when Riley walked in. 'Why do you have a bag packed?'

'I was going to leave town.'

'You were going to take me with you, weren't you?' she said in a small voice, the packet of chips dropping from her hand as I shook my head.

'Sorry, kiddo.'

'But...you always said you were going to help me,' she said, her voice straining with tears coming. 'You said.' She took a deep breath and whispered, 'Adam, I'm going to tell the police that it was my dad. I don't care anymore. I have to get away from him.'

I sighed. Definitely not the hero if I was breaking her heart with facts. 'There is no evidence to say that he killed her.'

Riley stomped her foot like a child. 'Am I not evidence?'

Silence.

She squealed, 'Why do you have to go now?'

I sat on my single bar stool and gestured to my head. 'With what Tempany did, what Cody is into now...I just...' I was a parasite. A plague. I turned everything to shit. I was meant to be a good guy but everything I touched was ruined. 'The gun and everything...I think it's better I leave.'

'You can't leave me, Adam,' she said with tears running down her face. 'Please. I can't live here without you.'

I shook my head. 'I can't take care of you, Riley. I'm not your legal guardian.'

'You can look after me.'

I buried my face with my hands. 'We're not doing that, Riley. No. That is not why I help you. You know why I help you.'

'You can't leave me alone with him!' she cried.

I looked up at her. 'It's fine. It'll be okay. I'm not leaving just yet. I've got to close up some things first.'

Her shoulders dropped and she sniffed. 'I don't want you to go at all.'

I couldn't tell her it didn't matter what she did. I would be gone at some point. My goal was to find the supplier, but also keep her safe. All I had to do now was make sure was safe.

To interrupt my dreams of Riley finding safety, my phone rang. The boss was calling. I answered it. He was being discharged and I had to come pick him up. He knew Riley was with me and I had to bring her too. I gave her the bad news and she wiped away her tears and set her face to stone.

I focused on breathing in my cigarette slowly to stay calm. I swallowed my anxiety and went to the hospital entrance, leaving Riley in the car, pushing the tendrils of her hair away from her face. I met the boss in the foyer with a determined expression on his face. He had been standing there watching me walk up to him. I felt cornered by the dark look on his face, like a little mouse. Even though I was walking to him, it felt like I was being hunted by his eyes.

'You brought Riley back?' he asked in a cool voice.

I gestured over my shoulder. 'She's in the car, boss.' I zipped up my hoodie right to my chin.

The boss stood still, staring at my face before he placed one hand on my shoulder, causing me to shiver. 'You're a good son.' I hesitated and shifted gently so that I was out from under his heavy hand. I held up my wrist as if to explain that I was in pain.

The boss gestured at my bruises. 'Find out who did that to you?'

'No, someone just needed a punching bag, I guess.'

He looked me in the eye, and I waited. He said quietly, 'Take us home.'


I drove him and Riley home and as soon as we arrived inside the house, he locked the door and leant in close to me. He said, 'The police came to see me. They seem to think you would answer their questions.' I laughed. He trained his eyes on me and lowered his sunglasses from his hairline. I cracked my knuckles and the boss sighed. 'You wouldn't, would you?'

'What?'

He growled, 'Tell them what you're really doing here.'

'I'm just working,' I stammered.

'So…what are you really doing here? With my family? With Riley?'

He sucked on his teeth. 'Because I'm starting to wonder where your alliances really are since you're always messaging someone else on that phone of yours…and you were bailed by someone.'

I shuddered at the venom in his voice. It seemed like he knew. He'd spoken to the police at the hospital, and it was worthless. I took a deep breath, and then said calmly, 'I'm making sure she's safe from you.'

He reacted quicker than I anticipated. He pulled me by my hair and shoved me, causing me to trip and fall hard on the floor with my hands outstretched. The pain travelled through my wrist and radiated relentlessly up my arm. I grabbed my wrist with my uninjured hand and cried out with torment.

'Adam!' Riley squealed.

The boss stepped over me and went to her. 'Get upstairs, Riley.'

I took many quick deep breaths before struggling, labouring, to stand up as Riley went upstairs with her eyes fixed on me. I followed the boss to the kitchen, and lingered in the doorway with fear. Riley paused on the stairs to listen.

The boss leant against the cupboard and pinched the bridge of his noise. He looked up and said, 'I'm beginning to think Rachelle didn't kill herself.'

I swallowed.

'It's war!'

I coughed. 'War? With who? The police?'

'Somebody came in to hurt my family!'

I threw my painless arm into the air in frustration and snapped, 'Nobody came in and hurt your wife! What would you even know about your family? You can control it but it doesn't make you know it! Your wife died after years of abuse by you. You're responsible for that!'

I prepared myself for the impact of his fist. I watched it glide towards my face with slow-motion detachment. I felt the sensation of it hitting my chin, but felt no pain. I was bunted backwards but righted myself quickly. I looked around and met Riley's eyes.

The boss took a step back from me and whispered, 'I think I get it now.'

'What do you get?' I asked.

'You're not my son.' His eyes were wide and glazed.

I shook my head. 'No, I never was.'

He lunged for me with a rageful roar. He pinned me down and he punched my middle. I flipped him over and held him down with gritted teeth. His hands found a cup and he smashed it against my head where I'd been beaten with the baseball bat. I cried out and pulled away but the boss grabbed me. I tried getting to my feet to run, but he gripped my ankle. Riley stood on the stairs with a terrified expression.

'Riley! Run! GO NOW!'

I hoped the desperation in my voice was enough to fuel her to finally go.

He glanced around at Riley and I stuck my tongue up hard against my teeth to stop myself from screaming with the effort of getting to my feet. It was now or never. I ran and made a dive for the door but the boss managed a firm hold of my elbow and reeled me backwards as if I was a fighting fish caught on a fishing line. I grabbed at the kitchen counter and accidentally knocked the hanging saucepans off their hangers. They crashed on the kitchen counter and clanged even louder when they hit the floor. The boss didn't let go. He pulled me down and kneeled on my thigh, corking the hamstring.

'Argh!' I cried.

There was a cold, stinging sensation on my neck and I realised it was a knife in his hand. He screamed, 'Fuck you!' The boss slammed me across the face with his fist and everything went fuzzy and numb.

'Oh, shit,' I murmured as black dots starred violently across my eyes and my vision went out like static on a television. My body dropped as I saw the outline of Riley sprint up the stairs.

Of course, she was going up the stairs. Of course, she couldn't just do as I told her and get the fuck away. The last thing I thought before I lost consciousness was *I had this coming*.

# 33 RILEY

RILEY! RUN! GO NOW!

His voice cracked he screamed so loudly at me. The shrill and the shake within his scream made my heart almost stop. I sprinted upstairs to hide. Why didn't I go out the door?

'Riley!' Dad's voice boomed and his footsteps bounced and echoed behind me. I dove under my bed with trembling hands and breaths coming so ragged I couldn't get enough air. I hugged at my chest and screamed when Dad came into my room and hauled me out by my ankle, making it pop uncomfortably. I slapped at his face and he sat on me saying 'Sssh, sssh, sssh,' before he managed to pin my hands together like he was hog-tying me.

I wailed, 'No, let me go!'

He crushed my fingers in his tight grip and shouted in my face, 'Just listen to me! He's a liar!'

I screamed as loudly as I could, and it tore my throat to shreds. He let go of my hands and slapped me across the mouth. I sobbed and turned my body and bucked him off with my hips, the carpet rug burning my arms and giving me welts. I peeled away from him and leapt to the balcony. Dad shouted, 'No, don't!'

I climbed over the rail and jumped from the second-storey.

I landed on the grass lawn right beside the patio – if I had been ten centimetres off, I would have hit the concrete edging. My knees squelched and burned with pain, but they did not break. I rolled a few times and got onto all-fours. I looked in through the window and saw Adam on the floor of the kitchen. I banged on the glass, screaming his name. As I saw Dad racing back down the stairs, I yelped and hearing Adam's voice echoing at me GO NOW, I limped away breathlessly.

I made it to the town centre and I couldn't walk any further. I huffed and puffed with an aching chest. Each breath tightened on my lungs, so tight it squeezed the life from my body.

I dragged my feet up a slope and stood under the protection of a bus shelter. I wrung the hem of my tee shirt as I peered down the road, expecting to see my dad's car zooming up. I had to rest. My legs hurt and my panicked escape had messed with my blood sugar.

The bus shelter was too close to the road if I was going to hide. I couldn't be spotted by my dad. Not now. I thought of Adam lying there in the kitchen and I almost burst into tears. Was he dead? Would Dad kill him if he wasn't? I stood stiffly and looked up and down the street. I could go to Tempany's, but she'd sent people after Adam to beat him for the cocaine. She couldn't be trusted, especially if Cody had gone back to her with the cocaine and told her I'd kept it from him. I'd kept it from him to save him. The way drugs changed people…it had changed my father, my mother and even Adam. I couldn't let Cody be changed, too.

I could see the seaside about a kilometre away, straight down the promenade. The sea was a dark blue-grey and seemed to join with the foggy sky like a blended oil painting. The sun was struggling to shine through the clouds, and it gave off a steamy warmth that often buzzed in the air after a storm. The promenade was not busy, still too early for the midday rush.

My legs were quite numb and unsteady. I rubbed my knees hard and they crunched. I was relieved I hadn't broken them or dislocated them in my effort to escape. I limped down the promenade in a daze. My head vibrated with the impact of each footfall. I made my way to the grassy park section near the beach car park and reached the picnic bench. I leant against it, exhausted. I stared out at the sea and thought hard about my options. Today I felt hopeless, and would give anything to have the abundance of options I'd had a month ago. This morning's prospect was bleak.

I shivered and rubbed at my face roughly, barely able to feel it. I was having a low. I should really be having an insulin dose but they were at home. Maybe if I just rested? It would come back up. I settled myself down onto the picnic bench and folded my legs in front of myself so I could hug my aching knees. Resting my cheek on my kneecaps, I watched cars pass on the road. They paid no attention to the lost teenage girl huddled on the picnic bench. I sighed, my lips tingling, and turned the other way so my attention was on the water. I could see the outline of a ship far offshore. I could relate to that ship, so adrift and detached from society. While my blood sugar dripped lower and lower, I drifted off into a twilight doze, just sitting and staring at the sea.

# 34 CODY

I banged so loudly on Tempany's door the booms reverberated through my gut and into my spine. There was no answer. *Damn it!* I felt like screaming.

I had the bag of cocaine stuffed inside my puffer jacket and I was sweating. I'd misjudged the weather when I'd looked outside before getting dressed. The grey Melbourne sky had fooled me like the trickster its weather was. I never thought I'd be walking the streets of our town carting a pack of cocaine like a dealer. My guts wanted to dissolve into diarrhea at the thought of being caught with it. Wouldn't Dad love to hear that? Delinquent son number two, addicted to drugs and walking around like an eshay with a bum bag and sideways cap.

Disappointed that I couldn't unload it back to Tempany (and have a snort or two in her company), I walked back outside and looked across at the bay. My heart leapt when I saw a girl sitting, hunched over, on the picnic bench. Brown hair, slight frame, slumped shoulders. Riley. Had she followed me? She hadn't been very happy when I'd snatched the bag off her last night and knocked her into the water. Would she try to get it back? I walked over to her. It was definitely Riley. She looked like she was asleep, but her eyes were open, staring out into space blankly as though in a catatonic state.

'Riley?' I tiptoed closer.

Her eyes roved and focused on me, but there was no recognition. Her skin was sallow and her hands were trembling. She had a new split on her lip and bruised hands. I swallowed hard and said, 'Would you like to come back to my place?'

She lifted her head and asked, 'What did you say?'

I wiped my sweaty palms on my pant legs, swallowed again with a gulping noise and repeated my question. Riley unfolded her body and stepped towards me with a confused glare. I took a cautionary step backwards. She asked, 'Who told you I was here?'

'I just saw you.'

She lunged at me and shook me with weak hands. 'You're lying!' I fended her off and she fell to the ground, grasping to my pants and moaned, 'I can't trust anyone.'

I crouched down beside her and thought to myself how misplaced she was; like a refugee whose house had just exploded in front of her eyes. I hesitated and placed my hand lightly on her back and patted her. She shifted and pulled me into a tight embrace.

'Cody, how did you know I was here?' she asked again, breathing into my neck.

'I told you – I just saw you. What are you doing out here all alone anyway?' I asked.

'Why did I come here?' she asked.

I shrugged. 'You tell me.'

She burped a little and said, 'I don't feel well.'

'What's wrong with you?' I asked.

She turned to me with tears welling up in her eyes. 'I need sugar, but I don't have any money.'

I unclasped her fingers from my pants and told her to wait there. I would go buy her a sugary drink and I did. I returned with a sugary can from the milk bar around the corner. She sipped at it, swallowing with little grimaces. We sat atop the picnic table in silence. Finally, she said, 'That's better. Thank you.'

'No problem,' I said.

We sat in silence again for what felt like hours. I kept looking back to the Vietnamese Restaurant to see if Tempany was returning but there was no sight of her.

'You keep looking up there as if Tempany is going to be there,' Riley said in a quiet voice. 'I think she left town.'

'Why?'

She gestured to my puffer jacket. 'It was either going to be her or Adam when you stole that from her.'

My heart sank. Did I really just put her life at risk? Just to prove a point to Riley, who probably knew all along anyway? Damn it. I thought of her running off, then thought of Adam. I asked, 'Did Adam run off too?'

She breathed heavily and said, 'He was going to.' Her lower lip trembled and she looked down at the can in her hands. 'I told him he could look after me.'

I laughed. 'No way. You didn't.' I said, 'Look, he's never going to rescue you, Riley. He's a con man and a drug addict. A degenerate. He left me – his own brother – and he has no remorse for anything he's done. He's a shithead.' I shrugged. 'He'll only drag you down. Look at what he's done to me.'

Her confused face softened a little.

I reached out and laid my hand on her shoulder. 'We Marshalls…we're just…misguided.' I added with a smile, 'We're a lot like you.'

'Well,' she replied with a quaking lip. 'I can't change who my parents are.'

'No, but you can get away.'

She stared at her hands and mumbled, 'He'll find me. He'll always find me.' Saying it aloud made her cry and I was stumped on what to do or what to say so I just sat there beside her with my hand on her shoulder.

I watched the water and lost myself in its depth and hypnotising movement.

'He threw my mother's body off a boat and watched her sink.' Riley's small voice suddenly said, interrupting my silent sea staring. I turned to look down at her so sharply that I almost threw my neck out. She was still hunched on the picnic table, her hair tangled about her face. 'I think it was my fault.'

I asked, 'Why?'

She finally looked up at me. 'He fell in love with someone else.' She buried her face in the square that her folded elbows on her bony knees supplied for her.

'Isn't there any other family you can stay with?'

'Nope,' she said with such emptiness that it gave me a chill. 'They all live in Sydney and I'd rather die than go with them.'

I shifted my weight and asked, 'Why do you think my brother can help you and look after you?'

She arranged her face carefully before looking me square in the eyes. 'I care about him and he cares about me.'

'I care about you…and him,' I said.

'Don't be an idiot,' she muttered. 'You don't care about him. You're too angry at him for lying to you and leaving.'

'Aren't you?' I asked with raised eyebrows. 'God knows what he's lied about to you.'

'It looked like you wanted to kill him, so I don't think you care about him at all,' she muttered.

I crossed my arms and bit my lip. 'Yeah, well…I guess love is complicated.'

She scoffed, 'Whatever.'

I stared bitterly at the bay with blood heating my face uncomfortably.

'We can't stay here,' she said. 'I'm going to go to Ben's Bar so I can hide out for a bit.' She gnawed at her fingernails. 'You coming?'

'Is that an invitation?' I teased.

She nodded and mumbled, 'I don't want to go alone.'

# 35 ADAM

My lips parted in a groan. My eyelids were heavy and a slog to open. I looked around and realised I was sprawled on the Flynn kitchen floor, wedged up against the wall.

I grabbed the architrave and pulled myself up with shaky arms. I leant against the doorframe and waited for my blurred vision to straighten. I massaged my chest with my good hand and looked around the room to make sure Dom wasn't around. I crept towards the staircase and peered up, listening for his movement. When everything was quiet, I eased myself down onto the bottom step of the staircase and pulled out my phone.

I texted Aldo. 'SOS, pick me up ASAP. Flynn house.' He had warned me that this would happen. For four years, it had seemed impossible. Yet being knocked out by him was a clear signal it was coming. Dom appeared suddenly at the top of the stairs, dressed in a royal blue suit and he had his hair gelled back. His cologne hit my nostrils and made my head thud. He gave me an expectant look as I pushed my phone back into my pocket.

'How do I look?' he asked.

'Suave,' I said with a swallow. Had I imagined that he'd punched my lights out? He was so chipper. Last I remembered, he was onto me.

Interrogating me. I stood so I wasn't as vulnerable when he walked down the steps. He loomed towards me and I backed into the wall with a small gasp.

'So did you call your mate?' he asked with a twinkle in his eye.

I didn't hide my shock in time because he sneered at me and grabbed my phone from my pocket and waved it in my face before smashing it against the marble floor. I ducked as it shattered into debris that flung up. He gave me a playful shove that was strong enough to knock me off balance and I had to grab the banister to stop myself from falling. He clicked his fingers and said, 'Come. Let's talk in my office.'

I followed him to the office and I sat in the chair opposite his desk, reminiscent of our first meeting. Dom carefully folded his hands together and held strong eye contact with me, with his head slightly lowered. 'If you keep betraying me, Adam, you may possibly see the end of your life through the bars of a prison cell. It won't be me who goes to prison.'

'I'm not betraying you,' I lied.

He silenced me by raising his index finger as if he were an orchestra conductor. He said in a steady voice, 'It didn't make any sense to me at first. Why wasn't she *grateful* for the protection I was giving her? I made sure she always had someone to keep her safe. Someone who knew my business inside and out so couldn't fuck it up.' I went to speak but he snarled, 'Someone I trusted!' I bit my lip and went quiet. He shook his head. 'Your habit fucking disgusted me.'

I thought, *just shut up, Adam, let him keep talking, you might be wrong. You might be okay. He might just be thinking something completely left of field. You know how crazy and unpredictable he can be. The years of dabbling in drugs has surely addled his senses. He's a desperate, violent man. Nothing more than a desperate, violent man. He isn't a murderer. You know he isn't a murderer.*

Dominic's eyes twitched at me as he grumbled, 'Always the little hero. Who was I to be fooled by this little hero with the eyes of a bloody saint?'

I sat silently, my body tensed, ready to run for it.

He sneered at me. 'Rachelle never liked you.'

'To be fair, I don't think she ever really liked you a whole lot either,' I mumbled, unable to stop it slipping out. Dominic arched his eyebrows at me. I shrugged and added, 'I just think that the way you go about everything is wrong, that's all.'

'What I do and how I do it is none of your business,' he replied in an arctic low tone.

I was emboldened by finally getting to say what was on my mind and challenged, 'Beating your wife and kid is acceptable, then?' His face twitched but he was still. 'No answer for that, boss?' I chewed at the silence then shook my head and snapped, 'Didn't think so.'

'I don't want to argue morals with you,' he said.

'That's because you have none!' I bit my tongue to shut myself up. I closed my eyes and sobbed. 'I'm sorry.'

Dominic got up and slid down into the seat next to me. He said, 'Adam, tell me it's not true. Tell me that you aren't working for that Elias character.'

I froze. I gaped at him. 'You think I'm working for Elias?'

'That's who killed my wife.' He exhaled through his nose and clapped me on the shoulder. 'I'm going to get that bastard.'

My heart gave a nervous thump as Dominic stood up and clapped me on the shoulder. 'Help me get him and bring Rachelle justice.'

'Where are you going?' I squeaked.

He glared at me scathingly, 'To get my daughter back – you know she jumped out of the bloody second-storey!'

A lump obscured my throat as I gasped, 'What?'

'Don't worry – I'll find her.' He winked at me. 'She's probably at your brother's place.'

I feared for Riley but more for Cody. If Dom thought Cody was using Riley to get him like he figured this Elias guy was, Cody would be in the firing line. Dom gave me a sardonic grin and said, 'Don't worry; I won't hurt your brother.' He paused. 'Or Riley.'

I asked, 'Do you really have to go get her?'

'Of course, I do. It's not safe out there with Elias running around, beating my people's heads in.' He nodded at my head. 'If that's who really did bash you.'

'But...she's safe with Cody, boss,' I said. 'He'll protect her.'

He snickered with amusement and slapped me playfully on the shoulder.

'I'm serious!' I snapped. 'Just listen to me for once, *for once!*'

Dominic studied me with concern, then smiled. 'No. I know best. Stay here.'

He left and I paced the office, where he had locked me in. I tried the window but it was nailed shut. The glass was reinforced and wouldn't break even if I shot at it. But for now, I sat in the chair and swore *fuck* over and over.

# 36 RILEY

My heart rate returned to normal as I walked with tender legs beside Cody to the bar. It was intriguing to have feared the outside world for so much of my life yet now I wondered why I had waited so long to run away. I should have run away before the incident with Mum. Why had I waited so long? Somehow walking beside Cody, my opportunities all opened up. I had a friend. I had someone who could help me and care for me.

Down the street to the bar, there was a scarcity of people and a few pieces of litter in the gutters. I grabbed Cody's hand and pulled him to the front door of the bar, eager to get inside and perhaps see Jess. Once we entered and I met Jess's eyes, she rushed over. 'Riley, what happened? Your face…' She hugged me and said, 'I'll get some ice.'

I brushed my fingers over my lip where Dad had re-split when he'd hit me before. My cheeks were hot to the touch as well. The part of my body that hurt the most was my knees. Jess came back with a tea-towel draped over ice cubes and I held the lumpy sack of material to my face before moving it down to my knees.

'What's happened to your knees?' Jess asked.

'Long story,' I winced. 'I sort of jumped out of the window, on the second floor.'

Cody's face went white and he said, 'Why didn't you tell me this before? You should go to the hospital.'

'I can't,' I said. 'He'll find me. The police will come. I'll have to explain it.' I waved my hand. 'It's too much.'

Jess guided me to a booth where I could put my feet up. The bar was empty except for us — the afternoon patrons hadn't come knocking just yet so I knew I could relax for a while. I knew Jess wouldn't call the police. She knew Adam and his connections to my dad's business. She also knew Tempany. She wouldn't want the police to come in and get me.

To my surprise, she said, 'I think it's time we tell the police what he does to you, girl.'

I snapped, 'I'm fine. I'm dealing with it.'

Jess and Cody stood above me, with concern on their faces. I fiddled with a coaster and avoided looking at them. They didn't understand what it would be like in foster care. If they thought my dad was bad, they'd hate to see the creeps I could end up in the care of. Old men who would sneak into my bedroom to fiddle with me and then have the old battle-axe wife blame me and slap my face. They could say what they wanted about my dad and how much of a cretin he was, but he would never hurt me that way. I needed to stay away from him until Adam could help get me away with his plan. The necklace was a bonus. Financial security.

Running away without any money or help was stupid. Though I thought of Adam lying there in the kitchen and my throat tightened. What if Dad had killed him?

Cody sighed and leant into the booth on the opposite side of me. He reached out for me to hold his hand. I held his. He said, 'Whatever you want to do...I'll do it with you.'

I had a strong urge to bawl my eyes out. I couldn't believe how nice he was being. He'd taken the drugs back off me but I could tell his intentions were good, just like Adam's.

Jess and I watched Cody playing pool in the corner of the bar with the kitchen hand. It had been three hours since we had arrived at Ben's Bar and it remained quiet. Cody had the black in his sights for the corner pocket and tapped it with his cue. It would have been a successful play, going down into the pocket and winning him the game, but Jess picked up the black ball up off the table mid-roll, ignoring Cody's exclamations.

'I have a quick question.' She looked to me. 'Adam and Tempany aren't coming, are they?'

'I don't want to talk about it, Jess,' I mumbled.

She frowned. 'Fair enough, but this is my bar so I have the final say.' She gave me a firm look from under her purple eyeliner and white eyelashes. 'Where are they?'

I looked to Cody who shook his head. I replied, 'I don't know.'

Jess looked at Cody and measured him slowly with her eyes. 'Why are you shaking your head?'

Cody's face reddened and he stammered, 'I just…we…don't know where they are. I'm shaking my head, like, nah, we don't know. You know?'

Jess put the ball back on the table and wiped her hands on the putrid apron she wore day in, day out. She shrugged. 'It's just…not like Adam to not come help you, Riley.'

She walked back behind the bar as customers came in. The kitchen hand shook Cody's hand and I stepped up beside Cody. He said, 'That was weird.' He watched the customers that had arrived and then asked, 'Should we go?'

'We'll wait until it's a bit busier,' I decided. 'Nobody will notice us leave then.'

Cody nodded and patted at his puffer jacket, before shrinking when Jess's eyes went to his jacket.

# 37 CODY

I used to love spending time by wasting it. Skateboarding instead of studying, the deck of the board firm under my shoes and always there to catch me after a jump. The scratching rumble of the wheels on the pavement as I rolled wherever I wanted to. The clackety clack like train tracks on the cracks of each paver giving me a rhythm to swerve and move my hips to, hands in the air like a flamenco dancer. Wasting time was sweet. Wasting time, sitting in Ben's Bar that afternoon however, was not.

Customers began filtering into the bar by three in the afternoon. They pretended to ignore the two teenagers sitting in the corner by the fire, but their eyes constantly darted to us. Riley wanted to not be noticed as we left, but the entire patronage was keeping an eye on us and as the afternoon wore into the early evening, we became somewhat of an attraction.

A middle-aged man with a potbelly spotted Riley and decided for some reason that her bruised face and oily hair were somewhat attractive. He stumbled over carrying his pot of beer and started a random conversation about fishing line sinkers. She listened politely but with raised eyebrows. I began to say something but the bloke blocked me by angling his shoulders, as wide as he was tall. I noticed the bloke's hand moving towards Riley's chest and I caught it sharply. He threw me off him and said, 'Get off, you cunt.'

Riley forced a smile. I went up to the bar and said to Jess, 'There's a creep trying to pick up Riley. Can you kick him out?'

She craned her neck and saw the man towering over Riley, who crossed her legs and had moved as far away from him as she could. She rolled her eyes and said, 'Bloody idiot. He's a nuisance.'

'He's a pedo!' I exclaimed.

Jess strode over and guided him away. 'Maybe leave the underage girl, alone, mate. Look for someone your own age.'

'Not cool, man,' I snapped at him as Jess led him past. His red face turned purple with rage as he stared me down. Jess led him away and showed him the door. I returned to Riley where she squeaked, 'Thanks.'

I scoped the bar and noticed that the patronage were all middle-aged guys who were swearing and getting drunker by the minute. It made my heart rate increase. There were far too many people.

I said, 'We should go now.'

'I don't want to go yet,' she said with a shrug.

It was getting dark outside and I didn't like the idea of walking around the town carrying a pocket full of cocaine inside my puffer jacket. I ignored her pleas and pulled her to her feet. 'Come on!'

'Cody, no!' She slapped my hand away. 'My legs hurt. It's warm in here. It's dry in here. I don't want to leave!'

I felt the bulge in my puffer jacket and felt the stress ride up my stomach and into my chest, before exploding out in my neck and jaw. 'I've got a bad feeling.'

'We can stay here!' She crossed her arms and sat down.

'Riley, please,' I begged. 'We should go while we can.'

She screwed up her nose. 'I want to stay.'

I gave up. 'I wanted to help you, Riley, but I guess you're fine helping yourself.' I snapped, 'Have a nice life!'

I went to turn away but she called, 'You're leaving me?'

I nodded, 'Yes.'

She pleaded, 'Don't – please!'

'Why should I stay? You don't listen to me. We have to go!' My blood flushed to my face as eyes began to land on me.

'We can wait for Adam,' she said. 'He might show up. He'll come get us.'

I exchanged a look with Jess. Her face was solemn. I said, 'Adam is a liar.'

Riley snapped, 'Just like you? You lied to me to get to know me. You used me. At least I know exactly who Adam is and what he wants from me!'

I held up my hand and said with a deep breath, 'You know what? Screw you, and screw my brother. Stuff it. I'm gone.'

I took open, angry steps. Jess called out to me but I ignored her. I walked away outside in the dim streetlights in the fading dusk glow. As I marched through the gravel car park, a car door opened and I stopped with a start as Elias got out of the car.

'Oi, you're that Marshall kid. Been looking for you.'

Before I could answer, he lunged forward and drove a screwdriver into my abdomen. I staggered backwards but he grabbed me. The pain in my stomach was worse than anything I'd ever felt. It was like I had stopped breathing and everything was on fire from my feet to my ears.

Elias tugged at my puffer jacket and grabbed the cocaine. I widened my eyes at him as the pain rippled through my body. He pulled out the screwdriver and I gagged.

Elias snapped, 'Don't fucking steal from drug dealers, kid.' He got back into the car and fishtailed away, spraying me with dirt and stones.

For a moment, I stood there in the cloud of dirt, thinking I had imagined it all. I clutched at my stomach that was giving me intense cramps and looked at the blood on my hands. Tears sprang to my eyes and I turned away, holding both hands to my wound, trying to stem the bleeding. I shuffled away with small gasps and grunts, leaving a blood trail smeared by my footprints.

I stifled my tears as best I could as I shuffled gingerly down the street. I just had to make it to the main road. Each step felt like my stomach was being cleaved apart and I kept dry-retching which made it even worse. I glanced behind him to make sure nobody was following me, terrified of being stabbed again. My mind went to Riley, alone in the bar. I couldn't afford to worry about her anymore. I had to get help.

I allowed myself a moan as I walked as fast as my desperation and adrenaline allowed. 'Oh, shit. Oh, shit. Oh, shit. Oh, shit!' I wheezed, feeling my hands getting warmer and wetter. I was losing too much blood. I wasn't going to make it. I couldn't hold back crying anymore and burst into sobs that tore my insides to shreds. I couldn't see through my tears, sweat, and fear but I knew I had made it to the main road. I staggered onto the roadway into the path of an oncoming car.

# 38 ACKERMAN

I gripped the steering wheel and slammed on the brakes as the headlights revealed a teenage boy staggering onto the road. The boy glanced over his shoulder at me and I saw his face wrenched I pain and fear. He was young but not too young judging by his height. I pulled up beside him and rolled down my window.

'Hey, mate. What's going on?' I asked, trying to sound less like a copper and more concerned citizen. The boy didn't answer but he moved his hands away from his stomach, drawing my attention to the widening red wound. His front was drenched with blood and I sprang out of the car – unbuckling my seatbelt, putting the car in park, and leapt out all while opening the door. The boy fell to his knees, sobbing.

I helped him lie down at the side of the road. I tore off my jacket and pressed it onto his wound. It looked like a stab wound. I pulled out my mobile phone out of my jeans pocket and pressed 000.

'Hello, my name is Senior Constable Ackerman and I need an ambulance sent to the corner of Pier Lane and Water Tower Road.' I named the suburb and said, 'Stab wound, teenage boy. Conscious, losing blood, losing colour rapidly. Applying pressure, code red.' I kept the phone on speaker phone and placed it down on the footpath beside us.

'Hang on, mate, you're going to be fine,' I told the boy who just blinked up at me, silent now.

I told the call operator that I didn't know his name but looking at him closer, I realised who it was. It was Adam Marshall's younger brother – the boy who had taken the gun to school. I kept eye contact with him, such a vivid blue, keeping pressure on his wound, willing him to stay alive. I promised him I would save him.

'You're lucky, mate,' I said in a shaky voice. 'You're lucky because I'm a copper, I know what to do...' I said this to remind myself because inside, I was gripped with a terrible feeling of helplessness that gnawed at my guts the way the wound gnawed at his.

He started to close his eyes and I shook him.

'Stay awake, mate! Stay awake, stay alive!'

# 39 RILEY

I limped out of the women's restroom after sitting in a cubicle and crying my eyes out. I always fought hard not to cry and it always overtook me. Why did I have to be such a weak person? All I wanted to do was be safe and strong. I washed my red eyes and tried to cool off the hot cheeks from where Dad had hit me again.

Jess met me as I walked out of the restroom. She put a hand on her hip. 'Cody left. What happened?'

I shrugged. 'He's going home.' I took a deep breath to dispel the horrible lump in my oesophagus.

'You had a fight, didn't you?' said Jess.

'Just leave me alone, Jess.' I went back to the table to put my hoodie back on. Cody was right. It was time to leave. The bar was getting dark, the ambient setting in for the night crowd.

Jess followed me. 'You should stay here. Let him go. You're among friends here, Riley.'

I looked around at the bar and saw familiar people, but no friends. No Adam. No Cody. But I corrected myself. I wanted Adam and Cody to be friends. Want was different from the truth. However, he had tried to help me. He had stayed as long as he could bear. He was at least telling me the truth when he stole the cocaine and he told me Adam was older than he said he was, which I should have figured out myself if I wasn't so bad at maths and dealing with the outside world. But the age lie had its reasons.

I shook my head at Jess and replied, 'I really should go after Cody.'

Jess sneered, '*I* wouldn't.'

A hush came over my ears and the way Jess's eyes flicked to the bar door unsettled me. Jess had been looking for Adam and Tempany. Jess knew Tempany. I thought of the stolen drugs in Cody's pocket and wondered if Jess had noticed them, and if she had figured out that he was Adam's brother. It wouldn't be a reach. Cody looked a lot like Adam.

I looked Jess up and down and replied, 'I'm not you.'

I walked out of the bar and scanned the dark parking lot but there was no sign of Cody. I heard the shrill siren of ambulance nearby and had a horrible sinking sensation that something bad had happened. Very bad. I began to jog to the road, ignoring the dull thudding in my knees. I glanced down at the ground and saw red smeared in with the dust and gravel. Was that blood? My breath came in raspy gasps. I looked up at the main road and saw the blinding bright red, blue and white lights of an ambulance pulling over near a parked car and two figures on the side of the road. A boy was lying on the road. Cody.

I sprinted towards the carnage, praying to whatever god would listen for Cody to be all right. I stopped as I got closer and could see that it was him on the road. A man was kneeling beside him, putting hard pressure on his stomach. His hands, and Cody's hands, were scarlet with blood. Two paramedics hurried over, talking in a language so alien to English.

'Cody!' I screamed and ran towards him.

The man at Cody's side turned and stood, stopping me from getting any closer. 'Riley, no, don't; he's not in good shape!' I recognised Senior Constable Ackerman, the cop who always seemed to be *right there*.

'What happened?' I gasped, peering around Ackerman's muscular arms to where the paramedics were stabilising Cody enough for him to travel.

Ackerman answered, 'It looks like he's been stabbed.'

My mouth opened and a sound like a wail came out before I could stop it. I clawed at Ackerman but he stepped into me more, forcing me back. I clutched at his arms and looked up into his eyes and saw how there were tears at the bottom of his eyelid. He was worried about Cody, too.

'It had to be someone at the bar,' I told him with a gulp.

'Ben's Bar?'

I nodded. 'He only just left, like twenty minutes ago. I was coming out to find him.'

'Did you see anybody?' he asked.

I shook my head and said, 'No.'

He held me a little tighter and murmured, 'It's okay, it's okay, we'll figure it out.' He stole a glance at Cody and I peeked around him. I breathed a sigh of relief when the paramedics moved him onto a stretcher. I was surprised to see Cody's eyes wide open as they lifted him into the back of the ambulance, looking wearily in my direction but not focusing. I watched the paramedics load him, hanging tightly onto his life and felt a crushing sensation of resignation. Reluctantly, I pulled away from Ackerman and mumbled, 'I have to go.'

He gently held me and reeled me in closer, and said, 'I don't think so. Come on.' He ushered me to his car. I sat in the front seat, too numb to pull away, but I looked around his car. The back seat had only a little space that wasn't covered with wetsuits, jackets, piles of papers, hats and jackets. There were numerous tools on the floor along with some rubber boots and a fishing rod.

'I better take you home,' said Ackerman, blushing about his disgracefully messy car.

I snapped, 'No, you can't take me back there.' My voice cracked.

He smiled. 'Back to Adam's?'

I thought quickly. How could I explain that Adam was at my dad's house and I both wanted to go there and check if he was okay, as well as never go there again? There was no way a cop, off duty or not, could leave me without adult supervision. I didn't have an answer to give him other than opening and closing my mouth.

Ackerman said, 'Once the team gets here, I'll take you to the station and you can chill for a bit and we can have a bit of a chat. Okay?' He gave me a caring smile and I stared glumly out of the windscreen at the gathering fog on the road.

Once his co-workers arrived, he squatted down beside me. 'Hey, so I'm going to stay here, but Senior Constable Burke – remember her?' He gestured to her standing on the footpath. 'She's offered to take you for a drive just to talk. Anywhere you want to go. If you feel like talking, talk. If you don't…she'll bring you to the police station and you and I can have a chat when I start my shift at five. Okay?'

'Are you allowed to detain me like that?' I snapped.

He shrugged. 'Well, you don't want to go home…We wouldn't really be detaining you as much as we'd be giving you somewhere safe to be.'

'What's going to happen to Cody?' I croaked.

'I'll check on him at the hospital before I start my shift in the morning. Okay?'

I nodded and got out of his car and sat in Senior Constable's Burke's car. Like, Ackerman, she was off duty. She was wearing grey track suit pants and a fluffy red jumper. She wore Birkenstocks on her swollen, red feet. Her car was immaculate compared to Ackerman's. It had neat floors and freshly deodorised suede seats. Air freshener the shape of a pineapple dangled from the rear vision mirror and choked me. She kept her eyes on the road as she told me, 'We spoke to your dad this morning.'

I asked, 'At the hospital?'

She nodded.

'What did you tell him?' I asked. 'He came home in a really bad mood.'

'Did he?' she asked.

I took a deep breath to steady my nerves. 'He made Adam come get him and then he…was so mad at him. I had to get away.' I looked down at my hands. My nails were turning blue.

Burke watched me in the corner of her eye as she said, 'My partner and I want to help you.'

I glanced at the Subaru that pulled up beside us with thumping techno music that vibrated the car windows. I explained, 'My dad's a bad guy.' I stared at the brightness of the red light so long without blinking that it began to bleed like Cody's stomach.

'Is he involved in the drug business?' Burke whispered.

I ran my hand over my head and pushed myself as far back in the seat as I could and returned, 'I don't know. He's just a bad man.' We drove along the road and I saw the sign for the scenic outlook of the spot where the bay met the wild ocean. Its high cliffs had always fascinated me and the currents mixing in their opposing directions always gave such spectacular water fountains. 'Can we stop there?' I begged.

She did as I asked. I got out of the car and stood at the cliff top so I could see the foamy white ocean below, crashing into rocks. Every now and then, there was a lull in the waves and all I could see was an inky blue until a large wave would surge up and climb the cliff face in a fantastic foam of water. I stared down at the dark sea and tried to keep my mind on the waves instead of on Cody and Adam.

Burke came up beside me and wrapped in a wool blanket over my shoulders. I shivered as she did so. She was going to be a really good mum. My heart ached for the mother I had lost before she had died. I nestled into the blanket that had dog hair on it, giving it a musky scent; it was fraying at its edges but it was warm. I sat down on a wooden bench and Burke groaned slightly as she perched next to me. I bet all her muscles ached just as much as mine did.

I studied her olive complexion and admired her brown hair, messy in a topknot but thick and healthy. I wanted to reach out and play with it and have her do my hair like mothers do. I asked, 'Did you have to call your husband to say you'll be out longer?'

'Yeah,' she breathed. 'He's very understanding.' She rubbed her hands briskly against her legs to generate a little warmth and reminded me, 'Riley, I need to remind you that anything you can tell me can be used as evidence.'

I cringed and wallowed under the blanket and felt the wind coming off the water. Hiding out in the darkness and staying silent was the safest, most secure way to stay. But thinking about Cody under the dim streetlight and the flickering colourful lights of the ambulance. His red hands made me think of my mother. If I had told her from the beginning about what Dad was doing with Tempany, where would I be now? Would I be sitting underneath a dog blanket next to a police officer who wanted to help but would ruin everything?

Memories of that day, the day my mother tried to kill me and herself came to my mind. She had sat in the bathtub, fully clothed down to her shoes. Where had Dad been? Why hadn't he helped? Hearing Adam behind the door making my heart lift in a swelling cacophony of my booming heart rate. Thinking of how ill I had been made me check my blood sugar level.

Burke watched me and asked, 'How long have you been diabetic?'

I chewed the inside of my lip. She was good – I could give her that. She must have been a police officer for a lot longer than her partner. She knew what kinds of questions to ask to get someone to share things. Too many things. She cared. It was off-putting. How could anybody care that much about a teenage headcase like me?

I shrugged and readjusted the blanket so it was wrapped around me like I was a toasty tortilla. She could probably just call a social worker and relieve herself of me. I stayed quiet.

'Why don't you talk to me?' she asked after eons.

'I haven't done anything wrong; I have nothing to confess.'

She nodded and said, 'Okay. I can understand why you'd think I'd be asking you things to incriminate you. I'm sorry.' She took a deep breath and tried again. 'Help me understand what's been going on for you at home.'

I said stiffly, as if it had been years since I'd spoken, 'My mum died.'

Burke nodded. I waited for her to give me the lines of sympathy like she had previously but she seemed to have learnt from her mistakes and just stayed quiet.

She asked after I went quiet again, 'How have you been coping?'

The openness of her questions had vanished. I could lie a lot easier with closed questions, but listening to the wind and the waves made me want to tell the truth for a change. I picked at my nails as I said to the wind, 'I haven't.'

'What has been the hardest thing?'

'Not feeling bad that she's gone.' Burke observed me and I blinked out at the water and the black sky. I added, 'I'm numb…and it makes me feel bad.'

Burke noted, 'I noticed.' She waited before asking, 'Were you and your mum close?'

'Super close,' I said. 'Until she did what she did.'

She leant closer and asked, 'What did she do?'

I snorted and laughed suddenly. 'I don't think I should say. I don't want you to think that I killed her or something.'

'What did she do?' Burke repeated.

I sighed dramatically. 'She tried taking me out with her…because she,' I used air quotations, 'LOVED me.'

Burke whispered, 'Love makes people do some crazy things.'

I murmured, 'Like lie…'

Burke said, 'Yes. If your family loves you, they'll lie for you.'

I snorted and said, 'I don't think my family loves me. Or anyone. If Dad loves me, why won't he show it? If Adam loves me, why doesn't he take me away out of that house? If Cody loves me, why did he lie to me and steal from me? If my mother loved me, why did she try to kill me?' My shoulders shuddered but I halted my tears. I needed strength and composure. I never spoke to anyone like this. I didn't understand what Burke had done but she'd opened the well and I couldn't shut up. I growled at myself and slapped my knees to make them hurt again. 'Nobody loves me!'

Burke placed a hand on mine to stop me from hitting myself more and made calm sounds to ssh me. She turned my wrist over to look at the old lines from my razorblade, my cold, reliable friend. She whispered, 'Life is never as bad as you think it is for you to do what you've done here.'

I scoffed.

'I'm serious. You can live for a lot more than this. You can overcome. You can be strong, Riley.'

I blinked at her, knowing she was right but the fear for Adam and Cody still wrenched and writhed in my gut.

She asked, 'Riley, who do you think stabbed Cody?'

I thought of Cody's goofy grin and how alike he looked to Adam, with eyes so blue they made you cold all over if you looked in them too long. I thought of the way Adam had told me in the bathroom. *There are a lot of bad people out there who would hurt you and your mum to get to him. That's why I look after you. I know he blows up, but he's trying to keep you safe.*

I hadn't believed him. I had, in general, of course, but I didn't believe those bad people would be looming outside the door of a local bar, ready to stab my best friend. I thought of Adam's insistence that Dad hadn't killed my mother, that it had been an accident. Nothing was an accident. Not really.

Had my father seen Cody as a threat and stabbed him? Or had it been these mysterious bad people *out there*? Or was he really the worst person of all? The true killer? Nothing was concrete in my mind, just thoughts.

I said to Burke, 'There are a lot of bad people out there.'

Burke looked like she understood more than I did. She said, 'Did your father stab him? He led Adam down the wrong path and now he's gone after Cody. He's unstable and you're scared to say it was him. You need to give a statement, Riley. All you have to do is come down to the station and we can get it on record. You can tell me everything.'

I looked up at her with a bored expression. 'Are you done?'

She stood and grasped my hands. 'Come on, Riley, you don't need to be afraid of him! Just tell me everything.'

I wrenched my hands out of hers and growled, 'I'm not telling you anything until you can guarantee my safety.'

She tried to nag me again but I jumped up, the blanket raining down off me to the ground.

'Haven't you been listening?' I screamed, tears cascading now down my face. 'I can't tell you anything because I can't! It's not safe for me to say anything!'

Burke picked up her ratty old dog blanket as I began backing up and it all poured out of me like a dam breaking. 'I have been waiting and waiting for Adam to get me out of there or help me. What am I supposed to do? What do I do now? I finally made a friend and somebody just tried to kill him. What is it that I'm supposed to do? Just what?'

A piece of my tooth chipped I had grit them so hard. My hand flew to my mouth and I felt the sharp edge. I sniffed and sobbed, 'She was supposed to protect me.' Burke stepped up to me and folded me into a strong hug, just as shell-shocked as I was at my outburst. I continued crying and yelling into her chest, 'She didn't tell me! She didn't tell me! She didn't tell me!'

'What didn't she tell you, Riley?' Burke asked.

'That she wanted to die,' I wheezed through my closing throat. It hurt after all. It hurt to lose your mother just as much as it hurt for your mother to betray you.

Burke's hands shook as she pushed me away from her so she could make eye contact with me. She explained, trying to hide the quivering of her bottom lip, 'Admitting they need help isn't something people are good at. Sometimes it's just easier for them to give up.'

'But I needed her,' I sniffed. 'And now she's gone and left me alone with him. The wrong person died that day.'

Burke said gently, 'What you need, Riley, is to feel safe. I can give you that...just come back with me and tell me everything you do know.'

I hiccoughed. 'I don't know if I can.'

'I bet you'll be surprised at how much you do know,' she said as she guided me back to the car with the dog blanket draped over her arm. 'Come on.'

# 40 ADAM

Locked in his office for hours, I pissed on his computer. My message to Aldo Iacopetta must not have gone through. The sun was setting and the room was getting dark. I paced up and down the window, heaving my body weight against it. The door was locked and I couldn't believe I was trapped in there like a mouse in a trap. The palm trees scraped against the spouting and made the hair on my neck stand up. I heard Dom return home and pause and listen at the door to his office. I stayed quiet, ear pressed to it.

'You still in there, rat?' His voice grated in my ears.

'Why you calling me a rat?' I asked, trying to sound casual.

He laughed sarcastically and his footsteps moved away from the door. I shook my head and pounded my elbow repeatedly into the door until it clicked. I froze. I looked at the lock. It had popped open. I could escape. But I'd be escaping straight into Dom. I hurried to the computer and started it up, wiping it first with my tee shirt. The cameras. They worked. I could see him in the kitchen, making a drink. Yes. Drink. His drink. He drank whiskey and swallowed too many sleeping pills. I'd wait for him to go to bed. Ever since Rachelle had died, he'd annihilated himself on the nightly. My heart raced and the plan was in my head, dazed and dehydrated as I was. I searched the office, breaking open locked cabinets and rifling through papers. There, under the papers in the bottom drawer of the black filing cabinet under his desk was a key, and a handgun. Its shape fuzzed around the edges. I held onto the edge of the desk to stop myself from passing out. When the room stopped spinning, I reached out and touched it. It was cold. Hard. Heavy. Loaded.

I stuffed it into the back of my pants and stood up so I could watch Dominic on the camera monitors. He paced the kitchen and stepped over each pot and pan that I had pulled down. He went up to my room, my eyes followed the cameras. Pulled apart the bedding, smashed the drawers against the wall. I glanced at the office. I had just done the same. My manuscript. He sat on the edge of the bed and read it. He paced the room until the pills kicked in. He lay on the bed and rolled to his side. I watched him. He stopped moving. He was asleep. I wiped my forehead and whimpered. I couldn't just leave while he had the manuscript. I had to get it from him. I could re-write it. Re-write the ending.

I crept out of the office and up the stairs. The lights were on, the LEDs blaring into my aching eyes. I drew my gun and pointed it down like I had been taught, crept one foot in front of the other in a crouched position. Into my room. Pausing with each step to quieten my breath. Stepped to the side of the bed. Take the manuscript, slide it out of his hand with a hush, then put it on the floor beside me.

The boss was out cold. I could solve this problem with one shot. I raised my shaking hands and took of the safety. Pressed the muzzle to his temple, sweat pouring down my face, my insides revolting against me. I tensed my body and tried to force my finger to touch – all it needed was a touch, a breeze, a jitter – but my finger locked at the knuckle and I pulled it away with a cry.

I fell back onto the floor and threw the gun aside, smothering my mouth with my hands to suppress the sound of a sob. I was about to murder a man in his sleep. A defenceless man. All I had ever wanted was to help people and fix things that were wrong in the world, and I was the problem. I sat there on the floor with tears streaming down my face and the realisation that I was drowning.

I would never be able to bring Dominic Flynn in for justice without implicating myself. Maybe he had made it that way, maybe he had known all along who I really was: the liar who had infiltrated his family to watch him. I was the liar who told his father he was dropping out of the police force because he wanted to be a mechanic, and got into using illicit drugs. The liar who ran away but really had gone deep, too deep, undercover.

Get information on his drug dealing, find out who his main supplier was, get out. Rachelle had been right when she'd told him that he shouldn't trust me. The poor woman was dead now for trying to tell him that there was something not right about me, and realising she was powerless because her husband would never listen to her. Never. Because he was too self-absorbed, too controlling, too unfaithful.

I'd been close to finding out the supplier. But Aldo tried pulling me out. Knew I was in too deep. They say once you start fucking a drug queen, you're going down the toilet. I think I would have been all right if I had got clean, and stuck with Tempany. It wasn't her that brought me down. Staying with Riley kept me longer than it should have. I felt so sorry for the poor kid that I couldn't get out even if I was dragged out. And her mother.

Rachelle. Poor Rachelle.

I'd been so stupid and desperate to keep her safe, keep her and Riley away from it all, that I'd become the thing they should have been kept away from. I'd shaken her, hit her head on the back of the bathtub. I panicked and let her drown when I could have saved her in the end. I didn't deserve to be saved for what I'd done to her.


I picked up my manuscript and tore out each page, flushing it down the toilet. I'd re-write the ending. The wrong person died that day. I'd re-write it right this time.

I snorted a line of gear then measured out a new line. I had already snorted six lines. All I could find in the boss's office. I'd leave no trace of drugs left in his office. I had gathered all the supplies from the office, sweating profusely and gasping for air.

I piled the gear up, line after line. It was how my descent had started after all – it should end the same way.

My life should have worked out differently – I'd taken this case on and given up my entire self with the white light of hope we have at twenty-two. I was supposed to be starting a life that would give me purpose and let me help people, but there I was murdering a woman by accident and dropping her body off the side of the super yacht hoping she'd stay down long enough for me to figure out how to bring Flynn down in the meantime. It had been four years of being a criminal – longer than my one month on the job as a police officer.

'You're baby-faced; you look like you're eighteen...we could use you in Narcotics.' The sergeant had placed me there and Narcotics had delivered me to Ben's Bar, where associates of Dominic Flynn hung out. It had all worked so well, until it hadn't.

So, let's just stop. I can't deal with this anymore. I am so far from what I wanted to be. I'm a scumbag. I'm a killer. I set out to be a hero and now that is just all gone.

My cover. Gone.

My purpose. Gone.

Rachelle's life. Gone.

My life?

G

O

N

E.

# 41 ACKERMAN

The call came in at 4:17 a.m. The Flynn House. Dominic Flynn on the phone, screaming and crying. I was getting ready for work, buttoning my pants when Burke called me and told me that Sergeant Doyle wanted me to come in as early as possible. There had been a big break in the Rachelle Flynn case.

'Where's Riley?' I asked, sitting on the edge of my just-made bed.

'She's sleeping in the sergeant's office. Poor thing was wiped.'

I told her I'd be there as soon as possible. I wouldn't have time to check on Cody like I had promised the kid. I packed my things. I brushed my teeth, two minutes exactly, and swallowed the lump of dread in my throat as I swung my duffel bag over my shoulder and grabbed my car keys. I got into my car and drove to town at 4:32 a.m.

I cringed as the windshield wipers scraped across the glass because I'd run out of washer fluid. I pulled up an intersection behind a truck and its red brake lights burned into my eyes. Lack of sleep was normal for police officers. It didn't mean it was right. I was on day eight of a ten-day week and the four-day break could not come fast enough. This Rachelle Flynn case had made me question my decision to move to Missing Persons. Being back on Highway Patrol seemed like the best option for me.

When I arrived at the station at 4:46, the sergeant ushered me into the conference room with Burke and the other two general duties police officers that were rostered on for the night shift. Sergeant Doyle, a man in his early fifties and a persistent cough from catching Covid in 2020, informed us that we'd had a death in the ranks and we needed to prepare for a shitstorm.

'Constable Adam Marshall,' he said. 'Was discovered deceased at the Flynn house this morning.'

Burke's jaw fell open and the two general duty officers bowed their heads out of respect but I knew that had no clue who he was. I flexed my jaw and Burke glanced from me to the sergeant, realising that I had known that Adam Marshall was an undercover cop.

I had no idea until this week. Doyle had told me when I'd tried putting through the remand for possessing the gun.

'Ackerman, you can't arrest him.'

'Why not?' I had asked.

Sergeant Doyle had given me the file and stayed silent, hand at his mouth while I read it. I'd thrown it down on his desk and stormed off. Having to hand Riley to him the day before had made my head swim. He was good. Was good. Had been good. He'd been a good liar, that was for sure.

The sergeant continued, 'He was working undercover with the Narcotics unit to find information on Dominic Flynn, whose daughter we currently have sleeping in my office.'

We all looked over to the frosted door of his office as if we could see through it to her.

'I believe Dominic Flynn discovered Marshall's true identity and he has met foul play.'

I raised my hand. 'I can bring Flynn in.'

'He has scarpered. He called Triple Zero and then he has left the scene. Paramedics are on-site, and Senior Detective Iacopetta from Narcotics is on-site.'

Burke mumbled, 'I've got to sit down.' The sergeant opened a chair for her. She thumped down into it, running her hands through her hair and shaking her head.

Poor Burke. I wished I could have divulged what I had known. It made me bite my tongue too hard to think of keeping that kind of secret. I was a terrible secret keeper. I hand to hand it to Marshall. The kind of turmoil he must have had, watching Dominic Flynn beat his wife and child and not being able to do anything alone would have sent me over the edge.

The sergeant sighed, which led to a minor coughing fit. 'I need one of you to go assist Senior Detective Iacopetta and the rest of you to go find Flynn before he skips completely out of the country. I will stay here and mind the girl until CPS comes to collect her.'

I raised my hand again. 'I'll go help Iacopetta.' I wanted to be the one who collected the evidence that brought that arsehole Flynn down for good.

Burke asked, 'How are you going to tell Riley that Adam Marshall is dead?'

The sergeant blinked at her. 'What do you mean?'

'They were very close, sir,' she said. I nodded in agreement. 'I think I should stay here with her.'

Doyle nodded. 'Okay. Then I'll hit the street and look for that son of a bitch with you two ratbags.' The general duty officers, Tui and Claire, nodded. 'Meeting adjourned. Let's go.'

Pulling in at the house by 5:40 a.m., I found Senior Detective Aldo Iacopetta at the door. Paramedics waited at the scene to get our clearance to remove the body. I went with him to the bathroom; the same bathroom Adam Marshall had supposedly rescued Riley from and where Rachelle was last seen.

Iacopetta took off his jacket and flung it on the hallway floor where it crumpled in a heap. His hands shook as he applied gloves. He muttered, 'Frigging told the lad he was getting in too deep. I frigging told him.'

I asked, 'You knew him well?'

Iacopetta shrugged. 'He was a good kid.' He cleared his throat. 'Didn't deserve this.'

My eyes went to the body, lying in the bathtub, bruised and bloody head resting to the side. I put gloves on and followed Iacopetta's lead of looking around the scene first. He brushed his finger along the basin and said, 'Cocaine,' as casually as though he were reading the weather.

'Did he take an overdose then?' I asked, looking at Adam's face. His eyes were closed and he looked like he was sleeping. There was no water in the bath. The lights shone brightly onto his face like a spotlight on a stage and he was the main act. The solo act that would break into a booming rendition of *The Greatest Show* at any moment.

'His heart would have given out,' Aldo replied, brushing the cocaine into evidence bags and walking out with a sigh.

I studied the base of the bath and noticed a notebook under his thigh. I reached and pinched it and tugged it out. I opened the notebook and found the writing to be messy and the pen had pushed through the paper in some parts as if he was aggressively writing it in a hurry.

There were pages ripped out early on in the notebook. I ran my thumb along the snags of paper. My eyes followed the lines Adam Marshall had written.

Good guys take a bow and exit stage left because they couldn't do right…I'm sorry but I'm the bad guy.

I gazed down at his face. The zip on his jacket was not completely up, lazily left undone. I could see a longer piece of his brown hair, curling around his ear and I swallowed a lump in my throat. It was not a homicide. Dominic Flynn had not done this, and he hadn't killed his wife either. I wanted to look away from Adam's face but I couldn't. The whiteness of the bath, the whiteness of the tile, the whiteness of the light and the whiteness of his skin fizzled in my eyes until I let a tear escape my eye and snap the notebook closed, shoving into my pocket. I was wrong the entire time. I guess I couldn't trust my cop gut after all. Case closed.

# 42 RILEY

I snapped my eyes open and found myself on the soft sofa with my legs folded up in a foetal position. I sat upright and felt all my senses fly from me faster than a falcon on a dive. I looked around and remembered where I was. I was in the police sergeant's office, with Burke's manky dog blanket over me. It was dark, save for the faint glow coming in from the light of the frosted door.

My chest ached and I was careful to not move too quickly in case the police officers heard me and came in. I needed to be alone to think through everything that had happened. A moment, all right. I needed a moment. I gripped the blanket and pulled it off me and dumped it on the floor. I placed my feet, now just in socks, down on the carpet that was such low quality it felt like shards of glass. The couch was positioned against the wall, under framed documents and newspaper clippings that included pictures of him shaking hands with important people. The desk was the nicest thing in the room. Mahogany and it gleamed with pride. Multiple computer monitors, black with a red light at the bottom right. Sleep mode.

I ran my hands over the goosebumps on my skin and rubbed at my knees, which ached with a dull presence to remind me that I had overextended the muscles and slammed the joints together. I wondered where Dad was now. If he had come after me. The police had been right about one thing…I was safe with them because he would never come near them to get to me. Maybe I had to change the way I thought about things. Maybe it wouldn't be so bad to be in foster care. Maybe it would be okay. Then I imagined an old man forcing himself onto me and I gagged. No, I had to find Adam. I had to see if he was okay and then I could be free and live with him.

I thought of Cody. I looked at my watch. It was 5:45 in the morning. He would have had surgery by now. Was he alive? Or dead? The quietness of the office left me with my mind reeling. In the distance, I heard a coffee machine starting to chug and steam and my breathing increased. It reminded me of home and it made my skin crawl. I blocked my ears and crawled under the mahogany desk and hugged my knees. I didn't want to go back there. I refused to go back there.

At 6:30, there was a soft tap on the door. Senior Constable Burke poked her head in and said my name softly. I pulled myself out from under the desk and pushed my hair back. 'You're awake.' Her lips twitched like she was trying to smile, but her mouth couldn't follow through. She rested her cheek against the door jam and asked, 'Would you like something to eat?'

I nodded and followed her out into the hallway where the police desks were not as extravagant as the mahogany desk. Panels and plastic chairs lined the hallway outside a wide-open room with a circular table. A label on the open door read CONFERENCE ROOM. I sat in the conference room with Burke and delivered my Bolus. I mumbled, 'I just have to wait fifteen minutes.'

'I'm glad you got some sleep,' she replied. 'You must have been exhausted.'

I nodded and admitted, 'I haven't really been sleeping since Mum died.'

'What you told me last night? That you didn't care that she was gone. Do you still believe that?' She passed me a cup of water and I drank it all without answering.

'What happens next?' I asked. I looked around. 'Didn't your partner say he was starting at five?'

Burke nodded. 'He came in and then had to leave for an emergency.'

I chewed on my inner lip and hoped it wasn't Cody. I wanted to know how he was but was too afraid that Burke would tell me that he had slipped away, unable to be saved, that he was gone.

Burke gave me a muesli bar once my fifteen minutes was up and I ate it despite it tasting stale and not really liking the sultanas that were littered in it. I wolfed it down then drank the hot chocolate she had made for me. She sat down next to me and took a deep breath. 'Okay. Now we need to have a chat.'

I took a deep breath. This was it. I had to make the choice. Did I ever want to be free of my father or not?

'I saw my father having sex with someone and Mum confronted Dad about it. He slammed her head against the back of the bathtub and then dumped her body out at sea.'

Burke blinked at me.

I stared her down.

She pressed record on her phone. 'Could you…repeat that for me? Slowly.'

I rolled my eyes then repeated it verbatim. She pressed stop and gave me a thin smile. I couldn't believe that I'd finally done it. Taken action. My word against his. I was sure Adam would back me up. Why wouldn't he? If I lied for him, surely he would lie for me.

'Riley,' Burke made sure I looked at her, 'I have some news to tell you and it's not going to be good.' Her chin tucked into her neck and her eyes darted side to side as if looking at each of my eyes one at a time. I braced for the news that Cody had died so hard that my face went numb. 'Riley, it's Adam. I'm am very sorry to tell you that Adam has passed away.'

Her lips were moving but the sound wasn't working. She just said Adam had passed away. Didn't she mean Cody? Adam was at my house. He was fine. Cody was the one who had been stabbed and he was at the hospital. But she said Adam. She definitely said Adam's name. She even said it twice. *Adam has passed away.*

I said with a breaking voice, 'Did you say Adam has passed away?'
Burke nodded.

I could feel the room around me closing in and crushing the air out of me. I sucked in air but none came. I gasped and tried to scream but colours blotched in my eyes and I heard a whistling sound as I crumpled off the chair into Burke's body. That roaring sound? What was it? I realised with a start that it was me moaning and wailing. Me. I didn't know I could make that sound. It hurt. It hurt so much. I clenched my eyes to black and clutched at my chest. Get out, hurt. Get out, get out. Why wasn't it getting out? Burke held me and rocked me like she would a baby and I cried in her arms until my body switched off and I collapsed asleep, shattered.

Burke stayed by my side all morning, giving me Diet Coke from the vending machine and little tea biscuits. I felt nauseous at the thought of swallowing solid food so instead just sucked on the lip of the can and the cups of water she brought me.

It was at least two hours later when I finally got the courage to ask what had happened. She told me didn't know and that she would do her best to find out for me. Did I want to see him to say goodbye? I thought of the last time I had seen him, on the kitchen floor, with his face contorting as he shouted at me to RUN GO NOW. So that would be the last time I heard his voice. Panicking, screaming at me to go. It made me sob to think he was so afraid.

'Did my dad murder him?' I asked with a hiccup.

Burke paused. 'I don't know. Your dad called it in to Triple Zero. I think he found him.'

'I think he killed him,' I said with a clear voice. 'They were fighting when I last saw them. Adam told me to RUN GO NOW,' I winced. 'So, I did.' I swallowed and looked down at my feet. I should have stayed and protected him. Typical me. Weak as shit. Running away instead of helping Adam and it cost him his life. Tears came to my eyes again and I wiped them away ferociously. Stop crying you weakling.

'Sounds like he was trying to help you,' Burke murmured. 'He might have saved your life.'

I looked up at her. 'Excuse me?'

'He might have saved your life.'

Drowning in the sea, he had saved me. Then swimming the other day, him shouting that he had saved me. I never thanked him. I was too desperate to get him to get me away from my dad. Away from that house. Away from all the times my father had beaten my mother, broken her bones. Adam saved my life.

I nodded at Burke and said, 'He did. He was a hero.'

Burke told me Senior Constable Ackerman would be back soon and a social worker would be coming by, so I could go with them into foster care until my family in Sydney could take me on. My shoulders slumped. Live with Dad's family or live in foster care.

'How long will it take for my family to take me on?' I asked.

'They went overseas according to their voice message; I'm sure they'll return my call as soon as they can.'

My nose wrinkled automatically as I said, 'So I'm stuck in foster care? Are you serious?'

Burke shifted her weight in her seat and rested her hands upon the top of her pregnant belly. Her hands folded neatly together but her nails were unpainted. Clean, short. She must have been an organised sort of person. Normal. Had a bunch of girlfriends that would throw her a baby shower, had a husband who had given her an under-stated but pretty ring that she wore on her left ring finger that was sinking beneath a layer of skin that had puffed up, no doubt from the pregnancy. Her hair was shiny and straight, her skin clear and her eyes bright. A natural blush, straight teeth, lips that were not chapped or dry. A career, a man, a baby, her good looks, and her health. Epitome of safe and secure. My face ached from crying so hard for Adam and everything I had lost. Him, as well as my chances to be normal. Hell, my own body couldn't even function without needing a boost of insulin.

I couldn't find the energy to speak anymore so I lay my head down on the conference table and let the cool surface soothe my cracking face.

# 43 ACKERMAN

I kept my promises to people unless it was out of my hands. That was why I still went by the hospital, following the van that had collected Adam Marshall's body. His notebook in my back pocket. The sun was rising and was piercing the clouds in a brilliant tangerine and rose cacophony. I threw my sunglasses atop my head and made my way into intensive care where I asked how the young stabbing victim was going. He had just come out of surgery and would be sedated for quite a while. I thanked them and headed out, but was stopped by a doctor.

'Excuse me, did you just ask about Cody Marshall?'

I nodded and held up my badge since I was in plain clothes.

'Cody Marshall is my son.' The breath was knocked out of me and I braced for him to ask about his older brother, whom we had not notified about yet. My hand raised up to shake his but I could barely feel his smooth skin in my hand. 'The paramedics brought him in – they said that he'd been found, stabbed.' He stammered, 'He's the last kind of kid that would be mixed up in anything that would get him stabbed.'

I swallowed hard and scratched at my eyebrow.

'I saw him just as he was sent in to surgery, and I…' He thumped at his chest. 'I can't believe he's been stabbed. Is it true, officer?'

I nodded and uttered, 'I'm the one who found Cody.'

His father studied my face with imploring eyes and hovered his hands mid-gesture as if expecting me to tell him exactly what had happened but I had no other answer for him other than, 'It looked like he had been stabbed.'

'Somebody really *knifed* my kid?'

I shook my head and mumbled, 'The wound looked more typical to that of a smaller object, like a screwdriver or scissors.'

He looked down with a gulp then looked up at me, 'Oh, I didn't catch your name, officer.'

'Senior Constable Ackerman, sir. Nice to meet you.'

'Robert. Dr. Robert Marshall.' He narrowed his eyes and wagged his finger at me. 'Was that you that left a message on my voicemail about Cody being in trouble at school?'

'No, sir, that may have one of my colleagues.' I found myself backing into the wall, further away from him yet he followed.

He said, 'I will have to come down to the station and talk to them about that incident. There is no way that Cody was involved in that either.'

I whispered, 'You wouldn't venture a guess that the gun and the stabbing are related?'

The doctor snapped, 'Absolutely not.'

I asked, 'Has anyone contacted you about your other son?'

Dr. Robert Marshall waved his hand. 'Ah, he's a delinquent drug addict. He made his choices. Wouldn't be surprised if you fellows found him dead, lying in a ditch somewhere.' He shook his head. 'I tried and tried with that boy.' He squinted at me. 'You know, he was almost a copper, like you.' I remained quiet, dumbfounded with his apathy for his own son, his own son who was now beneath his feet in the morgue having a post-mortem to determine whether he indeed overdose or if he had been killed by the devil he was studying, all in the name of trying to get justice and stop drug trade. It didn't seem enough now. A life for that? The inequity made my teeth hurt.

The doctor sighed. 'He got into drugs. Ruined his life.'

I murmured, 'I met your son.'

'You what?'

'I said I met your son.'

'Yeah, you mentioned that you found him.'

'No, I...'

The doctor was looking off now, searching the hallway for some other person to question about his son. 'Never mind,' I muttered. I took a breath and told him some officers would be in touch with him. I walked off down the hallway, glancing back at him over my shoulder, wondering if I should have informed him about Adam or not. I would leave that for the sergeant or Senior Detective Iacopetta to do. Why should I have the trauma of delivering a death notice when I could give that job to the officers that put Adam in that position in the first place.

I couldn't imagine what it had been like that for the guy. His family had to believe that he had dropped out because he'd got into drugs. He was alone in the world. Sacrificed. I drove to the beach and threw Adam's notebook off the end of the pier, finding it harder and harder to swallow.

Burke met me in the locker room and said, 'I told Riley about Adam.'

I put on my uniform over my singlet and put my heavy police boots on, bending down to lace them.

'Ackerman, did you hear me? I told the girl.'

I snapped, 'Yeah, I heard.' I sat up, feeling the vertebrae in my back collide together in a click-clack like puzzle pieces snapping together. 'I imagine she took it...*well*.'

Burke nodded at me. It wasn't easy for a kid to lose everything; I knew more about that than most. You're in a vacuum. Everything is a blur and you have faces of all those people around you, clamouring to make sure you're well, fed, supported but as time goes by and you're not snapping out of it, you're quivering with rage at the world itself and can't see a way through, those people that were desperate to make sure you had everything, ebb away until they're gone like smoke stack in the distance, getting smaller with a haze of the setting sun on a hot day. The girl wouldn't be all right for a long time. Even when she got to my age, she would still have little left-over twitches and spasms that woke her in the night and make her lash out at those around her. Girls like her should grow up to be like Burke, strong and with a support network, surrounded with love and a life purpose. Instead, she would grow up to be like me, alone and constant need to change to blend in. But hopefully she would have a purpose, and an intrinsic need to make sure people were safe, because one day, she would be safe, too. One day.

Burke cleared her throat and asked, 'You grew up in a foster home, didn't you?'

I nodded.

'I think you should speak to Riley.'


I handed Riley a packet of chips from the vending machine that overcharged by at least fifty percent and sat beside her at the conference table. I watched her eat them slowly and she said quietly between nibbles, 'I wondered when you'd be back.'

'I'm sorry; something came up.'

'I heard.' She eyed off a chip before putting it back into the packet and giving them back to me. I picked at them and stole a glance at the wrists Burke had told me to look at. The razor blade that I had taken in evidence when Rachelle had gone missing. She had been damaged a lot longer. Her mother disappearing had been another punch. No wonder she was apathetic and cold.

Rustling the chip packet and scrunching it into a ball, I said, 'I checked on Cody.'

Her eyes looked up at me with the lower lid drawing down, like a Basset Hound. 'Is he going to be okay?'

'I don't know,' I sighed. 'I really don't.' I stood and disposed of the wrapper in the wastepaper bin at the door. I sat back next to her and leant on the table with my entire right side so I could peer into her eyes in the way my father had liked to do to me. It had always made me speak up.

'Who do you think stabbed him, Riley?'

She glanced down and frowned. 'I can't say.'

'Don't you think it's worth a shot?'

She sighed. 'I don't want to get him into any trouble.'

'He won't be in trouble.'

Riley whispered, 'Cody stole a bag of cocaine.'

'From your dad?'

She shook her head. 'No, somebody else. My dad always told us there were bad people out there that hurt us to get to him,' she whispered. I covered my mouth with my hand and listened intently. 'I think that he wasn't lying about that.'

'Do you think these people hurt Cody?' It made sense. If Cody had stolen their drugs, they would have gone after him.

She nodded. 'They beat up Adam because they thought he was the one that stole it.'

Iacopetta's voice replayed in my mind *he was in too deep*. Was this what Iacopetta had meant? Adam had begun to cross the line between cop and drug addict, dealing with rival dealers?

Riley sat stiffly and I moved back to take in a breath of air.

'Your dad...he called in Adam's death...' My voice stopped and she recoiled as if I'd hit her. I remembered the way that I'd found out my parents had died. My brother and I had been on a school camp and found out from the teachers that told us in their shaky, first year out of uni awkwardness that we had to stay back after the last child had been picked up, and led into the principal's office where the police officers and DHS workers looked down at us with patient, sympathetic gazes. Our house had been broken into and our parents had disturbed them. Aggravated burglary. Then they'd told us our parents had been shot and our childhoods had ended right there.

I ran my tongue over my teeth and tried again, 'Do you have any idea where your dad may have gone?'

'Is the boat still there?'

'Yes.'

'So, he hasn't run away…Then I don't know where he is.'

I scratched at my neck again and said, 'Social workers will come and meet you, soon.'

She gritted her teeth and retorted, 'I really don't want to go to foster care.'

I leant on the table again and asked why. She thought carefully and I added, 'It could be the best thing ever for you, Riley, if you give it a chance, since you're abused at home.'

She snapped, 'I never said I was abused.'

I replied quietly, 'The bruises make it pretty obvious, Riley.'

She muttered, 'Yeah, well, at least I wasn't abused sexually.'

I supposed it was what was fed to her. The idea that she'd be sexually abused in foster care didn't come to a young girl's mind unless it was fed to her. A lump formed in my throat and I thought of what would have happened to me and my brother if we hadn't been taken into foster care. The houses and the families that took us in over the years – there were three – were all different, but in my experience, they made us feel welcome.

'My brother and I grew up in foster care,' I told her.

Her eyes widened. I gestured to her. 'You'll be safe there. A lot of people would love to look after you.'

She scoffed and looked away. 'The only person I want to be with is Adam.'

I chewed on my lip as my mind raced with the memories of what I'd been through myself. I wanted so much to be that police officer that was the hero but knew that the hero in her eyes was Adam and he would always be that hero, even after he had become entrenched in the monstrosities of the underworld. I wondered if Riley knew what Adam had done, if she knew that he was really the one who had killed her mother.

'Riley, did you see anything the day your mum died?' I whispered.

Her blue eyes bored into mine. 'I saw everything.'

# 44 CODY

A beeping sound and shearing pain in my entire torso woke me. The scraping of a plastic chair nearby being pulled across the floor made me wince. I opened my eyes halfway and stared at the heart rate monitoring machine and the IV bag that was connected to the crook of my bruised elbow. My face was swallowed by an oxygen mask and tried to open my eyes more but they were puffy, a side-effect of the anaesthetic. My throat burned and I was heavy as concrete in the stiff sheets of the hospital bed.

I wondered how long it had been. I flexed my toes and felt my stomach tingle which made me tremble. Anxiety chewed at me suddenly and the pain intensified. I groaned and stared up at the ceiling, willing the pain to go away. I groaned again to see if it helped as an outlet, but it didn't.

'Cody,' croaked a voice next to me. I tilted my head and looked at my older brother sitting next to my bed. His eyes were red and he looked like he had too been gutted.

'How are you feeling, mate?' he asked with a nervous smile.

'Like crap,' I moaned, muffled by the oxygen mask. I huffed, 'What are you doing here?'

'I wanted to see you before I left,' he admitted, fiddling with the ragged arm of his jacket arm. 'So, you can finish kicking my arse, right?' He tried to laugh but fell short.

I ignored his attempts to lighten the mood and asked sadly, 'Why?'

'Why?'

'Why did you choose Riley and drugs over me?' I whispered, in more pain than the morphine could relieve.

Adam replied, 'Because she needed me.'

'I needed you,' I said with a sniffle. I gasped loudly from the pain.

Adam leant forward and said, 'Press that button and it will summon the nurse to give you more pain relief.'

I clamped my eyes shut and said, 'I'm done with drugs.' My entire body tensed as muscles in my abdomen spasmed until I gave in and pushed the button. Twice. A nurse in her late thirties came in. She smiled at me like I was her very own son and said happily, 'Well, well, hello, there, sleepy head; you're awake.' She had a thick Scottish accent. She brushed against Adam to check on my IV and said, 'I'll get you some pain relief, sweetie.' She stepped back. 'Would you like me to call your father down?'

I answered yes and she left.

Adam announced, 'I'm leaving, little man.'

I begged, 'Stay. Why do you have to run away?'

He looked down at me, his weakened little brother and answered just as weakly as I felt. 'You'll know why and understand soon. I love you little man.'

He bent down and kissed my forehead and I shut my eyes to squeeze out the tears. When I opened my eyes, a tear was rolling down my cheek and he was nowhere to be seen. My father was sitting beside me where Adam had sat, holding my hand. The room spun and I realised with a jolt that I hadn't even woken up before because the room was completely different. Even in my dreams, Adam was leaving me.

The hot tear punished my raw face like a landslide. 'Dad, I'm sorry.'

'It's not your fault, son. It's not your fault.'

# 45 RILEY

I gave a great, miserable sigh and a thick, hot tear dropped from my eye onto the interior leather of Senior Constable Ackerman's police car. I sat in the backseat clutching a black gardening bag in my hand as he drove me back to the house. Apparently, Adam had died in the bathroom and I did not let that slide as a coincidence. There was a reason why he chose the bathroom. The way he'd pulled me out the window when I was sick and the way my mother had sunk in the shallow depths of the bathtub electrocuted across my brain. He had died in the bathroom with her.

We pulled up and I looked up at the boarded window, still unreplaced from the day Mum went missing, the day she died. I got out of the car, stiffly shuffling. My knees hurt more now. I'd probably torn some ligaments or shredded my meniscus; it was unsurprising the way I'd flung myself from the balcony that day, the day that I had last seen Adam.

Ackerman slid on a jacket and followed me into the house, our footsteps echoing now in the lonely desert that was the white walls and white floor. Sanitary or sanitorium. I paused at the living room and my eyes gazed upon my baby photos, gleeful chubby cheeks and brazen blue eyes. Criminal to be so innocent in this house. There were photos of my dad holding up trophy fish on the yacht. I peered at the yacht and remembered the time Adam taught me how to drive it. He put a skipper hat on my head and I had felt so special. There were photos of my mother with her chin on my shoulder as we posed. My eyes vast as a lake – I had that detached stare that murderers had. I cringed at the way my mum's lips met my cheek in another photo. I reached up and took them all off the wall, putting them face down on the hutch where Mum kept teacups. Teacups for her tea that she laced with diuretics and laxatives. I wanted to smear my hand across the entire shelves and smash them all to pieces.

Moving across into the kitchen, I stood and remembered gallivanting across the yard, pretending I was a horse or pretending I was a jungle girl as I swung on the palm frond that extended from next door. I remembered sitting on the patio and Adam telling me things so I'd understand how the world worked and why I needed to trust him. He'd saved my life. Surely, I could trust him.

Into the office, to the secret hiding spot. Ackerman waited outside the door. I hesitated before pulling up the soil in the fake plant and putting the item I'd discovered in the bag. Kept my hands out of view of Ackerman as I moved upstairs and into my room. Ackerman waited downstairs. I listened for him, buzzing chatter coming across on the radio he had locked at his shoulder. I shoved clothes in the garden bag, rustling it loudly and taking one item out and into my pocket. As many clothes as I could grab, Mum's lipstick. I painted my lips in a rush and went to the wardrobe where I had hidden the necklace in a shoe.

It glowed at me like the epitome of hope. All was not lost. Millions in my hand. I put it around my neck and listened for Ackerman. The radio still chattered. I went to the window and climbed over the balcony, this time carefully making my way down the drainpipe and across the lawn, sprinting down the steps to the beach and across the pier. I could be out of there in no time, halfway across the world.

All I had to do was sail away.

I leapt onto the boat with a thud and a skid, finding my way to the cockpit, the key to the cockpit door in my pocket and a desperate grail grating my inhalations. I had to stand on tiptoes to see over the nose of the boat. The navigation keys that Adam used to switch on first were above my head.

I squinted to see which buttons. Tried to remember desperately which ones of the Q shaped buttons to push. Main batteries GREEN. Rudder, bow, main engine, davit, flaps, dashboard, electrical...My fingers trembled. Port, starboard. I pressed them all green, having to jump which made the pain in my knees ricochet down my legs and back up to my back.

I jogged to the stairs down to the kitchen. These awful stairs. I'd fallen on them once. I hadn't broken my arm. I swung the wheel to open the door to the engine room. Adam had told me to ALWAYS check the engine room. If something was broken, the whole boat would be ruined. You need to make sure there's nothing leaking out. Clam it up.

In the small engine room, the stench of diesel fumes and the scent of grease made my mouth pull back and my stomach turn. There was a crash of metal suddenly and Dad stood up from a corner where he'd been squatting behind a pile of buckets. I yelped and turned. He seized the back of my jacket and yanked me down, almost sending my head diving into the engine that hogged the room. He smeared his hand over my mouth and held another finger to his lips, 'Sshh. Don't scream.'

'What are you doing here?' I mumbled. 'The cops are looking for you.'

Even if I had screamed, Ackerman wouldn't hear. He was probably still in the house, giving me privacy while I packed my things. There I was trying to run from him and I'd run straight into my father's grip again.

His voice shuddered as he lowered his hand from my mouth. 'I'm not going to hurt you.'

'Right,' I said in disbelief. 'Tell that to my dead mother.'

He said, 'You're really trying to tell me that you don't know what happened that day.'

'My memory is fine,' I snapped.

'Nothing about you is fine,' he said. 'You're in deep shit. Why are you here on my boat?'

'I wouldn't be in this shit if it wasn't for you,' I hissed.

'Just…calm down,' he said in a shaky voice, peering behind me at the kitchen before looking to me and holding my arms. 'I was waiting until the heat died down before I took the boat. You can come with me.'

'Why are you running away if you're innocent?' I asked.

'I found Adam dead in the bathtub!' he shrieked. 'I found out who he really was and I…I couldn't…I wasn't going to hurt him. I was just SO ANGRY.' Spittle flung out and landed on my face, making me flinch. 'He lied all along. I woke up. Found him.' He sobbed. 'I loved him.'

'Bull shit,' I spat.

'What?'

'I hate you! I hate your stupid face, your annoying voice, your disgusting job, and I hate all your damn secrets and lies!' I yelled with such immense hatred that it made tears spring to my eyes.

He took a deep breath and said, 'You're my daughter and I love you.'

I shook my head and shouted, 'There's more of your lies. All you are is lies!'

He said testily, 'Tell me if this is a lie, Riley: Adam was a cop. I read it in his bloody memoir. His plan to get me arrested? Caused the death of your mother.'

My stomach did somersaults, crashing into my organs as I said, 'It was because of you that she tried killing herself, and me…and it's your fault that Adam killed himself so I'll never forgive you.'

He grabbed my arms again and shook me, right there on the floor. 'Why can't you understand what I do? They went after Adam! They were going to kill him for those drugs. It was only a matter of time before they came for you, too!' His eyes narrowed and he pushed away the top of my jacket. He grabbed at my necklace before I could hide it.

'This is your mother's…You stole it from her body?' His mouth made shapes I'd never seen before.

'It's mine!' I clasped both my hands on hips and tried to prise him off but he didn't let go. He squeezed until the necklace snapped and the diamonds scattered all over the floor like marbles. I shoved my hands into his face and leveraged him away from me. I clambered to my feet and ran, but tripped on the steps and banged my chin into the floor, making my vision waver for a split second before I bolted up the stairs, with him chasing me. I went to the edge of the boat and stopped, looking over. He stopped at the top of the stairs.

'I'll jump from here if you come any closer,' I said in a wavering voice.

'Why the hell would you jump?' he called. 'You stupid girl, why can't you understand? I need to keep you safe! I need to keep you alive!'

I screamed, 'You've ruined my life!'

'I'm saving your life,' he murmured. Adam's face came to my mind saying the same thing. All these men thinking they were saving me. I had been the idiot waiting for them to. I grabbed the gun from the plant I had stuffed into my back pocket.

'All I've ever wanted to do is get away from you. Now I can.'

I disengaged the safety, cocked it, and aimed it with a trembling arm. 'How did you know how to do that?' he asked with a stunned expression that had him step back.

'Adam taught me,' I hissed.

'Put that down before you do something stupid with it.'

I squeezed the trigger. The power of the handgun impeded my aim and the bullet grazed cleanly against Dad's shoulder and pierced the side of the boat. He grabbed the hot gun from my hand and returned the favour by pointing it at me. He growled in pain, 'What the hell are you thinking?' He yowled like an animal.

Tears streamed down my face. 'I don't want to be part of your family anymore.'

He shook his head and cried, 'I've tried to keep you safe, Riley! These people…they'd tear you apart bit by bit and laugh at you while you cried. All I've ever done…I just needed to keep you safe! Get away from the rail.'

I shook my head. 'No, I'll jump.'

'You won't. It's too high.'

I snarled, 'How would you even know?' I took a step back.

'Don't take another step!' Dad shouted. 'Riley, if you jump from there, you're going to hit the edge. Stop.'

I took another step. He aimed the gun at my thigh and fired.

The agony screamed within me from my leg, through my entire body and out of my cavernous mouth, then bounced along the beach, along the cliffs and out to sea. The shock made me fall and I slid downwards towards the rail edge. Dad dropped the gun and dived to the rail, grabbing my arm, and struggled as he attempted to pull me up.

I looked down and knew he was right. If I fell from there, because of the angle of the boat, I'd hit the edge. I grunted with the effort to pull myself up. Dad held my arm with one hand: the hand that had constantly hit me and held me down; the hand that just pulled the trigger on the gun. I gripped his forearm tightly and shut my eyes to squeeze out the pain.

Dad growled, 'Riley, hold on! Don't you dare fall!'

Without opening my eyes, I broke down and sobbed.

'Riley!' he growled again, trying to pull me up. I winced as purple flashes of pain cannon-balled across my entire body. Dad squealed, 'Riley, if you don't give me your other hand, I swear to bloody God you will die! I can't let you die! I need you! I love you!'

I snapped open my teary eyes and locked eyes with him. His eyes were almost on fire they were so desperate. He pleaded, 'Come on, baby, don't leave me. Come on, honey…Riley.'

I grabbed him with my other arm and he heaved me up and fell over, pulling me onto the deck with him and he sobbed. I lay beside him and listened to his sobs and shuddering breathing and accepted the throbs in my leg and the cramping to take over. My hearing was overtaken by a shrill tinny as I began to pass out. I watched with detachment as Senior Constable Ackerman launched onto my father and handcuff him. The boat pitched as if we were on the open water and I closed my eyes as I heard a faraway voice read my father his rights.

'Riley…' said a male voice, breaking me out of my sleep.

'Adam?' I said weakly, trying to open my eyes but it was like swimming through clay.

'It's Doctor Marshall.'

I managed at last to open my sticky eyes. They were heavy as lead and my throat ached with thirst. I had an awful taste in my mouth that made me nauseous. I looked up to see the blurry figure of a doctor beside my bed. 'Marshall?' I croaked, thinking of Cody and Adam.

'That's right. I'm Adam's father. Do you know where you are?'

I looked around at the white room and thought for a moment I was in my kitchen but then realised it was a hospital. 'A hospital,' I whispered. 'I was on a boat.'

'Yes, you were shot. I've taken the bullet out of your leg. Do you remember who shot you, Riley?'

I was overcome with tiredness to think clearly but managed to whisper, 'My father shot me,' and closed my eyes, tempted to sleep again. I added quietly, 'He killed my mother, too. I saw it.'

I listened to him leave and then wondered if he knew about Adam. I started to cry there in the hospital bed, bereft without him.

# 46 ACKERMAN

Cody Marshall looked remarkably well for someone that I'd thought was going to die in my arms a couple of nights prior. His eyes shone and his colour was good. He was perched by a stack of pillows and he even smiled when I entered the room to take an official statement about that night.

'You look good, Cody,' I said, easing myself into the chair beside my bed.

He grinned. 'Yeah; considering – right?!' He gestured to the IV stand on the opposite side of his bed. 'Just remind me not to get addicted to this pain relief.'

I smiled, knowing that he was trying to joke but he wasn't really joking. I asked quietly, 'Cody…has your dad spoken to you about your brother?'

Cody answered, 'No. Is he okay?'

'Your friend Riley was shot yesterday morning –' I began. His eyes widened and his posture straightened, panicked so I quickly added, 'In the leg. She's fine, Cody; she will be fine.' He relaxed so I continued, 'A lot has happened since you were stabbed. I was there when Riley was shot.' I hesitated. I should have kept a visual on her. I'd really let her down. My voice wavered. 'I should have…' I stopped to give myself a moment. Her father could have killed her on that boat and I would have been responsible. I would have been responsible if he had killed that kid.

'You saved me, you know.' Cody was watching me patiently. He nodded. 'I remember.' He smiled. 'Whatever you think you should have done better, you did a pretty incredible thing for me. Thank you.'

My mouth opened and only a garbled squeak came out and I laughed. Cody smiled, grimacing, trying not laugh too. I finally heaved a sigh and said, 'Thanks, Cody…I didn't even know I needed that.'

'You're welcome.' He smiled.

'So, the suspect who shot Riley is in custody.'

'It's not Adam, is it?'

My face fell. 'No, it's not Adam.'

'I'm not giving up on him,' he said with a faint grimace.

I sat in silence. I supposed his father had decided to keep the news from him to protect him while he healed, but it made it hard to ignore it when he said things like that. Kid was in for a whole lot more hurt. I had to stay off the topic.

'Riley says she has a fair idea who stabbed you.'

'She wasn't there.'

'She said you had a substantial amount of cocaine on your person when you were stabbed.'

Cody looked down at his wound and whispered, 'Riley lies, you know.'

I thought of the shredded note left by Adam, admitting his guilt and I couldn't disagree that Riley lied. In a way, I was glad she did. We all lied to survive.

I explained, 'We ran tests on the clothes you were wearing that night. There were traces of cocaine on your clothes, Cody.'

Cody bowed his head and picked at the threaded hospital blanket. 'Cocaine?' His breathing increased and he picked up his sick bag and was violently ill. I stood up and pressed the nurse's button.

'Want me to leave and come back?' I asked.

'No,' Cody said, wiping his mouth with the back of his hand. His lip trembled and he said, 'His name was Elias. The guy that stabbed me. He was a friend of Tempany's, who was a friend of my brother.'

'Elias…Tennison?' I said, remembering seeing the name from the whiteboard of the conference room.

Cody shook his head. 'I don't know. I never knew his last name.'

'If I brought you a picture, do you think you would recognise him?'

'Definitely.'

The nurse came in and tended to Cody, giving him an oxygen mask. His face was swallowed up by the contraption and he looked embarrassed. I squeezed his hand. 'You just rest and get better, Cody.'

I walked out and went to Riley's room. She was joined by a security guard. I exchanged a wave with him and continued on past. She was still asleep.

I went back to the police station where we had Dominic Flynn in lock-up. He sat with his head between his knees and weaving on the bed. Tui brought him into the interview room. He saw me and his face stiffened.

'Mr. Flynn, a couple of questions and then you can go back to resting your shoulder.'

He eyed Tui, then me. 'Where's your girlfriend?'

'You're in a bit of trouble, old mate,' I said.

He looked down at his hands. 'Guess so.'

'You shot your kid.'

'I didn't want to. I was just trying to get her off the edge of the boat. I was trying to save her!'

'Did you have anything to do with your wife's death?' I'd never forget what Adam had written, but I wanted to see if Dominic Flynn knew if Adam had been the one who killed his wife. Whether he knew his daughter had already made a statement that she'd seen her father do it. I would never tell if he didn't.

'No.'

'Were you aware that you were being investigated for selling narcotics?'

He sighed and shook his head. 'I'm not going to do this with you. You're an angry little son of a bitch and you're out to get me.'

'Uh huh; Do you know Elias Tennison?'

He stared ahead with glazed eyes. I cocked my head and repeated myself. He nodded. 'He's a drug dealer.'

'Your supplier?'

Flynn sighed and said, 'Look, I'll tell you everything but you have to stop interrupting me all the time. It's rude.'

Tui stifled a laugh so I glared at him. I turned back to Dominic Flynn. 'Why did you run away after you found the body of Adam Marshall?'

He rubbed his face with the back of his hands and said, 'I...knew you coppers would blame me. Think I'd done it.' His voice cracked as he added, 'I mean, this whole time you thought I'd killed my wife.' He jiggled his leg furiously, trying to compose himself. 'So did my own kid.' He huffed. 'All I ever tried to do was keep my family safe from the psychos that are in my field of work.'

'Riley will be going into protective foster care. You're under the arrest for the endangerment of a minor, child abuse and trafficking an illegal drug...and murdering your wife.'

His brow furrowed and his mouth opened. 'But I didn't.'

'Witness says otherwise. Have a good day, Mr. Flynn.'

Tui led him back to the cells. I stood outside the locked door and heaved a deep breath. He hadn't killed his wife, but he may as well have. For everything he had put his child and wife through, he may as well have. He was likely looking at fifteen years at least. One year for each year of his daughter's life. Maybe she would spend the next fifteen years finally being safe. It was worth lying to get that for her.

I called Burke and let her know that Dominic Flynn was read his rights.

'Where are you?' I asked when I heard voices in the background.

'At the hospital. I wanted to make sure Riley is okay.'

I nodded and said, 'Good.' She needed a mother figure at a time like this. I couldn't always be the person that saved the day. That was okay. I may not have become a hero for Riley, but I'd been a hero for Cody, after all.

So, this must have been how Marshall must have felt. He had sacrificed his morals to keep that girl safe. Running my tongue over my teeth to erase the rotten taste of the lie, I understood. A good cop doesn't always mean being a good person.

# 47 RILEY

I woke up to someone gently brushing my forehead, stroking my hair.
I opened my eyes and pulled away. Senior Constable Burke was beside
me.

'Ssh, it's okay, Riley. You're safe now.' She stayed by my side and I
relaxed again and let her stroke my head the way I had wanted her to
what felt like forever ago. I sighed.

'Is my dad in jail yet?' I asked in a whisper.

'Yes. As soon as you're well enough, and can testify that he shot
you and murdered your mother…He'll be sentenced and sent to
prison.'

I closed my eyes and swallowed. 'Good.'


The next day, I had the television on in the hospital room as I got
dressed. My leg plastered from my hip to my ankle, rigid and
uncomfortable. With my eyes on the television, I pulled on a light
cardigan over my singlet. The pier with the boat was on the screen. A
woman reporter was telling the camera all about the suspicious
activities that had taken place on this boat – in the background, police

went off and on, carrying out evidence. A photo of my dad and my mum came onto the screen and I switched off the television.

I made my way slowly through the hospital on the crutches to Cody's room.

I was exhausted by the time I got there. My armpits rubbed and my hands ached. I had to lean against the wall outside Cody's room to catch my breath before I entered. Cody was sitting up reading back issues of gossip magazines. He looked up and smiled when he heard me clunk into the doorway.

'Hi,' I breathed. 'Can I come in?'

He patted the bed beside him. I went in slowly, awkwardly, and I even felt a little embarrassed. I sat on the edge of the bed at an angle so I could stick my bulbous cast out and leaned the crutches against his bed.

'Does it hurt much?' he asked.

'Surprisingly not,' I smiled. 'My dad's going to prison.'

'I heard you'd been shot. Did you dad do it?' He rolled up the magazine and placed it under his pillow.

I nodded.

Cody asked, 'Have you heard from Adam?'

I searched his face. He wasn't joking. Queasiness hit me.

'What's wrong, Riley?' he asked, the colour draining from his face. 'Has he done something? Is he going to prison, too?'

I fought with a thumping nerve in my neck to allow air to pass through to my lungs. 'You don't know,' I said.

'What do you mean I don't know?' he gasped.

I started hyperventilating. I couldn't breathe.

'Head between your knees.' Cody struggled to force my body down. He reached for the call button beside his bed. 'Hang on, I'll call the nurse.'

I slapped his hand away and shook my head. 'No, I'm okay.' I gasped for air and it slowly came. I sat up and tried to breathe normally. In one, two three…Out three, two, one.

'What did Adam do?' he asked.

I grabbed the crutches. I went to get up and said in a rushed voice, 'I have to go,' but the crutch slipped on the waxed floor and I almost went with, but caught myself on the edge of the bed. I managed to coordinate the crutches to escape from Cody's room where I fell into the wall with a heaving, wracking cry that I couldn't stifle. How could I go on without Adam? How could anyone not told Cody his brother was dead? That his brother decided to die? If I had told him, he would have hated me. He would spend the rest of his life re-living the last time he saw Adam and hate himself. Adam's lies had bitten him in the arse after all that time.

I was unable to suppress a wail and my knees buckled, my exterior caved in – I slid down to the ground, my rigid leg sticking out in front of me and my crutches banging me in the cheeks.

I heard Cody cry from his bed, 'Riley, what's going on? What happened to my brother? Riley!'

I clamped both hands to my ears so I couldn't hear him and I screamed until nurses flocked to me.

The wrong person died that day. I know that.

Adam shook my mother so violently she hit her head on the back of the bathtub. My mother got what she wanted. Can you be a good person even if you kill someone by accident?

I lit a cigarette and smoked it in the shade of an elm tree. Senior Constables Burke and Ackerman waited nearby. They would be taking me to foster care. To safety. Safety and security, and away from my father. It was what I had hoped for all along. I put all my trust in Adam and it destroyed him. Now all I had were these two cops.

I guessed I had to believe in them since it was all I had left. They didn't want me to go to my family in Sydney anymore because Dad would know exactly where I was. I was to be hidden, just in case he got out and decided he actually did want to kill me. Or Elias Tennison or Tempany might find me. I smoked quietly, thinking of all the people I had to leave behind in this town. Cody. Burke. Ackerman. They'd really done a lot for me in the end.

All I'd had to do was trust them.

I'd spent my entire life with my trust betrayed. How was I meant to trust people? Yet it was only by trusting new people that I got out. I'd sailed away. I'd dived off the edge of the pier and chosen life.

I had testified that my father killed my mother. That I saw everything. Adam had rushed me to the hospital because my father had tried to kill both of us. My own father. I hated him enough to be able to lie. But then again, I was a liar. If Adam could re-write the ending, why couldn't I?

I laid the packet of cigarettes upon Adam's tombstone in the cemetery and limped away with my cane, tears coming to my eyes. But I wouldn't cry. Only weak girls cried. Burke wrapped her arm around me and Ackerman held open the door to the police car. Onwards to my new life. Safe. Secure.

I would not cry anymore.

# ABOUT THE AUTHOR

Ava Dunn is a debut Australian author. She resides on a farm in Victoria, with her partner Rick and pets. When she is not writing, she is teaching, riding her horses, or surfing. I Lied For You is her first novel.

# I LIED FOR YOU

www.ingramcontent.com/pod-product-compliance
Lightning Source LLC
Chambersburg PA
CBHW010442100726
47904CB00008B/2446